WICKED IN THE PINES

CELESTIAL HAVEN
BOOK ONE

L.R. FRIEDMAN

Wicked in the Pines

ISBN 979-8-9862079-9-5

Edited by The Editor & The Quill

Cover by A.T. Cover Designs

To those who feel lost—
May this just be another beginning in your endless evolution.

AUTHOR'S NOTE

Wicked in the Pines is the first part of a supernatural MMF why choose paranormal romance duet. It contains some explicit content best suited for readers over the age of 18.

While Wicked in the Pines could be considered slow-med burn...in part 2, Midnight with the Hexed, all bets are off. This is your not-so-subtle warning.

For a comprehensive list of content and possible triggers for the duet, it can be found by turning to the very last page of this book.

CONTENTS

INTRODUCTION

There's a long and winding road that leads *nowhere*.

That is, if you don't know where you're heading.

Many have traveled its unmapped black path. The one flanked by bushy pines that cradle the moon above, as if spelled to hold it in place.

For minutes, they'll follow its glittering beacon, drawn toward something they don't understand. That is, until they're deterred by the thick fog that blots away their visibility. Or until they pull on the emergency brake before they slam into the wayward tree trunk left discarded on the pavement.

Yes, the average person sees these obstructions, shifts gears, and finds themselves heading wherever they came from.

Never looking back.

Never finding themselves on that road again.

As if it disappeared from existence. Or was merely a figment of their imagination...

Then there are the others.

The ones who smirk at the first sign of fog; at its smoky claws beckoning their cars in the moonlight. The ones who press down on the pedal, speed kicking up with a violent pulse, spearing straight toward the brittle trunk strewn across their path.

Yes, those are the blessed few that shriek in giddy fits of laughter as they vault through its sacred bark, pulled where the oblivious never land.

Car humming down the blissful path, past the illusions set for the world they've left behind, they edge toward one of the few places forged into existence for their kind. A utopia, hidden away from prying and persecuting eyes, tucked within the heart of Washington's Artemis District.

A partially rotted sign floats on the side of the road, crystals hanging from the thick cords nailed across its top.

Welcome to Celestial Haven.

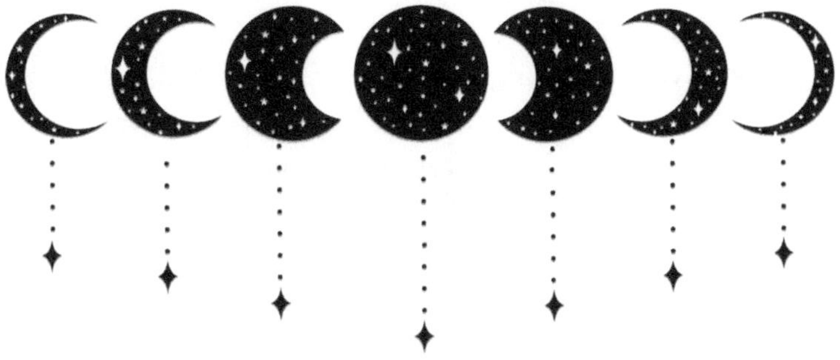

Ivy vines snaked along its exterior, wild grass sprang up from the soil, and the budless rose bushes with gnarled limbs creeped past the windowsills. Twigs, leaves, and yellowing newspapers from last May were heaped on the porch.

Forgotten.

Like all the other houses on the street, its roof and shutters were black and blended into the siding—a magnificently macabre construction. Its only peek of color came from the rich evergreen door inlaid with pebbled glass twisting in abstract swirls lined in gold.

The gloomy house tarnished the otherwise beautiful row.

Number 15's imperial purple door groaned open, its tenant, Ruby Cove, giving it a *tsk* when the autumn wind nearly swung it shut. Her gray strands whipped about as she pushed her way outside before hobbling across the porch, arms clutched tightly around her bag. She sat down on the floating loveseat and summoned her knitting needles and spool of yarn—orange to match the maple tree's leaves out front.

Knit four, purl two.
Knit four, purl two.

Knit four, purl two.

The loveseat swung gently as she worked, eyes cast anywhere but her hands. She watched the realtor walk down the street, a SOLD sign tucked under her arm, bold-red lips pressed in a firm line.

Another new neighbor.

Ruby rolled her eyes.

Clacking her heels against the pavement, the realtor's brunette tresses billowed behind her in the breeze. She brushed along the lapels of her polished blazer, a peek of a mesh floral corset underneath earning a scoff from Ruby.

Knit two, purl four.

Knit two, purl four.

Knit two, purl four.

"Hello there. I don't believe we've formally met. I'm Hazel Brooks." The realtor introduced herself with a pleasant smile.

"Ruby," replied the older woman, who watched curiously while the realtor struggled with the ward obstructing the door's knob.

"Just stopping by before moving day. Landscape crew will be here tomorrow to cast in preparation."

The elderly witch lifted her gaze, hands still knitting with deft precision. "What can you tell me about them?"

Would they be a blessing or curse?

Only time would tell.

"Funny you should mention that," Hazel said, clearing the path with a wave of her hand before the ward dissolved in a puff of smoke. "It's me! Isn't that exciting? Finally decided to snap up one of these beauties for myself. Hopefully my sister, Oakley, and my nephew, will live here too—if I can convince her."

"Oh really?" Ruby said, trying to hold back her surprise.

"A single witch from the city opting to move out to the suburbs?"

It was rather odd, but people often were.

"Yes. Finally planting some roots. Figure I'm here enough showing houses, might as well make the commute a snap."

"Might as well," the older woman agreed with a shrug, brows knit tighter than the yarn in her hands.

"Still got some hot dates lined up, though," Hazel added, giving her new neighbor a wicked grin. "Plus, this place was a steal."

"Yes it was, considering the location."

Starry Night Lane had boasted yearly victories for being the Stellar Street: the best one to live on in the Celestial Haven community since the neighborhood's inception. This was due in large part to their diligent yet elusive HOA.

"It was just too good to pass up," said Hazel, finally cracking open the evergreen door and giving Ruby a friendly wave. The elder witch went back to her knitting, eyes scanning around the rest of Starry Night Lane as neighboring doors *snicked* wide and *thumped* shut.

The hovering streetlamps extinguished as the coven wandered out to begin their daily routines. Some climbed into shiny cars, wearing black suits and carting briefcases, while others jogged down the street with their headphones on or shuffled in their slippers toward Café au Luna's coffee truck, where the *crackle* and *drip* of their morning brews summoned them.

As the evergreen door snapped closed, its insides rumbled, seemingly satisfied with no longer being empty.

Maybe things would work out better than they had for the previous tenants.

We'd find out soon enough.

CHAPTER I

OAKLEY

R ancid green liquid seeped between my fingers.

Scrunching my nose, I tried not to inhale the stench. Panic scratched its jagged nails along my insides, and I pushed it down, forcing it to retract its claws.

You can do this, Oakley.

Gurgles reverberated through the empty house, echoing off the stacks of boxes still taped shut and perched throughout the living room. They were followed by a piercing screech that would likely alert the neighborhood watch—if they existed here—that something was amiss at 13 Starry Night Lane.

I ran to the sink, avoiding touching anything with my desecrated hands, holding the putrid fabric in front of me. Using only my elbow, I turned the water on. Steam billowed from the sink, and I scrubbed and washed and repeated the process over and over, waiting for a knock at the door—for someone, *anyone*, to come.

To rescue me.

I shuffled to the mirror, heart ramping its rhythm, stammering against my ribs. The woman looking back at me was unrecognizable. Eyeliner was smudged into deep crescents beneath her eyes and her hair was pulled up into a messy auburn bun with pale streaks crusted through it. Her once white T-shirt was smeared with assorted stains.

I reached up to touch the unidentifiable moist stripe across my shoulder. It was pale yellow and sticky, sending a shiver through me. Bringing my hands back under the steaming water, I washed once again before drying them on the sink towel and turning toward the door.

It was open just a crack, enough to allow a sliver of moonlight into my bedroom. Each tiptoe closer, I could feel my lack of sanity bubbling over, one fluid ounce at a time. Peering through the crevice, my gaze drifted toward the foot of the bed. A roaring gurgle followed by a pungent odor, musty and foul, sent me staggering back a few paces into the hall.

Surely only something summoned from the depths of Hell smelled like that.

Taking a deep inhale and exhale, I gripped the door with one hand, bracing myself on its frame with the other.

Be brave.

I chanted it in my mind on repeat like some powerful incantation.

Steeling my spine and holding my breath, I slipped inside to face the fiend within.

(((●)))

IT HAD BEEN TWENTY-FOUR HOURS OF THE TWO OF US FACING OFF IN this house alone, my little demon winning by a poopsplosion-landslide.

Mommy: 0

Aspen: 63—at a minimum.

My sister's date must have gone *really* well because Hazel

still wasn't back a day later. *Good for her.* How she ever found these sex gods that could last for *days* was enviable.

I barely had enough energy to wash my hair.

My gaze dropped down to my shirt's replacement, already mottled with damp spit-up. Partially covered by the fabric, a tiny fist beat impatiently against my breast. Our matching chestnut eyes locked, the only feature he'd gotten from me, and I stroked Aspen's hand with my finger, garnering a gummy grin and a soft coo in response.

The pure joy of it snatched the breath from my lungs.

As I bent down, I greedily inhaled his sweet witchling smell, savoring it before giving him a kiss on his chubby pink cheek.

"You're lucky you've got me spellbound."

A knock at the door jolted me from his enchantment, instantly souring my mood.

Who knocks on a door after nine o'clock at night?

Hazel had keypad access with our newly installed home system, so I knew it wasn't her. Whoever it was, they were lucky Aspen wasn't sleeping because I would hex someone in a heartbeat for waking him at this point.

Not that I *actually* could with so little magic flowing through my veins, but it was the spirit of the sentiment that counted.

It'd been just over a week since we moved in with Hazel, and mortal-style unpacking while caring for a newborn was near impossible. Thank Goddess she said she'd use the enchantment she'd found on the dark web to make it a snap once she was back. In the meantime, boxes glared at me from every corner as if to say, *yes, witch, you're a mess.* I'd managed to unload most of Aspen's things by hand, but I needed to find the rest of my clothes—the real adult ones that weren't stained—along with a slew of other items.

I popped Aspen off my nipple before wrangling my partially deflated boob back into my nursing bra, snapping the clasp shut. What I wouldn't give for an underwire to hike these puppies back up to their former pre-pregnancy glory.

"One minute!" I shouted to whoever was at the door, pulling down my shirt. One of the many ways having Hazel around was helpful: her Precognition made it pleasantly unsurprising when people showed up on our doorstep.

I scrambled to my feet, throwing the muslin blanket peppered in inky evergreens on my shoulder. Shifting Aspen on top of it, I patted his back a few times, hoping he'd burp now versus spit up all over me later. At least having him situated like this would hide my lopsided chest.

Heading to answer the door, my nerves were in hyper-drive, surprised to have someone coming by so late. Maybe they were here to see Hazel? It would be awkward if I had to tell them she was still on her date from over a day ago, but that was Hazel. When she worked, she worked hard, and when she let loose to *play*, the same was true.

Tugging at my shirt one last time, I gripped the knob, twisting it to open the door a few inches. The evening breeze smacked me in the face, along with the sight of the handsome witch standing on my porch, his sandy-blond mop of hair shimmering in the buttery moonlight.

Great Goddess, he probably *was* here for Hazel.

Lucky witch.

I pulled the door the rest of the way open, trying not to gawk at the muscles that peeked from under his fitted gray T-shirt and ripped jeans. From the few crinkles edging his eyes —a brilliant shade of sienna—I'd guess he was also in his mid-to-late thirties. Salt and pepper mixed into the blond stubble along his sharp jaw, framing a big grin so perfectly pearly it nearly blinded me.

My gift's dusty remnants perked up in response.

"Hi." His voice was calm, sultry, but with a pinch of gruffness that had my body prickling with heat. Lifting his oven-mitted hands, he held a covered dish with steam trapped under its glass lid.

I wasn't sure which was the hotter dish.

My throat dried, warmth spreading through my chest and neck until I was sure my cheeks were painted pink. I tried not to think about the fact that I was covered in various stains and hadn't bothered to shower.

May the Moon Goddess bless whoever conjured up dry shampoo.

"Sorry, I didn't mean to bother you." He lifted his shoulders, giving me a warm smile, eyes twinkling. "I got tied up at work but wanted to bring this by and welcome you to the neighborhood."

Where had my words gone?

This was the first neighbor I'd met since moving in. Hazel already knew many of the neighborhood witches who she'd sold houses to. She'd probably introduced herself to everyone here before I'd even arrived. It had been a while since I'd interacted face-to-face with another adult who wasn't her.

"I'm Lynx, over at 16," he continued, cutting through my tongue-tied awkwardness. I couldn't remember the last time a supernatural had me speechless. He pointed at the house diagonal from mine next to the coffee truck I'd been dying to check out. This late at night, its only discernible features were its rustic-looking turquoise door and fairy lights that hovered over its wraparound porch, illuminating a floating onyx loveseat.

"This is for you," he continued, lifting up the covered dish. A delicious combination of sausage, biscuits, and rosemary filled the room. "It's a breakfast casserole. I figured breakfast is good at any time of the day and you could easily reheat the leftovers in the morning."

That boyish grin returned, and he tossed back his head, trying to get the mussed hair out of his eyes. The urge to brush the wild strands made my palms twitch. Were they as silky as they looked?

"That's really thoughtful," I said, going to reach for the casserole before remembering I was one-handed and the dish was too hot for me to handle comfortably with Aspen in my arms. "I'm Oakley."

"Why don't I drop this on the counter for you?" he offered, taking a step forward before pausing respectfully, waiting for me to invite him inside. I nodded, patting Aspen's back.

"And who is this little pumpkin?" Lynx asked, shoulder brushing into me as he made his way over to the kitchen. The rich scent of cedarwood and chai spices curled around him, sending a prickle of my gift wriggling up my spine to the nape of my neck.

"This is Aspen. He's just shy of five months." I kissed the faint tuft of dark hair on his otherwise bald head. "I'm sorry if you hear him screeching from your house. He tends to get pretty vocal when he isn't pleased with the service around here."

Lynx chuckled and placed the dish down. When he turned around, his attention snagged on the stacks of moving boxes and confusion etched his brow. "Doesn't look like he's been too helpful with the unpacking."

"Yeah, he's not earning his keep just yet."

Aspen giggled along with me before spitting up onto my non–burp cloth-covered shoulder.

Fuck me.

Lynx snapped up another burp cloth that was draped over

a half-unpacked box and brought it over, dabbing up the mess on my shoulder and wiping some out of my hair.

This is exactly the first impression I'm going for.

I let out a heavy sigh, stifling the heat of embarrassment, the inescapable pressure of repetitive sleepless nights making tears an all too real possibility right now.

"If you need any help with unpacking or just an extra set of hands to put things together, I'm free off and on during the weekdays when I'm not in sessions."

"Thanks. You don't have to do that, though."

"I really don't mind. Do you have anyone else to help you?" he asked, cocking his head to the side.

Was he asking because he wanted to know if I was single or because I looked that desperate for help?

I glanced down at my soiled self, the latest smear on my shoulder still drying.

Probably the latter.

"Where's Hazel been?"

Duh. He already knew my sister. She probably sold him the house.

"She's been busy with work. Lots of people moving in and out of the area lately."

"I didn't realize she was normally out so late being in real estate."

"Oh, she isn't," I replied, my bouncing picking up speed. Aspen's eyes widened, the opposite of what I was aiming for with bedtime. "She's on a date. You know, just enjoying a few moments of single life without her little sister and nephew cramping her style."

Why am I word vomiting everywhere?

"I'll definitely let you know if we need any assistance. Thanks again for offering," I added, trying to sound less socially impaired.

I didn't want to come off like a helpless damsel needing some knight to rescue her. This had been my choice. I had opted to be a single mom, to let my magic dwindle, and I refused to have my decisions burden anyone else. Not my sister and definitely not this *way-too-handsome-to-be-hanging-out-with-my-spit-up-covered-ass* stranger.

I could do this on my own, even if I lost some sanity in the process. I already felt like enough of a moocher living with my sister in this beautiful house hidden away in one of the most affluent parts of the country.

"Hmm...so Hazel, Oakley, and Aspen? Sounds like your family has a thing for trees."

I couldn't stop the heat from rising to my cheeks. "It's been a tradition in my mother's family for as long as I can remember. Her name was Willow." I chuckled. The sadness that came with saying her name was not nearly as cutting as it had been a decade ago when we'd lost our parents a few months apart. "It just seemed appropriate to have this little witchling follow suit."

"It's a great name," he said, smiling at Aspen, the gentleness of it highlighting the nearness of him, quickening my pulse. Despite my heart's heady rhythm, his presence was like a comforting blanket, instantly enveloping me in its calm.

"May I?" he asked, pointing to the aspen tattoo spanning my forearm. Hazel and I had gotten matching ones after his birth. I nodded, breath hitching when the pad of his finger met its inky bark. Lynx traced the trunk and delicate branches, sending electric heat through my skin. "What a sweet way to commemorate your growing family."

His gaze dropped to his feet before he placed a hand at the nape of his neck, smirking with amusement for whatever reason.

Strange.

It made me wonder what his gift was. But I couldn't ask. That would be rude.

Only magically blessed witches were allowed to live on coven-allocated streets. Spread throughout Celestial Haven were areas dedicated to shifters, vamps, Nephilim, and even a waterfront section for mermaids, sirens, and other sea inhabitants. Some streets were intermixed, but it was a place we were free to be ourselves and be *safe*.

Our community had been through enough when magic rocketed into our world over fifty years ago. And while some supernaturals still lived among the mortals, many preferred to openly embrace their powers, moving to designated hidden districts that were overseen by the Council of Magical Welfare.

I rubbed Aspen's back and paced side to side, keeping a bounce in my step. I was shocked he hadn't cried since Lynx's arrival. On one hand, I desperately wanted this witch to stay so I could enjoy the quiet—and I had to admit, looking at him was a cross I didn't mind bearing. But on the other hand, I didn't want to drown him with the perpetually rising level of hot mess here.

"What do you do?" I asked, curious what gave him such a flexible schedule.

My social meter was running low. I'd probably forget the entire exchange in about thirty seconds, but I wouldn't stop this conversation if it gave me a few extra moments of peace.

"I'm a personal trainer."

Of course you are.

Just by looking at his chiseled arms and chest accented by his fitted shirt and the perfect way his jeans hugged him, it was obvious he knew his way around a gym. His outfit left little to the imagination, and I couldn't decide if that was a good or bad thing for me right now. The dusty particles of my gift tingled beneath my skin, parched and eager to come out and play.

"Do you train at a gym in town?" Cutting into my own thoughts, I slapped a blanket of calm-the-fuck-down on my dried-up ability. It was latching onto my attraction and being much too encouraging.

"I used to but now I have my own business in the neighborhood. I do group training three times a week in the mornings outside the community center and then have private clients."

I bet he had lots of clients wanting one-on-one sessions.

The idea of working out seemed impossible when I could barely think straight most days, much less try to move my body in some coordinated way.

His jaw ticked a moment, accentuating the steely angle edged in blond-and-silver stubble. It also didn't help that this entire exchange had made me acutely aware of the fact that I hadn't had sex in many moons.

Many, many moons.

Sweat beaded on my forehead, and I smoothed it back into my hair. *Is this what a hot flash feels like? Would it be awkward to start fanning myself right now?*

Yes. The answer was a big freaking yes.

"That's amazing. Maybe once I get my life together..." I laughed at my current state and how silly I must look trying to carry on a conversation with a hot trainer that probably had clients throwing themselves at him all day, begging him to demonstrate hip thrusters.

Not that I was currently imagining him doing hip thrusters...

Fine, maybe I was.

"You should join in for our morning group. It would be a great way to meet other people from the 'hood. You can even bring the witchling with you," he said with a wink that sent a jolt straight down my spine. "There are a few other moms who come and really enjoy it."

Of course they do.

"I'll think about it," I replied with a smile that curled into a sleep-deprived yawn.

"I'm so sorry if I disturbed you from getting some much-deserved rest. Enjoy the dish for breakfast, dinner...whatever. It's meant to be enjoyed anytime, really." He flashed a small but dazzling smile, and I had to remind myself the dish meant to be enjoyed was the casserole sitting on the countertop.

"Thank you," I choked out, trying to wrangle my gutter-wandering mind.

Curse you, hormones.

Lynx beamed, a glint in his eyes that was all too knowing.

Could he hear my thoughts or read my gift? I had never met a witch who could but that would be super awkward right now.

Aspen began to fuss over my shoulder, and I picked up my bouncing again.

"I almost forgot. Let me put my number in your phone. That way if you need any help unpacking, or anything at all, I can pop over," he offered.

Yes, because I'm sure you want to spend your spare time with a sloppy new mom and her tiny banshee.

Just before I was about to politely let him off the hook, he added, "I'm happy to do it."

"Okay, cool." I cradled Aspen into my chest, bouncing as I searched for my phone, not remembering where I'd put it last. Lynx spotted it first on the counter and brought it over to me to unlock. He tapped in his number and handed it back with a smile so magnetic it would be impossible not to want to be pulled into his orbit.

Heat coursing through me, I switched Aspen to my other shoulder. Then I watched Lynx walk out the door, slowly closing it behind him. Once shut, I leaned up against it, shaking my head at myself.

What the hell was that?

I looked at my phone.

LYNX CAVEN

I probably would never use the number, but it was nice of him to offer. At least I had a name to go with the fantasy.

Swiping out of my contacts, I checked to see if there were any texts from my sister.

> ETA? Neighbor brought over food for us. Will you be home tonight?

I stared at the phone for a few minutes, waiting for the triple dot to pop up before Aspen started crying in long, over-tired wails. Putting the phone down on the counter, I broke out the soothing butt-pat move that seemed to help him calm down while I paced back and forth. Motherhood was definitely training me to up my multitasking game.

About ten minutes later, I brought a finally sleeping Aspen back into my bedroom and placed him in the bassinet. I cringed when I heard a *ding* on my phone, but he didn't stir.

Thank Goddess.

I tiptoed slowly out of the room, taking my time to shut the door as quiet as a ghost. Shuffling to the counter, I inhaled the smell of breakfast for dinner. This momma was *starved*.

Apparently in more ways than one after tonight's visit.

Yawning, I picked up my cell to see when Hazel would be getting back.

ATLAS

How's the new place? Still good for this weekend's visit?

New place is great. Still good.

I debated if I was being too short with my ex in my responses, weighing out what might send mixed signals. Instead of writing anything else, I sent along a video I had taken of Aspen giggling as I made ridiculous faces at him from behind the camera.

ATLAS

Looking forward to it! Thanks for the video.

Miss you both.

See you Saturday.

I exhaled, pushing off the unease that was aimed equally at him and myself. Every time I saw Atlas, it was all too confusing to juggle things between my heart and my mind.

I dished out some of the casserole: a blend of fluffy bread, cream cheese, sausage, and cheddar, and a few moments later, I had eaten two servings and was ready to pass out from a carb-induced trance.

Sneaking back into my room, I looked over the side of Aspen's bassinet and watched him sleep. How come I always missed him so much when he slept but prayed so many times throughout the day that he would nap long enough for me to regain an ounce of sanity?

It'd been a few days since I showered, and I maybe had twenty-four more hours to get away with relying on dry shampoo. Now was as good a time as any to try to squeeze one in.

Throwing my clothes into the hamper, I moved through the steam, pulling my messy bun out and letting my auburn tresses fall around my shoulders. The hot water beat down on me and I let my mind drift to Lynx, clinging to those momentary prickles I'd felt when he'd been here. The warmth from the billowing steam reminded me of the electric feel of his finger when he traced the tattoo on my skin.

The way his shirt clung to his body.

The way his eyes didn't seem to need to search to understand.

The smile that felt like it was meant just for me.

And much to my surprise, long-forgotten impulses stirred within me.

CHAPTER 2

OAKLEY

I woke to the sound of Aspen's coos, pulling me from the sienna eyes peering back at me in my dreams. My boobs were like boulders, my chest uncomfortably tight. I rubbed my eyes and yawned, glancing up at the illuminated numbers on the clock. 2:32 a.m. That meant I'd gotten two more extra glorious hours of sleep than usual with his feeding schedule.

As I rolled over, my excitement dissolved, spotting the dark wet patch beneath where I had been sleeping.

Great.

Lifting Aspen out of his bassinet with a yawn, I sank to the ground, using the bed as a backrest before shifting my shirt. I adjusted my position until he latched lazily onto me, suckling happily and relieving the pressure that had me leaking onto the sheets. I snagged my phone from the nightstand, hoping to have a message from Hazel.

Nothing.

The approaching full moon made our sexual appetites more ravenous, and I was feeling the effects of it too, considering the steamy shower thoughts and dream I'd had about our neighbor. I was sure Hazel was having an amazing time, but I already missed her being around.

> You coming up for air over there?

> They better have a ribbed tongue or something.

Putting the phone on the ground, I stroked Aspen's back as he fed, slowly shutting my eyes...

A tiny fist smacked my breast, jolting me back to alertness. I fumbled for my phone, then switched him to the other breast. Swiping the screen, I started typing out another message, probably sounding crazy already texting her again.

She would definitely be making fun of me later.

> Atlas is coming in a few days. Think you'll be back before then?

> I don't want the house to look like a shit show. You know he'll see it as an opportunity to swoop in and play hero.

Once Aspen finished feeding, I got up with him, throwing on some *Gilmore Girls* reruns and dozing off in small increments on the couch while he hung out in his play center. After a handful of episodes, I loaded him into the stroller, figuring that walking the length of our neighborhood about five times would burn through some of my nervous energy.

Where was my obligatory text from Hazel letting me know she had found a sex wizard and that his magical staff had dickstracted her the last two days? Hopefully by this time tomorrow she would be sitting across from me at the table, regaling me with her sexcapades while we laughed over cups of coffee.

When my phone buzzed from the stroller basket, I halted,

dipping down to dig under my diaper bag and extra blanket to grab it.

Thank Goddess.

Chuckling to myself about whatever ridiculously salacious message awaited me from Hazel, I tapped the darkened screen to see what she'd written.

The laughter quickly vanished, my gut clenching when I saw who the next was from.

ATLAS

Anything I can bring for Aspen or the house this weekend?

I think we have everything handled.

Don't be a dick, Oakley. He's clearly trying to make the best of our situation.

Thanks for asking. Surprised you're up in the middle of the night.

ATLAS

Work's been crazy lately. Think of it as co-parenting solidarity since you're up with our son.

He was coming to visit Aspen and see how we were settling in since I'd made the decision to move us to Washington. My pulse quickened at the thought of him being here, seeing all the boxes strewn about. Seeing how much I didn't, in fact, have it handled. But Hazel would be home by then. She'd be able to use her magic and would be the perfect buffer so I didn't do anything stupid like run back into the arms of my ex.

I put the phone down before I continued to overthink my responses. Turning toward our house, I strolled along the sidewalk while the lanterns bobbed above us, casting their golden light onto the sidewalks. The street was completely silent, most of the houses shrouded in darkness. Guess no one else was sleep deprived and anxious enough to be out at four in the morning.

Only one house seemed awake against its sleeping brethren—the first along Blessed Crescent, a row of expensive luxury homes that looped around a paved, half-moon shaped street nestled behind the Coven Community Center. Nearly all the lights were on in the house, a silhouette flitting between the ones on the lower level. The lone *creak* of the home's front door halted me at the bottom of my driveway.

My night owl neighbor scurried to the side of her house, snipping herbs from the planters resting there. During the day, they would fly off to the best spot for sun or shade, depending on what each needed, returning home at sundown. The more finnicky plants resided within the community center's attached greenhouse, only summoned to their owners when needed.

Aspen screeched from the stroller and her head snapped in our direction. Our eyes locked momentarily, and she stilled, clearly startled to see someone outside at this hour, her hand clutched around her clippings. I'd probably be freaked out too if I saw a darkened shadow staring at me. She readjusted her spectacles, as if wanting to get a better look at us, and I waved to break up the awkwardness, getting a quick nod in acknowledgment before the witch pivoted and hustled to her door. Ascending the stairs leading to her porch, glittering outlines of wards contoured her shape as she passed through them.

Interesting.

It was unusual to see so many handmade wards on a house. Most of the homes around here boasted top-of-the-line systems. Apparently one of the witches who lived on Blessed Crescent owned a home security and maintenance tech company.

Placing my finger on our silver star-shaped panel stuck to the side of the garage door, I waited a moment for it to groan open. When the screen came to life, its red light blinked, reminding me what I already knew.

LOW MAGIC

I swiped through the automated messages, switching the house to manual mode until Hazel got back. I couldn't risk it taking the last dregs of my magic.

Looking over my shoulder, the brilliant waxing crescent stared down at me as if the Goddess wanted to remind me that the full moon would be here in a few days—like any witch ever forgot.

Our gifts recharged once each lunar cycle, absorbing into our skin from its swelling illumination. Seeing it used to bring up anticipation and excitement, signaling a great time of reconnection. Intimacy.

Now all I felt was dread.

If I skipped another full moon, another month would fly by without refilling my magical stores. Ticking away a few more after that spelled an even bigger problem...

Losing it completely.

Covens didn't want a magicless witch around, and I was already an outsider here. If I continued to let my magic wither, where would we go?

The mortal world?

Just the idea of that made me shiver.

Other than Lynx, I hadn't met anyone else from the coven. Hazel had said she would take me around when I got settled... which hadn't happened yet. I wasn't outgoing or assertive enough to insert myself into the goings on of the neighborhood. But the full moon was when they would traditionally gather and embrace its newest members.

At this point, that was probably when I'd end up meeting most of them.

I'd never been more out of touch with my gift or my body. They barely felt like *mine* anymore. The idea of recharging—especially after so many moons of dry spells—seemed daunting. I wouldn't even know where to begin if I wanted to. And there was still a huge part of me that was wary of inviting my gift back with everything that came along with it.

The magic, I missed. The gift I needed to recharge in order to access it—that was another thing all together.

I took a deep breath, trying to steady the nerves rioting through me. Atlas was going to be enough for me to handle in a few days with his...*Atlasness*. The fact that he'd be here during the full moon added a whole other layer of problems.

Luckily, Hazel would be back before then. She'd help me navigate what to do.

CHAPTER 3

LYNX

I dumped the second scoop of neon-yellow instant-energy elixir in my shaker cup, then glanced down at my watch. Thirty more minutes until my group training session. Double checking that my playlist was ready, I scanned my duffel bag to be sure I had everything I needed before walking out the door.

Last night was not what I'd expected. I'd gone over to meet the new neighbors, thinking I'd just hand off the casserole, quickly introduce myself, and then head home. Instead I'd invited myself in, hunting for any excuse to keep the conversation going—even offering to help Oakley unpack.

Anything to not have to leave without knowing more about *her*.

Checking my phone, I looked to see if she had texted. Unfortunately, aside from a bunch of work-related messages I'd have to decipher after class, there was nothing.

I passed by Café au Luna, giving a quick wave to Saros before heading toward the small outdoor pavilion set next to the Coven Community Center. I loved how convenient it was to get to work from the house, and even after a year of being in the neighborhood, I still had a steady stream of clients coming to classes.

Pulling out the portable weights, I swiped them through the air, releasing some magic from my fingertips before setting them down where they expanded to full size. As usual, once *they* saw me setting up, the Crescent Crew—as I coined them—made their way out of their homes. Did they just watch from their windows each day, waiting for me to arrive? They always came to class early, using it as an excuse to gossip and socialize.

There were five families that lived on Blessed Crescent, which looped behind the community center. Their homes were tall and imposing in comparison to the ones on Starry Night Lane. Each grew in size and luxury, their owners all an eclectic and tight-knit bunch.

Laurel Pierce was the first of the Crescent Crew to make it out this morning. She was wearing a black tank top, leggings, and baseball cap that she believed hid her Bluetooth earbuds during class. A river of pale-blue loneliness trailed her foot-steps. Her husband, Wade, was always away for work, and I was pretty sure it was the reason she attended bootcamp reli-giously while also training with me on the days class wasn't in session.

Every time I went to her house, I got to check out all the coolest Pierce Protections gadgets and security equipment on —and off—the market. Cameras were installed in every space inside and outside the house, which was both really cool and creepy as fuck. He was definitely an overly paranoid and cautious man, but in his line of business, I guess that came with the territory.

Cordelia and Brax Blossom headed down through the grass, passing the coffee truck and grabbing their usual bright-yellow shooters, dropping some cash on the counter without a second glance.

They'd made a small fortune through their BooTube channel, filming a weekly segment called Iris's Imaginarium where their daughter, whom the show was named after, would unbox and test out different magical toys. Parents making millions off their kids doing that shit appalled me, but apparently there was an audience for everything.

The Blossoms did *everything* together. They may have looked like the perfect suburban supernatural family but the sour scent of curdled milk that clogged my nose every time they were around told me otherwise.

"Ready to go?" Ace Irving called out to me as he came in for a high five. He and his wife, Heather, who was due with their sixth moon-blessed child, had moved to the neighborhood a few months ago after the previous owners left town.

"Always," I beamed, glad when he took a spot near the front, his energy waking me up with a hit of citrus. He was the hardest worker in class, and I could always count on him to help encourage the rest of the group.

"Hiya, Lynx," a sultry voice purred from behind me, self-confidence lapping over every syllable.

Please just go talk to anyone else.

"Hey, Aurora," I said nonchalantly, bringing the neon-yellow elixir to my lips in an attempt to avoid having to talk to her or witness the way she ogled me. Aurora Wells lived in the largest house on Blessed Crescent. It was easily over three times the size of mine.

Her husband, Fitzgerald, was Artemis's District Attorney, but with the ambition of a true politician. Aurora stayed home with their two teens, Atticus and Chrysanthemum, and ran the Nyx High School PTA and Athletic Boosters Club. Between her and Fitz, they were the epitome of a power couple in the supernatural community, always throwing elaborate neighborhood parties and hosting guests at their mansion.

She was also Starry Night Lane's coveness, the coven's matriarch—one of four within Celestial Haven. Which meant as much as I despised her attention, I had to play nice.

Snapping the shaker cup shut, I pointed to the rest of her *friends* that were already huddled together and chatting. "Why don't you go catch up? I'm just getting the last few things set up before class."

I bent down to reach into the duffel, not missing the leering tilt of her gaze following my ass. She wasn't even a little bit subtle about it, making my skin crawl. When she joined her friends, probably chatting about plans for the next neighborhood moonluck, I sighed with relief.

Slowly, the other residents of Starry Night Lane, where the ordinary witches like myself lived, trickled in. A few of their spouses dropped them off with a kiss before snagging coffee down at Luna's. Ivy Hendrix and Jade Fisher rolled their strollers to the back of the pavilion so they could stay by their babies while they worked out.

Forest Delta, who lived next door, jogged over in a pair of shorts and no shirt, as if it wasn't forty degrees and breezy at seven in the morning. He hopped around, never stopping his movement while he waited for class to start, probably because he was freezing—unless he couldn't feel the cold.

I was still trying to pinpoint his gift, among a handful of others' on the street.

The last few stragglers arrived and I told everyone we'd give it a few more minutes, craning my neck to see if any movement came from number 13. Maybe she was already out on a stroll? But when no foot traffic moved up or down Starry Night Lane, I called class to begin, trying not to let the disappointment set in that Oakley hadn't taken me up on my invitation to join.

"Keep those shoulders down, chests lifted," I directed while we warmed up with squats, feeling the release of tension when about half the group took the correction. For the few who didn't, I moved in front of them, demonstrating before rolling my shoulders back, a reminder to loosen them up and keep them down. "Make sure it's your legs that are doing the work. Your back will thank me tomorrow. Give me five more and then drop low and hold that deep position."

I made my way to the front of the group and bent low. "You should still be able to see those big toes out of the corner of your eyes. Now pulse." A handful of audible groans rang out, the best applause I could ask for. *Hate me today, love me tomorrow.* I always enjoyed the high I got pushing my clients and sensing those emotions alongside them as they overcame their struggles during the workout.

That's when I saw *her* walking swiftly down the sidewalk. She was dressed in leggings and a wine-colored zip-up jacket that hugged every muscle and curve of her body. Her auburn hair was tucked up in a bun. Hands gripped tightly around the handlebar of her stroller, dark-blue exhaustion swirled heavily around her mixed in with stress that clung to her with its gray static.

What was Oakley so worried about?

"How much longer?" Aurora asked, much too perkily, drawing back my attention.

I had no clue how long they'd been pulsing.

Whoops.

"Fifty more. Why don't you count us back?" I said to her, waving Oakley over. She stopped for a moment, startled and a bit confused, but then wheeled Aspen up the community center's walkway. "We just got started. Why don't you join us?"

"Umm. I wasn't planning on it," she said in a hurried voice, averting eye contact. Laced between the other emotions she was giving off, lust filtered through the air like a blissful cloud of powdered sugar. I took a deep inhale, smirking as it wafted in my direction.

"And?" I arched a brow.

Flirting? Really, Lynx?

Get it together.

Off limits.

Her wide chestnut eyes glanced down to Aspen, knuckles pale around the bar. I pointed over to the other strollers, their owners grabbing waters out of them and taking a sip, checking on their littles. "You won't be the only one. Why don't you park over there and you can tend to the witchling as you need?"

She picked up her phone and swiped at it a few times, lips frowning slightly. The gray static shifted into charcoal fumes. Disappointment. "You sure?"

"Yes!" I blurted, like a clumsy idiot.

Smooth, Lynx.

She was obviously hesitant and here I was pushing her, though wasn't that also my job as a personal trainer? I scanned over the class once more. The few who'd eased up on the exercise quickly returned to their previous effort under my gaze.

When my focus returned to Oakley, she gave a small smile that *cracked* through my chest like a whip. Then she walked over to the corner and parked her stroller alongside Jade and Ivy, my attention pinned to the tantalizing way she moved.

Fuck. Me.

"Alright, everyone, grab a resistance band and let's do

some bicep curls." I walked over, tossing an extra band in Oakley's direction. Cueing everyone, I tried to pay attention to the group and not this woman who, for whatever Goddess-known reason, hadn't left my mind since I'd dropped off the casserole.

She took the band and set up her form. The way she corrected her own posture before starting made it clear to me she was no stranger to working out. However, she remained in the back and didn't try to show off like *some* of the other group members who always wanted to be front and center. The only time she seemed to struggle was during our core work at the end when frustration curled off her curves with its pale-orange smoke.

I made my way around, correcting each person before finally kneeling next to her.

"Sorry, I'm just not as good at the core stuff anymore," Oakley said, cheeks tinged pink. The pale-orange smog thinned out, mixing with charcoal fumes.

"You're doing great," I encouraged, willing my palm to my side instead of reaching out to touch her like it so desperately wanted.

She lifted her head, as if trying to listen for Aspen, and I waved her back down, giving her a thumbs up while pretending to peek over the side of the stroller. I didn't need to. I could smell his lavender contentment from here. "He's doing great too, Momma."

Relief washed away some of the hesitation crowding her, filling me with a strange sense of pride. Clearing my throat, I went back to the front to lead the cooldown.

I couldn't help but listen in when Ivy turned to Oakley and pointed to the stroller behind her. "Is he your first?"

"Yeah."

"How old?"

"Nearly five months," she said, smiling, sending another *crack* beneath my ribs. The pink glow illuminating every line of her face when she talked about him could light up the night sky.

"Great job, gang!" I yelled, giving a few claps of approval. "Same time Friday for those of you who can make it."

The class dispersed to their smaller groups as they packed up to head home.

"Why don't you grab some coffee with us?" Ivy asked Oakley. "It's our post-workout treat."

She hesitated a moment before nodding. "I could definitely use some coffee."

When they strolled toward the coffee truck, I couldn't take my eyes off her, as if enchanted. But that was quickly stifled by the green pin-pricks emanating from her. There were so many warring emotions coursing through her at any given time that it sometimes made it hard to decipher exactly how she was feeling.

Maybe that's part of what intrigued me so much about her.

Off. Limits.

"Lynx," called the all too syrupy voice from behind me, this lust drenching me in its sickly sweet aroma. "Are we still on for my private session Friday?"

"Yes, Aurora. I'll be there at ten."

She gave me a smile that was more predatory than pleasant. "Great. I'm looking forward to it."

I wasn't.

CHAPTER 4

OAKLEY

My fingers fidgeted with the stroller bar as I stood in line with Ivy and Jade at Café au Luna. There was still no word from Hazel. I thought maybe she'd come home or text back while I was in class, desperate for the distraction, but nada. Nothing.

"How are you liking the neighborhood so far?" Ivy asked, picking up her witchling and rocking her back and forth in a football hold. Her little one was precious, wearing purple pajamas with tiny crescents stamped onto the fabric.

"It's really nice. I'm glad Hazel convinced us to move here with her."

"That's awesome. We were happy to finally see the house occupied again." Jade waved over to her husband who was coming down their driveway, toddler in tow. "It was such an eyesore before Hazel got it fixed up."

"She's pretty amazing like that." And she was. Sometimes I wondered if her Precognition helped her see the potential of the houses and people around her. She could always squeeze lemonade out of the sourest lemon.

I took my phone out from the cupholder on my stroller and sent off another message.

> I don't care how good the sex is, Haze. If I don't hear from you by tomorrow, I'm going to go into full-on panic mode.

Just as I went to slip it into the cupholder, it buzzed. *Finally, she'd gotten her phone charged or something.* Relief washed through me. I'd missed her so much these last few days.

LYNX

> Glad you came today!

While my heart sank at no update on Hazel, I couldn't stifle the flutter at my fingertips or the smile on my lips. I couldn't believe he'd already texted me. Class had basically just ended, and he was out of sight, but he'd thought to send *me* a message. Not that my intrigue would go anywhere but it was nice to pretend.

> I will definitely be back, but I may need to wait a week to recover.

My nonexistent stomach muscles and legs were cramping. I regretted everything about that workout...aside from the eye candy.

LYNX

> Haha

> Fair enough.

> How's unpacking?

I thought back to the cardboard city in my living room

and grimaced. There was no way I was going to make much of a dent in it before Atlas came into town.

Unproductive.

Hopefully Hazel would turn up before then—I needed her here so I wasn't on edge the whole visit more than usual. She understood why I'd made the decision to turn down his proposal and then, months later, finally come out to Washington.

I needed her.

LYNX

Why don't I come by tomorrow and help? I'm free in the afternoon.

The thought of being alone with Lynx for *hours* had heat creeping along my collarbone. My mind wandered to all sorts of scenarios I had no business contemplating. Not that it mattered. The last thing he'd want to deal with was a post-partum single mom with baggage.

Sure. Thanks!

Fortunately, Aspen would be there. No easier way to keep the naughty thoughts at bay than having an infant attached to you and likely being covered in spit-up and Goddess only knew what else.

Just text first so I can unlock the door for you in case Aspen is sleeping.

LYNX

Sure thing.

"Next," a rich yet gravelly voice called from the coffee truck's window. "What can I get started for you?"

His short black hair was shaved close to his head, a small crescent-shaped bald spot parallel to his right ear, and he wore a fitted evergreen Henley that I realized, when he handed me the menu, matched his eyes. His well-trimmed stubble framed the sharp angle of his umber jaw. "Do you know what you want?"

My throat went dry.

Mind blank.

What did he just ask me?

"Um. Sorry. Mom brain," I said, tittering awkwardly and fumbling over my words. "What did you just ask?"

"What would you like to drink?" he repeated slowly, eyes narrowing.

"Oh. Duh." *Of course, you idiot. He wants your order.* "This is my first time here."

"I know," he said, lifting the menu a bit higher until I took it in my hands.

I wasn't sure whether I should thank Hazel or chastise her when I saw her again for landing me in a neighborhood full of attractive yet unattainable men. It was like the worst version of window shopping.

Especially troublesome for a witch like me.

"What do you recommend?" I asked, overwhelmed, glancing back and forth between the selections and the specials written on the chalkboard attached to the truck's side.

"Hmm..." He thumbed over his stubble and looked as if he were sizing me up. "Do you like chocolate?"

"I do." The intensity of his gaze drew hot streaks across my skin, making my dusty gift crackle and fizzle beneath it.

Needy bitch.

"How about our midnight mocha? It has a splash of locally sourced raspberry syrup."

"Sounds perfect."

"Name for your order?"

"Midnight," I said instinctively, thinking about the coffee I'd soon be inhaling.

His brows furrowed. "It'll be ready in just a few, Midnight, if you don't mind waiting over there," he said, no humor in his tone, then gestured to the side of the truck where a handful of neighbors stood.

"Oakley. I meant—my name is Oakley." Apparently remembering my own name wasn't even possible anymore. The corner of his mouth peeled up a smidge, but he said nothing else as I paid for my drink. Then I moved off to the side with Jade and Ivy. Aspen started to get restless, so I took him out of the stroller and bounced with him, my quads raging at me.

"Ivy!" the brewista called out from the truck, and she headed over to grab her coffee. I kept an extra eye on her stroller where her daughter, Parker, slept soundly. There was just something so comforting about watching the rise and fall of the chest of a sleeping witchling. I nuzzled my nose into Aspen's hair, inhaling his perfect smell.

"Mmm... Leave it to Luna's to always have the best brews," Ivy said, taking a sip from her cup before placing it in her stroller. "Just another reason why we are the best neighborhood."

"I'm sure they are the reason the houses sell like hotcakes," I teased.

Ivy laughed alongside me. "We were so excited to find a house here. Had to get a plot with the great location and school system for the kids. We have three."

"It's absolutely beautiful. I understand why the area is so

sought after," I said, scanning the rows of black houses with their telltale doors and gilded numbers. "Have you lived here since the neighborhood opened up?"

"Yes. My husband, Bear, and I bought the house when it was just a slab of concrete. We live next door at 11."

"Jacob and I also moved in when the neighborhood was being built. There have been a handful of folks to come and go since then but a fair amount of the neighbors have been here from the beginning," Jade added. "We're just across the way at 12."

"That's amazing. I'm hoping we will be around for a while. I'm excited for Aspen to attend the schools here."

"Yes. Gardner Elementary is incredible. They even have a pre-K program that your little guy can go to when he turns four," Ivy said, smiling and tickling Aspen's tiny wrist.

"Midnight!"

I internally face-palmed myself on my way over to the truck's window to grab my mocha.

"Enjoy," the brewista said, the side of his lips curving up in a sensual half smile.

My face flushed.

"Thank you." I gripped the cardboard cup, bringing it up to my nose and inhaling the rich aroma of coffee, chocolate, and the tiniest hint of raspberry.

He didn't reply, already focused on brewing the next drink.

I looked down, shaking my head as I walked back toward my stroller to enjoy my coffee with the other moms. A moment later I realized I never even learned his name. How rude of me, considering he'd be integral to servicing my caffeine addiction once I stopped nursing. When had I gotten so awkward I couldn't even make it through an introduction?

"You witches ready for this month's blackout bash?" Ivy asked. I placed my coffee back in my stroller and sat down on a bench to feed Aspen under his thin blanket.

"I am. Last month's was so fun. Bummed you didn't make it," Jade replied, giving Ivy a frown. She used the other end of the bench, laying out a long mat and changing her daughter, Petunia, with the finesse of a pro. She was not a first-time mom—I could tell by how relaxed she was about everything.

And here I was just trying to not look awkward hunched over with a boob out under my makeshift nursing cover. One false move and every witch in the vicinity was going to get their *café au lait,* and not in a way that was appropriate for being neighborly.

I fussed about with the blanket, making sure everything was hidden from view.

"Yeah, Parker was a real gremlin, and I just needed to get some sleep once I got her down," said Ivy.

"I get that." Jade nodded.

"What is a blackout bash?" I asked, realizing I was still having a conversation with other adults where I could actually vocalize my question and get an answer.

"We have a neighborhood new moon get-together. Aurora started with the other wives on Blessed Crescent when she became coveness, and it's been slowly growing in size over the years. We usually meet up a few weeks after we've recharged under the full moon and do some casting as a coven," Ivy said, picking up Parker and lifting her shirt to nurse her without taking a beat, her breasts somehow magically discreet despite being in public.

Obviously another mom expert, Parker was perfectly placed and latched in no time. If I tried to do the same thing, Aspen would probably unlatch and turn to give every witch a wink for getting an eyeful of my now porn star-level boobs. Being a part of the DD club before pregnancy, I didn't need all the *extra* that most women saw as a perk of breastfeeding.

"Gives us some girls' night fun since the full moon usually brings about other sorts of activities..." she added with a smirk to Jade.

I swallowed hard.

"That's nice," I said, then gave myself a silent pat on the back for being able to follow the conversation.

"It is," Jade replied, walking back from throwing a dirty diaper in the trash can. "I'm sure you'll get an invite soon."

"I'm pretty much a homebody."

Plus, I'd need to recharge under the full moon to join in.

"Oh, if you're out here, you're not a homebody." Jade picked up her daughter and gave her a kiss. "We already have one of those."

"The one who lives in the last house?" I asked, pointing at 1 Blessed Crescent. "I saw her out yesterday, but I haven't met her yet."

"Don't be surprised if you never do," Ivy piped in. "That's more of a sighting than many of us have seen in weeks. Acacia doesn't really do the whole coven thing."

"I thought that came with the territory in Celestial Haven's witch-designated sections?"

The whole appeal for most supernaturals living in tight-knit communities like these was having others who understood the challenges that came with a magical life. The capital where I'd lived with Atlas was different, same as the city's supernatural sections, but these hidden oases boasted the collective.

"It is, but apparently when you have enough money to buy the big houses, they don't seem to care." Jade shrugged, taking a sip of her coffee.

"She was some important supernatural geologist who lived on the East Coast." Ivy let down her sweaty white hair before tying it back up in a messy knot atop her head. "Discovered something big there, apparently."

"What brought her to Washington?" Most people stayed on their coast. Moving wasn't very common, especially for those with a successful career like it sounded like this witch had.

Rummaging through her stroller, Ivy grabbed a pacifier and wiped it on her sweaty tank top before popping it into Parker's mouth. She made motherhood look effortless—something I both envied and admired. I was still trying to let go of the mom guilt of not being able to do a sterilization spell when Aspen's pacifier fell to the ground. Without my magic, it would only make me more tired, more drained...

Like I needed more of that.

Ivy gave me a smile before she continued on. "I believe it was for work, though no clue what she was doing because after her first moonluck, she never showed her face again. That was... How long ago, Jade?"

"No clue. Maybe two years?" Jade supplied, alternating guzzling down her post-workout elixir and sipping at the coffee she'd just ordered.

"Don't even worry about her though. You'll get to know all the others. Aurora makes it her business to include every witch in the neighborhood," Ivy said with a chuckle.

"Her husband is the DA, and she's the president of basically every neighborhood and school organization." Jade nodded over her shoulder to the massive house that stood out among the rest. It dwarfed the ones on our street and the cul-de-sac and was much larger than the others on Blessed Crescent. "You could say they are couple goals."

Modern glass windows encased the middle level, showcasing an extravagant living area and kitchen. An onyx table ran the length of the window spanning the dining room. It was beautiful and bold, fully on display for all the neighbors to see. The rest of the house was shrouded in glamorous black siding, only the deep-purple door and a silver star in a windowsill standing out against it.

I rested Aspen on my shoulder, rubbing his back until he elicited a satisfied burp. Then I strapped him back into his stroller, looking once more at the magnificent 5 Blessed Crescent. How nice it must be to have it all together. To live in such a picturesque home.

When we strolled back in the direction of our respective houses, I pulled out my phone, checking once again to see if Hazel or the police department had called or texted.

Nothing.

I heard a shout from behind me. "Midnight!"

Hopping out from Café au Luna's truck, the broody brewista strode toward the bench we had been sitting at, Aspen's muslin blanket laying there. I met him halfway with my stroller and watched while he folded it with near perfect precision. Then he came and handed it to me, our hands grazing before he recoiled. It was subtle, but still noticeable.

My breath caught at his reaction and I waited for some magic to hit me. Did he burn me with a flame ability? Or did he see that terrifying future for me like Hazel had?

"My name's Oakley." I laughed, still embarrassed from earlier and trying to play off the confusing moment.

"I know." He kept his gaze averted, the hand that had touched me held by the other.

"Well, thanks," I said, giving him a half smile, half grimace before pivoting and speed walking to catch up with Jade and Ivy.

Odd.

When I glanced back in his direction, he was watching me warily, but there was something akin to awe in the way his evergreen eyes sparkled. It was basically the opposite of being disgusted by me, like his reaction suggested, and I wondered what had happened when he touched me...

CHAPTER 5

OAKLEY

After a sleepless night followed by a lazy morning, I decided enough was enough.

Yes, Hazel had disappeared for days before, regaling me with her carnal exploits, but she'd never gone this long without responding to a text message. I didn't care how good this guy was, no one was that good.

No reason could outweigh my gut feeling that something wasn't right. Not when Hazel was usually attached to her phone in case she heard from clients. She kept portable chargers in her purse, and one in her car, at all times. Her phone was basically an extension of her.

Where the hell are you, Hazel?

I grabbed my phone off the coffee table and sent off the text I'd been avoiding. Maybe she'd make fun of me for over-reacting later, but I'd exhausted all the rationale my frazzled mind could muster.

About ten minutes later, a *ding* came from my phone, a text popping up on the screen that Lynx would be arriving in two minutes.

Shit. That was less of a warning than I thought he'd give me.

I unlocked the door and then carried Aspen over to the bouncer then scurried into the bathroom, quickly brushing down the loose wisps of hair before checking for any massive stains on my T-shirt.

Why was I even primping myself? Lynx didn't see me like that.

But, for whatever reason, I did it regardless.

The door groaned open, making me freeze. I took a deep breath, and with one last glance in the mirror, I headed out into the hallway. Lynx was in light-gray, *fitted* sweatpants with a Luna's coffee cup clutched in each hand, like an incubus sent to lure me to my ruin.

Settle down, Oakley. He's just being neighborly because he took pity on you.

No wonder he had so many private clients. One look at him in those and I was about to ask if he had any openings in his schedule, despite the fact that I could barely move after yesterday's class.

His eyes glinted, and I tried not to stare too intensely.

"You look great," he said, holding out one of the drinks, a smile playing across his lips.

I laughed, taking it from him as I attempted to play off the compliment. "The wonders of a stain-free shirt and dry shampoo."

Walking past me toward the counter, he looked around at the boxes stacked into their own little cardboard city lining the walls. He sipped his coffee, put it back on the countertop, and then clasped his hands together. "Okay, where did you want to start?"

The bedroom.

The dried-up particles of my gift crackled deep beneath

my skin, perking up at that thought. Tomorrow was the full moon, a chance for my magic to recharge through my gift, and it was begging to be used, to come out to *play*. It was so weird to be moon-blessed with an ability that affected every romantic relationship I'd ever had.

I was sleep and sex deprived, and my emotions were playing tricks on me. Tricks involving this beautiful man and the bulge I was trying to be casually unaware of. In my defense, it was hard not to notice in those sin-inducing sweatpants.

"I was thinking the kitchen. I've only gotten through about half the stuff I brought."

A *ding* came from my back pocket. "Sorry. Do you mind holding on just a second?"

He nodded over to a few boxes, and I waved him on to go ahead and start unpacking.

ATLAS

You sure it's not just Hazel being, well, Hazel?

She hasn't responded to a single text in three days.

ATLAS

...

I sat there, waiting for the tiny dots of torture to disappear and tell me whatever he was thinking.

ATLAS

That is strange for her. I'll get in touch with my contacts and see what I can find out.

Thank you.

"Sorry about that," I said, slipping the phone in my back pocket. At least I felt slightly more validated with my concern now. With innumerable resources at his disposal, Atlas could definitely get answers if there were any to get.

"Everything okay?" Lynx asked, eyeing me curiously. He was holding up the unpacking charm instructions Hazel had found and printed off, probably wondering why I hadn't used them.

"I'm sure it's fine," I said, mostly to reassure myself. "Hazel went on a date a few days ago and she's just probably having an amazing sexathon..." My face heated as the words came out of my mouth. "And while *that* obviously isn't something to worry about, I just haven't heard anything from her, which isn't like her. I'm hoping I'm being paranoid."

"I don't blame you for being worried. I would be too if it was my sister." He twisted the knob on the stove, lighting the burner beneath the cauldron there. "When was the last time you talked to her?"

"When she was getting ready to go on her date. She was picked up around eight, and I never saw her after that. Our location sharing app won't load either."

"Do you know who the date was with?"

"No. I've been a little distracted." I waved at Aspen in his bouncer. "Which I know makes me sound like a shit sister... I think she said it was a former client."

I tried not to let the guilt gnaw at me too deeply that I didn't have more answers.

"Well, that doesn't narrow it down too much, considering she's the only realtor for the neighborhood," he said, brow furrowed. Then he ran a hand through his sandy-blond hair.

"The more time that's passed without a response, the more concerned I get."

"I'm so sorry, Oakley," Lynx said, walking over and placing a hand on my shoulder. The weight in my chest lifted a bit, and I wondered if it was his sincerity or something *more* causing the instant relief. "If you want, I can get in touch with my contact at the Artemis Police Department later for you? I know some of the folks that work there."

"Thank you. That would be great." A few stray tears tracked down my cheek. "I'm sorry. I'm such a mess."

"You're just worried about your sister."

That only seemed to make the tears flow harder, finally feeling like the nagging voice at the back of my head was justified. He pulled me in for a hug—one that felt protective, soft and firm all at once. I couldn't remember the last time I had been held like this and sank into the unequivocal calm of being in his arms, sobbing into his navy-blue shirt.

When I lifted my head up, a wet patch of tears had been left behind. He ran the palm of his hand along my cheek, swiping away the droplets with the calloused pad of his thumb. My heart pounded, my gift crackling beneath my skin.

His jaw tightened.

Could he sense the effect he had on me?

Another *ding* from my phone snared me from his grasp. "Sorry, I have to check."

"Of course," he said, clearing his throat before stepping back, putting a body's worth of distance between us. Then he shoved a hand in his pocket, the other brushing through his hair while he scanned the room. "I'll get this charm situated so we can get you unpacked. Which cabinet has your casting supplies?"

I pointed to the last cabinet, and he went and opened it, finding its shelves stocked with jars of dried herbs and crystals. Grabbing my phone from its charger I took a deep breath, hoping it was Hazel making a fool of me for being worried.

ATLAS

Before you tell me you're fine, I already asked my assistant to rearrange things so I can come tomorrow. I'd really like to be there with you and Aspen.

I closed my eyes, willing away any frustration that bubbled in my chest. I didn't want him coming a day early, especially with Hazel gone—and around the full moon no less. On the other hand, I was glad to have someone who cared about us here, and I couldn't hold it against him wanting to spend some time with his son.

Okay.

ATLAS

Be there in the morning.

When I turned around, setting the phone down on the counter, Lynx was holding Aspen in one arm. He giggled with joy as Lynx bounced him and continued throwing ingredients into the cauldron.

My throat went dry.

If there was anything sexier than a gorgeous witch in gray sweats, it was a gorgeous witch in gray sweats holding my heart in his hands. Lynx genuinely seemed to enjoy hanging with him.

My fingertips prickled, begging to be used, but I swiftly stuffed them into the pockets of my joggers.

Lynx's gaze met mine, softening as he paused his bouncing. "I would ask if everything is okay but we both know it isn't."

The sharp tingles in my chest brought me back to my reality. "If you don't mind, I just need to feed him."

"Not at all. I can finish up this charm while you do."

Lynx handed him over, and Aspen's thin brows furrowed, as if disappointed. Then his body jerked excitedly, and he rooted around my shirt, leaving little circles of drool. Lynx politely averted his attention, shuffling over to the cauldron.

It was about to be a bit more awkward in here as I lifted up my shirt to shift my breast out. I looked around for Aspen's blanket but didn't see it, so I tried to strategically angle myself and the baggy shirt to be as modest as possible. "I feel bad taking away your afternoon. I'm sure there are more exciting things you could be doing than helping me unpack and hanging out with a witchling."

"You have trouble accepting help, don't you?" Lynx said, raising an eyebrow.

"I'm so used to being the one taking care of everyone else. It's strange to be on the receiving end of it." I watched Aspen's tiny fist unclench. "I like having my independence."

"Needing help doesn't make you less independent. It makes you normal. Well, as normal as any of us supernaturals can claim."

He was right...in theory. I was always helping others and I never minded. The only person I ever let take care of me was Hazel, and even that was a battle. Why was it so hard for me? I never felt burdened taking care of my friends or family but for some reason, the idea of *needing* help made me feel weak. Incapable.

It had taken Hazel months to convince me to move here with her, and even then, she never once mentioned wanting to help me. She probably knew I would have said no. One day she just showed up at my apartment saying one of the houses had become available, insisting it would be too big for her to live in alone. Plus, she argued that Atlas would approve of the neighborhood, knowing his son was growing up in one of the best supernatural school districts in the country.

It was time to switch Aspen over to the other breast, so I maneuvered him to my shoulder, patting his back and rubbing it until he let out a satisfied burp. Then I moved him to the other side.

The cauldron sizzled. Lynx waved his hands over it, yellow mist rising from its depths. They streaked toward the boxes, slowly opening them one at a time and setting the items in the correct room before disappearing the box and moving onto the next one below it.

"Sorry. I hope this doesn't make you uncomfortable," I said, fumbling around a bit. Nursing had gotten a lot easier since Aspen had turned about twelve weeks, but it had been a struggle off and on leading up to that. Even so, I still lacked the confidence of other mothers I saw who could do it with so much grace and not an ounce of spit-up on their wardrobe.

"Not at all." Lynx was still respectfully keeping his eyes on unpacking the boxes in the dining area. "Can't blame a witchling for wanting to be well fed." He smirked to himself. "Can I get you anything?"

"My coffee would be amazing."

"Of course." Doing a few more swishes of his fingers for his casting, more wisps of yellow mist swam out of the cauldron, this time heading for the nursery and my bedroom.

"You seem to have a knack with kids. Do you have any of your own?" I called over to him, trying to not be too loud as I noticed Aspen's lids flutter.

Thank Goddess. A nap was in sight.

"Nope. Though my sister has two and my brother has four, so I've had a lot of practice with my nieces and nephews.

Plus, kids are much easier for me to understand compared to adults."

"Do you get to see them a lot?" I asked.

He was quiet, the usual upturned quirk of his lips morphing into a straight line. "No. Unfortunately they don't live near here. They are in Oregon."

"Is that where you're from?" I felt Aspen pop off my breast and knew he was asleep. Peeking through the neckline of my shirt, I caught him dozing with his open mouth pulled up in a slight smile. I refastened my nursing bra, leaving him to nap in my lap, stroking his cheek with my thumb.

"Yeah, I grew up there." Lynx headed to the counter, taking a sip of his coffee before grabbing my cup to bring it over to me.

"I'm from there as well. Which community did you grow up in?"

"None actually." He shrugged. "I was raised in a mortal neighborhood. My mother is one. So are both my siblings."

"Oh, wow." It was very unusual for supernaturals to build families outside of the magically blessed community, even stranger to raise supernaturally gifted children there. Thanks to leaders stepping up into what eventually became our own secret government decades ago, we had found a way to live around mortals while still being under the radar for the most part. I'd never lived in the mortals' territory, but I did visit it plenty of times with Atlas when we both lived in the city. "What was that like?"

"Different, but I'm grateful for it in a lot of ways."

I eagerly took a sip of my coffee, enjoying the chocolate and hit of raspberry and the fact that it was warm. "A midnight mocha. How did you know?"

"Saros has an impressive memory."

Well, at least now I could stop calling him *the broody brewista.*

"I asked what you got yesterday, and he hooked me up." Lynx tapped his black to-go cup with mine before taking a sip. Café au Luna's crescent-shaped logo was stamped on the cardboard band around it. "When it comes down to it, mortals aren't that different. They have all the same fears and feelings we have."

"That's true. I'll admit, I haven't had a ton of experience with mortals. I was raised in Arbor Sanctum." Hidden within Oregon's mortal capital was our own, the epicenter of supernatural magic in a veiled, thriving metropolis.

"Oh, *the* Arbor Sanctum? My dad grew up there before he met my mom, and I worked in the capital for a while."

"Small world." I smiled and took another sip, savoring the warmth as it traveled down my throat. "A hot cup of coffee is very rare around here. By the time I remember I have some and get Aspen to sleep it's usually room temp if not frigid."

"Well, cold brew is very trendy," he replied with a wink that made my gift sizzle in all the right places.

I laughed, then quickly cut myself off, remembering that I still didn't know where Hazel was. How could I be laughing and enjoying anything without knowing for certain that she was all right?

"It's going to be okay, Oakley," Lynx said, grasping my hand gently. He ran his thumb back and forth, stroking the space between mine and my pointer finger. Lifting his hand, he traced along the line of my jaw until I looked up at his face. His sienna eyes shone with such gravity that all I wanted to do was drown in their glittering pools. My heart raced, gift prickling beneath my skin, parched and eager, driving me closer.

I bit my bottom lip, and his lashes dropped to the action, lips parting.

I hesitated. Could my gift be doing something to him?

No. That would be impossible. My ability had been dormant for months. Even if I could feel it layers deep, it didn't work. Couldn't work.

Which meant...

Nope. That was equally impossible. There was no way he was looking at me like I thought he was. It was a trick of the light. My desperate gift nudging me to act on my attraction to him. I was in a baggy shirt, covered in drool, with a messy bun and an underwireless bra. There was no way—no freaking way—he'd be interested.

The grating chirp of the phone ringing pierced the silence, pulling me back from my trance. Aspen gave an annoyed grunt from my lap. *You and me both.* I carefully lifted him, setting him in the bouncer where he curled into its embrace. Then I shuffled toward the phone.

As I drew closer, I realized its screen wasn't lit.

"Okay, I'll be there in thirty," Lynx said from behind me, sounding frustrated with whoever was on the other line.

When he hung up, he helped me put everything that had been unpacked into its rightful place in the kitchen. Every so often, when our bodies grazed each other or our eyes caught for a moment, the remnants of my gift would flit up beneath the surface of my skin, desperate to latch onto something. Someone.

This witch was going to be a problem.

"I am so sorry I have to run for a bit, but I'll be back in a few hours to help you get more done."

"You don't have t—"

"I *want* to. We've got the living room, and I saw the nursery needs tackling. Got to give this wildling a cave to call his own." Lynx gave a quick smile toward Aspen, who was still asleep. "In the meantime, I'll go ahead and shoot that text over to my contact at the police department and see if he knows anything."

"Thanks."

With a nod, he opened the door and shut it gingerly behind him.

My Desire sizzled impatiently, all *too eager* for his return.

CHAPTER 6

OAKLEY

A few hours later, Lynx returned, toting a small paper bag. "I come bearing treats."

My mouth watered, about a fifty-fifty ratio on the cause being the man in front of me and whatever was in the bag wafting of flour, butter, and all things sugary and good. "Thanks! Smells delicious."

He stepped inside, moving fluidly toward the cabinets like he was right at home. Taking out a plate and setting it on the counter, he snapped his fingers, the assortment of muffins and cookies piling up on it. "Go ahead and grab something to eat. I know it's rare to have a moment to yourself when you're a new mom, I hear it all the time from Ivy and Jade." His eyes scanned the rooms, as if taking inventory of the things we still needed to do. "I recommend the pumpkin streusel muffins with cinnamon cream cheese filling. You'll never find anything else like them."

Two of them sat side by side on the plate, and I quickly scurried over and grabbed one, along with a paper towel. Sitting on the barstool, I brought the treat to my lips, inhaling the sweet spices before taking a bite. The perfect amount of cinnamon cream cheese oozed from the fluffy pumpkin muffin. With buttery, crumbly streusel on top, it coalesced in a decadent blend of flavors and textures.

I moaned, unable to control myself.

"Right?" He smirked, lifting a framed photo of Hazel and I from when we were teenagers. Holding it up, he looked at me for direction. I pointed to the wall across from the couch and he took it over, placing the photo in various positions until I nodded in approval. Then he released some magic, adhering it to the onyx wall.

Watching him move so effortlessly to get all this done really made me miss having my magic. It was always on my mind: whether or not to summon it back the coming full moon. It was hard to know how many more I'd have left before it was decided for me. Maybe one to two.

I took another bite, then swallowed it down, suddenly full despite not having eaten much all day. "This could be the best muffin I've ever tasted. Where did you get them?"

"I made them." His chest puffed up with pride. I raised my eyebrows in surprise. "You've got a little..." He pointed to my lips, and I lapped up a few stray crumbs, not wanting to waste a morsel.

"Better?"

"Almost. May I?" His brown eyes twinkled in the dim light. I froze, my head the only thing moving as I nodded silently. He brushed his thumb along my lower lip, and I jolted at the unexpected static prickle, starved for more.

A wail echoed off the walls, snatching my attention to the open bedroom door. Aspen was up.

Were we about to kiss, or did I just imagine it in my sleep-deprived state?

"Mind if I grab him?" Lynx asked, clearing his throat and hiking his thumb toward the room.

"Umm. Sure?"

He headed to the nursery, and I tried not to drool over the ripple of his back muscles or the way the gray sweats hugged the biteable globes of his ass. Pausing in front of the slightly cracked door, he rested his hand on it, a smile curving his profile before he slipped inside.

A series of shushes quieted Aspen's crying and replaced them with contented coos as Lynx walked back out, a small bounce to his step. Aspen clutched his chest. "Why don't I finish up out here with him while you enjoy that muffin and get started putting things where you want them in the nursery?"

My chest ached seeing how at ease they were around each other in such a short time.

He's just being neighborly.

I whispered the words to myself like a spell to calm down my overactive libido. He could tell I was struggling, probably from the bags under my eyes, the cityscape of boxes in my house, and not having Hazel here right now. I was obviously seeing things that weren't really there, the ghost of my Desire taunting me in its attempt to revive my magic.

Lynx's hand caressed my shoulder, and a sense of calm washed through me like the ocean spreading over the shore.

How was that possible? A second ago I was spiraling—

He gave me a light squeeze. "Empath-blessed."

There were a multitude of Goddess-given gifts that witches could possess, and even within a specialty, there were many differentiations.

"How does your gift work?" I asked, quickly adding, "You don't have to tell me if you don't want. I don't mean to pry."

Some witches were very touchy about their gifts. I was one of them, but it didn't make me any less curious.

"My Empathy allows me to sense emotions." His chin

dipped to Aspen, whose eyes were darting from him, to me, to around the room. "Like right now, this little guy is feeling mischievous."

"But just then, when you touched me"—a slight twinge of heat rippled across my cheeks—"my emotions settled almost instantly."

"I can shift emotions, mostly when I'm touching someone. It's not something I do often because emotions are meant to be experienced and I don't want to do anything detrimental, but there are times I can't resist."

He lifted his hand, as if to touch me again, before clenching it and then rubbing Aspen's back. "I can't make someone feel anything they don't already have within them, I can just...turn the volume up or dial it back. Your emotions were spinning out, so I gave them a short-term sanctuary."

"Oh." Now my chest was flushed too, embarrassment creeping through at his acutely accurate assessment.

"I'm sorry, Oakley," he rasped, eyes falling like stars plummeting from the sky. "I shouldn't have done that, especially since you didn't know about my Empathy."

"I appreciate it anyway. My mind has been doing that a lot lately, and you were only trying to help."

The stars in his eyes returned, blinking back at me. "Thanks for not being mad."

"Don't mention it." I just hoped he didn't expect me to tell him what my gift was in return.

He nodded toward the nursery. "I'll be there in a bit."

"Sounds great," I agreed, heading into Aspen's room.

Phew! I was grateful for the subject change before things got awkward. Though I had a feeling he could possibly sense my Desire, I was too mortified to really contemplate it much.

⊂⊂⊂⊛⊃⊃⊃

THREE HOURS LATER, THE CRIB HAD BEEN ASSEMBLED AND ALMOST everything in the nursery was set in its place. Aspen was passed out in his baby swing, rocking back and forth, the classic instrumental of "Paint It Black" crooning from the speaker. A set of small pine trees and moons hovered at varying lengths, circling above him.

"Let me go grab the stuff from the dryer." I headed out into the hallway to load up the laundry basket full of clean clothes and linens.

When I walked back toward the nursery, Lynx was sitting on his knees, watching Aspen sleep. The corner of his lip quirked upward, as if in awe. My chest ached at the sight.

"He's so precious," Lynx whispered, not taking his gaze away but startling me nonetheless with the fact he knew I was watching. "If you don't mind me asking, are you and his father..." He tilted his head, not fully finishing the question but not really needing to.

"No, we aren't together," I replied, placing the basket on the floor between us and taking out the crib sheet. Lynx stretched it over the corners of the mattress, not taking his eyes away from me. I began folding up a pair of jammies with little painted skulls and vines in a sweet shade of sage on them. "We were. He actually proposed when I was pregnant."

"But?"

"It just wouldn't have worked."

Couldn't have.

The cost wasn't worth it.

"I see." He remained quiet a few moments, as if processing what I'd said.

Then, kneeling next to me, he grabbed some more of Aspen's clothes, holding up a tiny sock and digging through the basket for its twin. We worked in silence, folding up play-suits and onesies before Lynx handed them off to me in piles to place in the sable dresser set against the wall, copper foxes jutting out from its drawers for handles.

Lynx's phone lit up, and he grabbed it, quickly swiping to see the message. "I texted my contact at APD after I left here. He's filing a missing person report and will keep us updated."

A pebble's worth of weight lifted off my chest. "Thank you so much. I know I probably sound crazy."

"Not at all. You just sound concerned," he replied, typing into his phone before slipping it back into his pocket.

I grabbed my own phone, checking for any messages. 12:04 a.m. shown on the lock screen. "I can't believe I kept you here so long. I'm sorry."

"Don't be," Lynx replied, standing up. "I'm glad we were able to make a good dent in things. If you need more help over the weekend, I can come by tomorrow or Sunday after the full moon."

"That won't be necessary." My gut clenched at the reminder that Atlas would be here and that I'd be spending the weekend working especially hard to avoid my gift's lusty lunar demands.

"You okay?" Lynx asked.

I forgot he could sense my emotions. That was going to take some getting used to. Well, if we spent more time together. Not saying I wanted that, or that it would happen but—

"You're spinning out again," he said, lips pursed and hands clenching his gray sweats, leaving even less to the imagination.

Woof.

"You didn't touch me this time," I replied too quickly.

"Doesn't mean I didn't want to." His eyes darkened, voice so low and husky I could have sworn it licked me right in my most magical spot. I took a step closer and drifted my free hand along his jaw, half convinced this wasn't real.

But he didn't pull away.

Aspen's shrill wail sliced through the moment, demanding little demon that he was. Blinking a few times, Lynx pressed a lingering kiss to my forehead and started toward the door. "I better get back home. Goodnight, you two."

"Goodnight," I replied, still trying to catch my breath.

Grabbing Aspen from the swing, I took him to the rocking chair, my mind now racing with even more than it had before. While I desperately craved to see what would have happened without his untimely interruption, I was grateful for it. If by some insane stroke of luck Lynx *was* interested in me, he still had no idea of the consequences involved if I ever gave in.

CHAPTER 7

OAKLEY

I watched Aspen snooze in his crib, enjoying his first night in the nursery. Staring at the staticky green-and-black image on the baby monitor screen made dozing off near impossible. Every time my eyelids fluttered closed, they'd inevitably pop open to make sure he was okay. Between that, thinking about Hazel still being MIA, Atlas's arrival, and my budding attraction to Lynx, my mind whirred in every direction.

Sleep wasn't happening tonight. What else was new?

Rolling out of bed, I tiptoed to the corner of my room, gently taking out some supplies from the partially unpacked box. Grabbing the tasseled throw off my bed, I laid it on the ground, setting out the various crystals and herbs in front of me before pulling out my mortar and pestle.

Just like my gift, they'd become dusty.

I'd had to shut down my online shop. Temporarily. Well, at least I'd planned for it to be temporary while I was on maternity leave for a few months prior to and after Aspen's arrival.

Now almost eight months after fulfilling my last orders, people probably didn't even care about Full Moon Emporium anymore. I'd stopped posting on social media because who wanted love potions, sex and fertility tinctures, and spell-infused crystals from a magicless postpartum witch? My feed was full of sexy lingerie and alluring boudoir shots peppered with products. The last shot was a cropped image of my belly about six months pregnant, strands of crystals draped over its swell with Atlas's hands strategically beneath it.

Where was that confident witch now?

How was I supposed to feel sexy?

Desirable.

It was as if I was staring at someone else in that photo, as I stood here in a stretchy bra stuffed with nursing pads that was held together by snaps under a shabby sweatshirt that, if it didn't have stains on it already, would within the next hour.

I shook away the shiver creeping up my spine, walking over and grabbing the monitor to lay it next to me while I inventoried my supplies.

Rubbing my face with the palms of my hands, I opened up the small jars of herbs, sniffing each one to see if it was still good enough to use and setting aside the ones I'd need to eventually replenish if I opened the shop back up.

If.

There were still a few days left until the full moon. In order to reopen, to offer anything, I'd have to recharge my magic. Which meant feeding my Desire. Which meant...

A pit lodged in my stomach at the thought before I flicked it away. That was a problem for future Oakley. Today's Oakley had enough shit to tackle.

⟨⟨⟨●⟩⟩⟩

I was already up and dressed when the black SUV rolled into the driveway the next morning, its copper crest containing symbols for each of the supernaturals circling its hood: a pair of wings, a paw print, a spell book, a shell, and a heart.

A watercolor emerald tunic was strategically draped over my stained tank top, paired with some leggings and leather combat boots. I'd dressed Aspen in a black playsuit, tiny constellations scattered across it, but he'd managed to pass out right before his father was due to arrive. Of course.

From the moment Atlas stepped out of the car, I had to continually remind myself why I had turned down his proposal. His aqua eyes glinted like they always had as he combed back his near black hair with his palm. He walked up the driveway slowly, adjusting the collar of his black button-down.

He was handsome, his power spreading from him like an energetic beacon, catching the gaze of every witch who was out. Some of the neighbors were even peeking over their fences, and a few gawked out their kitchen windows. Their curiosity made me uneasy, and I shifted uncomfortably before waving him inside, away from prying eyes.

The last thing I needed was to give the neighborhood something to talk about.

"Great to see you," he said, with that grin that nearly had me falling into old habits: pulling him in for an all-consuming kiss, pushing him against the wall, exploring each other in every way while my Desire drove him wild.

"You too." I croaked out, my resolve already weakening at the nearness of him.

His chest brushed against me in the doorframe, and the moment our bodies touched, I was transported: watching us lying on the grass under the full moon after one of our monthly midnight picnics—the few times I would get Atlas all to myself with his busy schedule. Half-empty jars of moonshine sat off to the side, along with picked-over plates filled with cheeses, fruits, and breads. My hands threaded through his hair, tugging as he traced crescents up my thigh with his tongue before licking up my center. Hips bucking to meet him, I jerked against his—

"Stop that," I said, my underwear becoming damp at the mirage he'd created and the memories it brought up.

"Stop what?" He chuckled with amusement, looking down at my crossed legs, his vision vanishing just as quickly as it'd appeared.

Fucker.

"You know what." He shifted toward me, but I took a step back before he could touch me again, accidental or otherwise.

"You used to enjoy when I pulled out our little time capsule."

"I did." I crossed my arms. "But please don't make this any harder."

"If I remember correctly, you also enjoyed when I made things harder." He sighed. "In fact, I'm pretty sure that little highlight kicked off the Goddess-blessed night of Aspen's conception."

"Yes." It was all I could manage to choke out. My eyes darted to the nursery. Too bad there wasn't a spell to make a baby cry when you needed an escape.

Atlas had a rare gift. *Illusion.* If he could imagine it, he could manifest it in your mind. As long as he was touching you. A visionary of sorts. It would feel real, but only temporarily. And he was using it to take me down memory fucking lane.

It had a fun side, which sometimes equaled mind-blowing sex. We could be on a beach somewhere without the messy sand clean up. Or spread across a paint-covered tabletop in a cabin. Or in a stadium with crowds of people watching—

A cry rang out from the other room. *Thank Goddess.* Aspen was awake. At least this would give Atlas a distraction so I didn't have to be taunted with the reimagined highlight reel of what I had given up when I'd rejected his proposal and broke things off with him months ago.

He didn't even fight me on moving across state lines with our son. An argument he could have easily made—and probably won, knowing his connections.

It would have been better to hate him. But I didn't. I knew this witch loved both of us. Would do anything for us.

But I needed to keep my distance.

"Have you heard anything on Hazel?" I asked, changing Aspen in the nursery.

Please tell me you have.

"I should be hearing from my contacts in the next forty-eight hours. I'll let you know when I do, especially since I'll be here anyway."

Like I need the reminder.

"Thank you." I hadn't wanted to bring him into this, but I was desperate. Atlas had influence and ability to get answers in the supernatural community, and I needed to know she was okay. "You know Hazel—she might get a little wild and let loose, but this isn't like her."

"You're right. It isn't." He had been close with Hazel when we were together. Before her premonition. Before he proposed.

And when I'd said no, she'd understood. She had seen why, after all.

"Hopefully my people will have some leads," he continued, arms outstretched for his son, grinning as he took him from me.

Looking at him with Aspen, my heart swelled. Just one prick of regret and it would burst.

I pushed those thoughts away, savoring the moment. He tossed him into the air, eliciting an excited squeal from our son before swaying back and forth with him. Aspen's eyes lit in wonder, making me curious what Atlas could be showing him.

"That hike we went on a few years ago and all its wildlife," he said, answering my mental question with a smirk. "Trying to show him some of Oregon for whenever you both come out to visit."

"Us, come to Oregon?" The thought hadn't even crossed my mind since I'd been so focused on the move and then Hazel...and surviving on minimal sleep.

"I know you two are still getting settled." His eyes drifted around to the mostly unpacked house, seemingly surprised. He'd probably assumed he'd be helping me get things together this weekend, but thanks to Lynx's assistance and sleepless nights, I'd gotten the majority of it done. "I was hoping maybe you'd make it out there in the next few months. I would fly you both out, of course. Hazel too, if she wanted. My family would love to see Aspen, and I wouldn't dream of separating you two with him being so young."

That seemed fair. He was just wanting Aspen to get to know the rest of his lineage. One that was integral to the supernatural community. Plus, he'd taken me into consideration. "Once things are settled and I know Hazel is okay, I think that sounds very nice."

"Why don't I grab us some coffee? You guys can bond a bit without me," I added, needing some Atlas-free air.

"You sure?" He seemed surprised, but a hint of pride lingered in his tone.

"Of course. Let me feed him before I go, otherwise he'll be a hangry little witch."

"Well, we wouldn't want that." He chuckled.

I slipped my tunic to the side and unclasped my nursing tank and its attached bra, nodding over to the burp cloth. I thought about covering up, but it was just a feeding, and this man saw me birth our child, for Goddess's sake. I looked down at my chest. "I know, terrifying right?"

"I don't know about *terrifying*," he said, expression turning curious. His eyes went slightly wide when he saw my breast, half-assing his attempt to avert his gaze. "They are a little more *intense* than I remember..."

"They look like they could have their own sideshow at the carnival," I said, snapping my fingers in front of his eyes to get his attention back from my over-engorged boobs.

"Don't be ridiculous. Your tits will always be the main attraction."

My face and chest heated, any sort of clever retort dissolving on my tongue.

"I get what you mean, though." He chuckled once more before regaining his composure. "And I'm sorry. I didn't mean to make you uncomfortable. Honestly, I am just always in awe watching you feed our son."

"It's okay. I know things are kind of strange between us." I shrugged, the prior heat dissipating into gentle warmth.

"It doesn't have to be. I feel like there's so much I'm missing out on... I miss you both. I miss us." His aqua eyes shone brighter than usual, sending me a silent plea.

"Atlas..." How could I explain why I couldn't be with him without hurting him? Based on something that hadn't even happened yet. *The future isn't set in stone*, he'd argue. And I couldn't. I just couldn't go there with him right now. My mind was too tired, and my magic was too depleted.

Atlas's phone buzzed in his pocket.

"Let me take this, it could be news on Hazel," he said, heading out to the porch, effectively ending the conversation.

Blessed timing.

CHAPTER 8

LYNX

T he door opened the moment I stepped on the welcome mat, just as creepy as the first time I came here a few weeks after we'd moved into the neighborhood. Aurora had been the first one to rally the rest of the coven to my classes. Initially, I'd been grateful for the coveness's help, wanting to fit in and find my footing after relocating to Celestial Haven.

After a few private sessions, I quickly changed my mind. What most of the neighborhood wives envied when it came to Aurora Wells was a façade. I'd seen the real power couple of Blessed Crescent. After a very awkward encounter where I learned firsthand that Fitz had a thing for watching his wife with other witches, I had made it clear that while I loved that they were such an open couple, I was not interested.

It wasn't that I had anything against group activities or sharing. I had no interest in joining *them*. Just because you were into something, which I suspected they knew about me for whatever reason, didn't mean you were into it with every witch. And I was not about to become the third for their sexual escapades.

Not then.

Not now.

Not ever.

I'd seen more than I wanted anyway. Their glass-encased house overlooked ours, and they rarely turned the privacy setting on for their windows, so I'd witnessed them fucking numerous times. What took place when they actually wanted to be unseen?

"I'm upstairs," Aurora heaved, sounding like she had already started her workout without me, as usual. Sometimes I wondered if she even took a break after class before hopping on her spin bike or dreadmill.

I climbed the first staircase, heading down the hallway to the sounds of the *swish, swish, swish* of the dreadmill's rubber mixed with the pounding of her feet. When I got inside the room, she was busy running, eyes glued to the large screen in front of her, an almost life-size simulation of a forest.

"Which one is this?" I asked, genuinely curious what she'd picked. It was dusk and changing directions so quickly that nausea churned my gut from watching the camera angles shift.

"10k mating moon hunt," she heaved out at the same cadence she ran. "I normally choose the pack alpha but was a little more tired than usual, so I went with the beta."

She began to slow, the wolf getting closer and closer until she pressed pause right as it lunged at her.

"Have you ever seen a mating moon hunt?" she asked, arching a brow before she toweled off her face. "They're brutal beasts, but there's nothing like it to get you in the mood."

"I haven't," I replied, keeping my tone as clipped as possible, wanting a new subject.

"Their alphas scent their mates in the pack each new

moon and have only that night to find them and claim them. Then they have two weeks to court their prospective mate before they choose to accept or reject the bond." She chugged down a tube of bright-pink elixir, no doubt concocted in her Brewrig. "I would even call it beautiful to watch if it wasn't so Goddess-damned bloody. I've never seen a bond-claiming ceremony on a full moon, though... I'm usually busy with... other things."

The air thickened between us, like molasses. Lust. I grabbed my phone, swiping to my playlist and syncing it to the Bluetooth speaker so we could get to work.

"You should check it out sometime. They usually run around two in the morning."

"Good to know," I said, trying to ignore her as I flipped through my notebook to the page with today's session plans. Moving to her weight rack, I set out some stations, quickly walking through each thing she would need to do for the circuit. "I'll be right back, just need to use the restroom. I've set the timer for five minutes to do as many rounds as you can, so make sure to keep track."

I flashed her a half-assed smile and then dashed out to the hallway. Heading into the bathroom, I pulled my phone out, eyes darting around to see if I was alone. With all the cameras nestled in corners, I felt like I was always being watched. Were they kinky enough to extend their top-of-the-line home system into the bathroom?

I hoped the fuck not.

Though nothing seemed off the menu for those two.

Getting down to business, I quickly scanned the message from headquarters.

UNKNOWN

New Moon

Fuck.

Through the wall, I could hear Fitz schmoozing on the other line, unable to make out more than a scramble of words. I washed my hands and pressed my ear against the wall.

"This doesn't look good. We've worked too hard for word to get out about these disappearances," mumbled Fitz, presumably into the phone as I listened in. "Look into it but keep a low profile."

With the Wellses' power-couple status and Fitz being the District Attorney, coming here each week was the best shot I had to get more intel on Starry Night Lane's coven. I'd spent a year gritting my teeth and smiling through personal training, doing what I could to see how much they knew. This finally confirmed what I'd hoped wasn't true: that Fitz and whoever he was talking to already knew about the disappearances and were investigating it, albeit discreetly.

The alarm from my phone went off, and Fitz's discussion halted.

Shit. I needed to get back to Aurora.

Just another glorious day on the job.

The one thing getting me through the next shitty hour of my life was mulling over what I'd do the next time I was alone with the new intriguing addition to Starry Night Lane. Someone close to our most recent victim, Hazel Brooks.

CHAPTER 9

OAKLEY

As soon as Aspen had finished feeding and I'd learned the call wasn't Hazel-related, I left the house, beelining for Luna's. I needed a few moments to think by myself, not within arm's length of Atlas's overly immersive touch.

Since Aspen's birth, I had been able to keep my distance for the most part, figuring it would be easier once we moved away. But with him here, my resolve was wavering with every memory of us together he could reproduce and every word that alluded to wanting us to be together as a family.

But I couldn't tell him what I knew.

Atlas didn't subscribe to premonitions. He would refuse to accept that if we stayed together, he'd seal his fate. A fate that ended with his blood on my hands.

I shook away the image before it wandered back into my mind.

The autumn wind whipped into me, the scent of withered leaves, pine, and sage tickling my nose. Looking around the neighborhood, I noticed how quiet it got here in the afternoon. It was basically a ghost town, aside from our elderly next-door neighbor who sat outside knitting a bright-mustard sweater.

Pulling out my phone, I called the Artemis Police Department and left them a voice message to get an update on the case. Then I sat on the bench next to the coffee truck, trying to collect my thoughts.

I took a deep breath, reminding myself that Atlas was here to help and to see his son. He just happened to be here during the full moon. That didn't mean he expected to win me back, even if only for a night.

...Did it?

Shit.

To recharge my gift would mean using it beneath the full moon's light, its swelling radiance refueling my depleted stores. What that entailed was slightly different for each witch, depending on their gift. But with my Desire, it felt especially nerve-wracking with Atlas here, whether I involved him in its *use* or not.

Beyond that, while I missed my magic, I wasn't even sure I wanted my moon-blessed ability back—

The sound of a throat clearing grabbed my attention. A black cardboard cup was poised in front of me, the smell of cinnamon wafting in the steam seeping from its lid.

"You okay, Midnight?"

I trailed my gaze up toward that deep voice, drinking in the fitted navy thermal with rich brown skin peeking out at the chest, along with part of a tattoo. A constellation, maybe? I wondered what the rest of it looked like.

"I'm fine," I lied.

He passed the cup in his hand to me. "It's not your usual, but it's more comforting. Apple pie latte. Looked like you could use it."

"Thanks."

I reached for my wristlet to take out some money, but Saros moved his hand to stop me, hovering it over mine. "It's on the house."

"You don't have to do that."

His mouth snagged into a frown for a split second. "I know."

"Thanks," I said and inhaled the spices coming from the warm cup clutched between my hands. "What's in it?"

"It's the Starry Night Weekly Special. Just a bunch of apple pie spices and brown sugar with bourbon maple syrup thrown in, but don't tell anyone—it's supposed to be a secret family recipe," he said, the corner of his mouth lifting up in a smirk, exposing a sliver of pearly white teeth.

Blowing on the steam and staring back at the house, I took a small sip, enjoying its warmth surging down my throat. I missed Hazel so much. Hopefully, I was just overreacting, but at least now Atlas and Lynx were helping me, and neither of them had made me feel ridiculous for worrying.

"Want to talk about it?"

I took a generous swig, wishing the bourbon maple syrup actually had some kick to it. "Just needed a mental moment."

"A mental moment?"

"You know," I said, placing the cup down on the bench and leaning forward with my elbows on my knees, clasping my hands together, "a few minutes to take a breather. Clear your head. Let the thoughts stop swirling and settle."

"Ahh, I see." He sat next to me, clasping his own hands together. "Where's that little twinkle of your eye?"

"He's being watched at the house," I replied, more defensive than I'd intended. *Did he think I'd leave him alone?* "Why?"

"I'm just not used to seeing you without him." His evergreen eyes locked with mine, sincerity softening their crinkled edges.

"We are a package deal at this point." I sighed, sipping my coffee again and savoring the blend of cinnamon and spices with the subtle bourbon undercurrent.

"Nothing wrong with that." He gave a slight smile that stopped just at his gaze, a tinge of ruefulness laced in it. For whatever reason, I wished I knew the cause. There was something about him that came off equally bitter and sweet, like the coffees he served. His very presence made me want to scoot closer and scurry away. I couldn't put my finger on it, but it was as if my Desire—as rusty as it was right now—was both magnetized and repelled by him.

"I better get back home," I said, lifting the cup toward him with a pleasant smile, the best one I could muster, considering everything going on in my head. "Thanks again for the coffee."

"Of course." He nodded, evergreens narrowed on me. But then he turned and strolled back toward the coffee truck.

What was his gift, and why did my gut pull me in two very different directions about him?

It was a sensation I'd never experienced. But to be fair, most of my recent sensations when it came to what was left of my dried-up magic were unusual. This could easily just be another side effect.

Either way, right now I had enough on my plate to contend with, like an unaccounted for sister and an ex who was currently in our house about to stay the night.

CHAPTER 10

OAKLEY

"Hey, beautiful momma," Atlas said, waving Aspen's tiny hand at me when I walked through the door. He beamed down at the miniature version of himself. "What kind of coffee did you grab for me?"

His attention went straight to my empty hands.

Shit. "I'm sorry. I was a bit distracted."

He sighed. "Well, I guess I can just walk over with Aspen and get some."

"They're already closed for the day," I spat out quickly, almost defensively, though I didn't know why. "I can whip up something for you here."

Atlas's eyes narrowed into slits, but before he could say anything, a tiny fist gripped his shirt. Aspen giggled as his father nuzzled their noses together and tickled the rolls climbing up his chunky thighs.

Hunting through the cabinets, I grabbed some coffee and began to brew it. Then I pulled out some oat milk, maple syrup, and lavender, mixing it together into a homemade creamer. Atlas watched each step, sharpened gaze softening when I handed him the pumpkin-shaped mug. One he had gotten for me the first time we'd met at Phil's Pumpkin Patch.

"I did hear from my contacts, and they are looking into Hazel's disappearance," he said before inhaling the relaxing scent of lavender then took a sip. "They are trying to work backward as to her whereabouts that night. Do you happen to have your phone with the messages you sent? It would help us flesh out the timeline of when you last spoke and when you stopped hearing from her."

"Do you really need to see them?"

"Is there something incriminating about them?"

"Not in the way you're thinking."

He transferred Aspen onto his hip, holding out his free hand. Waiting.

"Fine," I said, pulling out my phone and handing it to him.

He scrolled up a few moments and smirked, then his brows furrowed. *Oh fuck.* Of course he saw *those* messages.

"Ribbed tongue, eh? That would be something. I think the incubi over on Eclipse Street have that feature." He chuckled, and my face heated.

"Not going to comment on the other message?"

"Oaks," he said, handing me back my phone. I took it, stepping quickly out of his reach, not in the mood for more illusions or trips down memory lane. He averted his gaze, looking at Aspen and tickling his tummy, eliciting giggles that shook his entire tiny body. "What is there to say? You know what I want. And yes, I'll happily swoop in and play hero any day when it comes to you and Aspen."

"I—"

"Look, I'm not going to push anything."

Aspen latched onto his shirt, leaving a messy trail of drool. At least it wasn't just me that he left his mark on, though I didn't see any spit-up stains gracing his button-up.

"Here," I said, taking Aspen and grabbing my nursing pillow with the other hand before sitting on the couch. It hadn't been that long since he'd last eaten, but maybe he was cluster feeding. I unlocked my home screen and tapped on the app that would tell me about all the developmental milestones to expect right now. *Yep.* A growth spurt was right on target.

When I pointed to the opposite side of the couch, Atlas moved to join me but then halted, pulling out his phone instead. "Why don't I get some dinner for us? You still like sushi?"

"Love it."

"Great. I'll put in the order." He tapped into his phone, bringing it to his ear, the faint ringing echoing through the room. Aspen continued to feed as I stroked his little wisps of dark brown hair that were finally coming in. "Hey, I'd like to do a delivery. Send us your ten favorite specialty rolls... Yes, surprise us... 13 Starry Night Lane. Here's my card info..."

About five minutes later, there was a knock on the door, one of the wonders of UndeadEats and their speedy delivery. Atlas opened it, handing a teenage witch some cash before taking the plastic bags from him.

"Thank you, s-sir," the boy said, eyes wide. "Y-you're the..."

"Atlas Thorne." He flashed a charming smile, the one I remembered all too well from attending numerous events with him.

"Would you mind if I got a picture with you? I'd never think to see you here in our neighborhood. My mom is a huge supporter."

Atlas was eating this up. He acted humble, but I knew

better. He secretly loved the attention his well-earned position of Salem's Archon, one of the nine districts' council members, granted him.

"Of course." He twisted, placing an arm around the young witch's shoulder, smiling when the flash went off on the phone before turning back to face him. "And what's your name?"

"Hedley Haycox, sir."

"Well, Mr. Haycox, it was a pleasure meeting you tonight. Make sure to thank your mom for her support, and I hope you both make it out to the polls in a few years when you're able."

"Of course, Archon Thorne."

I rolled my eyes, settling Aspen on my shoulder to burp him with no success as he pushed to look for his father.

Atlas shut the door and took the bags to the kitchen, arranging them on the counter and pulling out the plastic containers filled with various colorful rolls of sushi. My mouth watered. "That looks amazing."

Aspen yawned. Perfect timing. Maybe I could actually enjoy a hands-free dinner—a rarity for me.

"Here, let me," Atlas said, taking him. As he walked him toward the nursery, creamy fluid spurt from Aspen's mouth all over Atlas's shoulder.

Oops.

Stifling a chuckle that I'd been the one to dodge that spit-up explosion, I headed over to the cabinets to grab some plates. Then I poured a few glasses of water and set them out, along with the chopsticks that were at the bottom of the bags.

About five minutes later, Atlas crept out of the nursery. "Where's the baby monitor?"

"My room," I said. "I can—"

"No worries, I've got it." A minute later he was back,

standing the monitor on the counter next to us. Then he unbuttoned his spit-up covered shirt, bunched it up in a ball, and left it on top of the laundry machine. "I'll grab my overnight bag after dinner."

Part of me wanted him to go grab it right this damn minute because as I shoved a spicy roll in my mouth, a whole different sort of fiery hunger coursed through me. I couldn't stop myself from staring at the panes of his tanned chest or the trail of dark curls that led below the waistband of his trousers.

The effect he had on me...it was still there.

Luckily, I was also starving for food. I quickly shoved another roll, something topped with avocado, into my mouth.

Get it together, Oakley.

Once again, I wished my sister was here. In addition to worrying about her and missing her, I knew she would run interference. But there was no one else to hide behind at the moment.

I gripped my sticks around another sushi roll, barely done chewing the last before I popped it in my mouth.

"Have you been eating enough?" Atlas asked, looking slightly concerned at how fast I was inhaling sushi in front of him. "If you need me to hire someone to cook for you—"

I held up my hand, stopping him as I swallowed down that last roll. "That won't be necessary."

I'm trying to fill myself up on food right now so I'm not tempted to fill myself up with you.

Who was to blame for turning me into a horny teenage witch, my weakened magic or the surplus of hormones? Or was it the full moon closing in, amplifying everything?

"How are things back home?" I asked, trying to change the subject.

"Good. Work has been insane, as usual. Lots of big changes coming in the next year or two, and I'm trying to keep everyone happy."

"I'm sure it'll all work out. You've always been good at keeping everyone satisfied."

"I'm glad you think so," he replied with a wink before eating another bite of sushi.

I choked on my dragon roll, chest heating in embarrassment. Dropping my gaze, I avoided thinking about all the ways I knew he could satisfy me and the tiny scraps of left-over Desire flitting within me. I clenched my thighs, hating that I felt this way, especially with him.

If I gave in, I'd be leading him on, and I'd never forgive myself. We had a son to raise together for many moons to come. Plus, there was that whole I-almost-kissed-the-neigh-bor-and-I-liked-it issue too.

Remaining in a permanent knot for the rest of dinner, I was grateful when Atlas excused himself and went to grab his bag. He didn't even give my room a second glance, instead setting it right by the couch. "Got any spare blankets? I brought my own pillow."

I nodded, heading to the linen closet, pulling out a few flannel throws, and handing them to him.

"Do you have milk stored in the fridge so I can let you sleep if he wakes up?" Atlas asked, taking the baby monitor. "I figure you probably haven't gotten much sleep, considering... well, everything."

"I don't, just because I haven't had a chance to stockpile anything since we moved in. But if you're sure—"

"I am," he said with the authoritative tone he used in his position as Archon.

"Okay." I scanned the room for wherever I'd managed to put

my pump, finding the bag tucked off in the corner of the kitchen. "I'll pump in a little while before I go to bed. He'll still probably need me at least once since I think he's having a growth spurt."

"That works. Get the sleep while you can. I'll bring him to you if he wakes again after the first feed." He pulled out his laptop, setting it on the couch before grabbing a small bag and walking toward the hallway bathroom. "I'm going to go ahead and get ready for bed. Need to do a few things for work before I go to sleep anyway."

I went into my room, calling the Artemis Police Department and leaving another voice message before grinding up some herbs. Collecting the grains in the tiny capsules, I set aside the nursing supplements. I'd been tempted to make some full moon suppressants, but upon further research realized they weren't safe to use while breastfeeding. I'd just have to think long and hard about if and how I would go about recharging my magic tomorrow night.

Grabbing the pump, I sat on my bed, wrangling my breasts into the cups. Then I held my hands over them, thinking through the spell a handful of times. It took a few tries, and I could feel another sliver of my magic gone—possibly never to be replenished—but a moment later, the cups suctioned against my chest, taking long drags, relieving the pressure that had built there.

There were other kinds of pressure coiled within me, albeit lower, that I vowed would get no relief tonight with Atlas here.

Thank Goddess in less than forty-eight hours he'd be gone.

Unfortunately, this ache wouldn't be. With each passing day, my magic dwindled. From the way my Desire was thirsting after every attractive witch we'd come in contact with in the last few days, it was getting desperate to replenish.

And *I* desperately needed to stay away from Atlas with the full moon's arrival tomorrow.

It was going to be a *long* weekend.

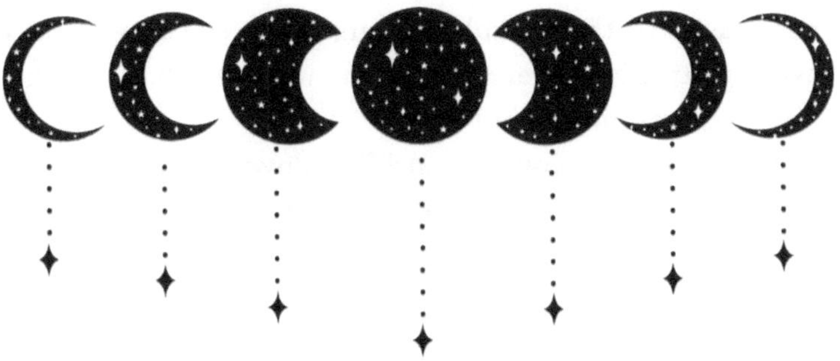

Preparations were underway for her worship, with each household celebrating the occasion in their own way—some merrier than others.

Number 1 sat ominously still. Its maw clamped shut with four locks twisted securely into place along with seven protective wards. Such crude security measures but what made Acacia Mirabel feel safe was her own choice, even if that choice was wholly unsophisticated in comparison to her neighbors'.

She'd come here in search of answers, the window to her study forced to keep its eyes wide open into the late evening and early morning hours. She never left in the daylight. Never attended events under the moon.

Not since she'd finally discovered what darkness truly lay hidden within Celestial Haven.

How it'd gotten that way.

Acacia watched as Heather Irving waddled out onto number 2's front porch, shutting the door quickly behind her as quietly as she could. A mug resting atop her belly, she sat on the loveseat, sipping from it for three to twenty minutes, however long it took for a child to spot her and start banging on the window or smudging images of funny animals onto the glass with their stubby fingers. Then she'd head back inside, getting her older children out and to the bus stop, the little ones toddling behind them.

But it was the coveness striding down the driveway of number 5 that really drew Acacia's attention as she jotted notes.

"The caterers can't be here a minute after seven, and please send *extra* linen this time. Last time was disgraceful when a cauldron bubbled over and there were not enough napkins to pass out with the pumpkin crème brûlées," she said in a tone wholly pleasant for the unpleasantry of her words.

She looked as if she were talking to herself, walking along Starry Night Lane and clutching a black thermos filled with her custom brew. When she passed Ivy Hendrix and Jade Fisher pushing their strollers down the sidewalk, she remained engrossed in her conversation as they waved eagerly in her direction before she was out of view of Acacia's observation.

Standing up from her windowsill, Acacia grabbed the paper, spelling it into the orb she held in her hand. The words were sucked inside, curling around its edges until the paper had disappeared.

Another day, another orb.

And if tonight went as planned, Acacia would get another answer.

CHAPTER II

OAKLEY

I woke up the next morning, my chest aching. Staggering out of the room, rubbing the sleep from my eyes, I startled when I found not only Atlas—whom I'd forgotten had stayed the night—but also a man I'd never met before seated on the couch in the living room, the two chatting quietly. The man was tall with brown hair and a tailored black suit. When they looked up, the stranger flashed a pleasant smile.

Was this Atlas's contact he'd been in touch with?

"Hey..." Atlas's eyes zipped to me, gaze dropping to my shirt. I crossed my arms over my chest, knowing they hadn't missed the darkened circles over my nipples from where I'd leaked. *Just great.* "We didn't want to wake you. This is Fitzgerald Wells, Artemis's District Attorney."

"Nice to finally meet you, Oakley. I'm actually your neighbor, so please call me Fitz. Everyone around here does."

"Nice to meet you, Fitz."

"Have you met my wife, Aurora?" he asked. "If you haven't, I'm sure you will soon. She makes a point to reach out to all the coven's new additions as its coveness."

"Are you here about Hazel?"

"No, I actually came to invite you to tonight's moonluck at our house before I headed over to file some paperwork at the police station," Fitz said.

"I've called the police station twice to get an update on her missing person report, but it just keeps going to voicemail."

"I know you're worried, but hopefully it's nothing other than Hazel up to her usual wild antics."

"Oh, do you know my sister well?" Maybe Fitz would know who she'd been on a date with.

"I wouldn't say well, but since we are heavily involved in the community and she sold us our house, we've spent a fair amount of time together." He flashed another grin and then looked down at his phone, as if checking something, though he didn't touch the screen. "If you'd like, I'd be happy to take you along with me to the station. My business should be pretty quick so you wouldn't be away too long from your witchling."

Atlas nodded, "I'm happy to stay with Aspen while you go."

As much as I didn't like being away from my sweet little witch, it would be a lot easier to focus on finding out any information on my sister's case without needing to divide my attention.

"That would be great." Using my thumb to gesture toward the nursery, I kept my arms in front of the damp spots on my shirt. "I'm just gonna go feed him and get dressed, if you can wait?"

"Not a problem," Fitz said. "I'll go wait for you in the car and get some emails answered."

Shuffling into the nursery and cursing myself quietly, I gripped the edge of the crib, finding Aspen asleep, so gloriously peaceful. I didn't want to wake him, but I needed some relief and didn't want to deplete my magical stores with another pumping spell.

Slowly easing him into my arms, attempting to not jostle him out of his dreams, I sat in the plush chair in the corner, leaning back as I brought him to my breast. Laughter filtered in from the living room before the front door groaned shut.

Atlas's footsteps padded across the wooden floor, becoming louder until he appeared in the doorframe. He was in a pair of black flannel sleep pants and a matching T-shirt.

"So, he invited us to the moonluck?"

He walked over, kneeling down next to the chair and resting his elbows on its arm, looking up at me. "Yeah. Apparently, Aurora had meant to invite you when she saw you at your bootcamp class."

"She saw me?"

If she did, she didn't act like she noticed. Not that I minded. I wasn't really trying to draw attention to myself during that workout anyway.

"Yep. I told him we'd let him know. It's from five o'clock to moonrise."

"Well, that sounds great!"

This would be perfect. At least at the Wellses we'd be surrounded by other witches and Atlas would be so distracted by the attention he'd get that it would buy us lots of crowded hours. It would also stop him from trying to go down memory lane or plan any moonlit picnics.

Desire snapped painfully under my skin like a rubber band, stinging at the thought. And while I missed how fucking good it felt to have my magic, the idea of replenishing it tonight with Atlas here...

It would just be so wrong.

"Do I need to make something for it?" I asked, realizing you usually bring a dish to share for these things.

"I've got it covered." Atlas was already typing into his phone. "Getting groceries delivered within the next hour. I'll make my famous rosemary potato salad. Aspen can help."

My mouth watered at the thought. Atlas's cooking was exceptional. I never minded being his taste tester, and so many times those evenings of watching him cook turned into something much hotter than any oven—

Nope, nope, nope.

"Sounds great." My voice cracked through the lie I was telling myself: that I didn't want him anymore. But whatever happened tonight, I needed to stay as far away from Atlas as possible.

"I'm looking forward to meeting the rest of your neighbors," he said, heading out into the living room.

Another thought hit me, one that was even more terrifying... If every witch would be there tonight, that meant Lynx might be there too.

What if they met? How the heck was I going to handle them both?

I'd already explained I wasn't with Atlas, so it wasn't like I was hiding anything. And for all I knew, I could have been misreading things. But how would my ex take the idea of me with someone else?

I didn't know.

And I wasn't sure I was ready to find out.

)))●(((

THIRTY MINUTES LATER, WE ARRIVED AT THE POLICE STATION, AND I followed Fitz inside, watching as he greeted every officer he ran into. He truly seemed to know everyone.

"I'll meet you back here once I'm done," Fitz said, giving me a pat on the shoulder.

"Sounds good."

I headed toward the front desk, waiting for the officer, a tall woman with dark-brown skin and intricately braided hair that was tucked up into a bun, to look up at me. Her eyes remained on her computer, seemingly not seeing me standing right in front of her, chuckling to herself. Two long fangs glinted as she did.

Vampire.

My hackles were instantly raised. It was unusual to see vampires working in law enforcement, especially since most of their community was under the protection of the Vivaldi Syndicate, an underground criminal network that had dealings between the mortal and supernatural world. There weren't many supernaturals who would willingly let a vampire feed from them, so their kind often operated between our two worlds, both as a business strategy and as a matter of survival.

I couldn't remember the last time I'd seen a vamp. A few times when we lived at the capital, but it was rare. Any in politics were instantly a red flag for corruption, since it was rare to find a vampire not under Vivaldi's protection.

Either this officer was extremely bold or maybe the Artemis Police Department wasn't as irreproachable as I'd believed.

Anxiety thrummed under my skin. Regardless of the vampire officer in front of me, it had been too long since I'd heard from Hazel. I patted the counter, and her peridot eyes whipped up, suddenly aware someone was standing there. "I'm here to check on a missing person report that was filed a day or two ago."

"Name?" she asked, with a huff that told me she was

annoyed I was keeping her from whatever had made her smile.

"Hazel Brooks."

She rolled back her chair, rifling through a series of orbs organized on a board. Some glowed red, others yellow, and a few green. Her brow furrowed after she'd looked into a handful, then she pulled herself back to the counter and pursed her lips. "There's no report in our records for someone with that name."

What?

My body heated, hands becoming clammy and I gripped the sides of my pants to steady myself.

"Are you sure? I was told a report had been filed," I said, voice wobbly, worry cramping my gut. "Can you look again?"

She slid her chair back to the board, squinting into the crystal balls again. "Nope. No Hazel Brooks here."

My hands shook against the counter, so I clasped them together. "I-I called three times and left voice messages. No one answered or dialed me back."

The vampire, whose badge said Driscoll, frowned, pointing to the blinking phone in the corner. "We get over a hundred calls a day. And every time someone comes in, it goes to voicemail." Just like clockwork, the phone began to ring, and she stared at me as if to show me firsthand how short-staffed they were.

A hand on my shoulder made me jolt, and I turned to see Fitz scanning me over, concern etched in his forehead. He turned his attention to the officer, whose spine straightened, and frowned at her. "Everything okay?"

"No," I said, tears springing to my eyes. "Everything is definitely not okay."

Arm around my shoulder, he walked me outside the police station, the fresh fall air drying the tears on my cheeks.

"I know I probably shouldn't say this, but the truth is the APD is woefully understaffed, and the new crops of recruits don't have the tenacity to go after cases like this," Fitz said, voice just above a whisper. His eyes darted around to ensure no one at the station heard him, a very different demeanor than the man who'd been smiling and waving at all the officers fifteen minutes ago. "I'm happy to go back in with you and file a missing person report but honestly, Archon Thorne's contacts have much more funding and resources at their disposal to look into it. I can even send you the number of a private investigator I've worked with before if you'd like."

Based on how apathetic Officer Driscoll seemed about her job, he was probably right. Atlas had contacts across all the criminal and technology departments as one of our government's Archons. And he cared about Hazel. He had planned for her to be his sister-in-law at one point, after all, and she was the sole aunt to his child. He'd have more incentive to find her than anyone in the Artemis Police Department.

"I'd rather you just take me home. But I'll definitely take that contact information."

"Of course," he said, walking me toward his car.

All my previous worry became more and more clouded by another, more inflamed emotion. Anger.

Lynx had told me he'd contacted the APD. That they had filed a report.

Why did he lie?

I didn't know, but I sure as hell was going to find out when I saw him at the moonluck tonight.

CHAPTER 12

OAKLEY

5 Blessed Crescent boasted all the grandeur you'd expect from a power couple living in the center of the supernatural suburbs. It was three stories tall, one side completely covered in glass, showcasing the home's internal awe. The moonluck was already bustling with just as many witches and their families out on the lawn as there were inside.

Pushing the stroller along the long, curved driveway nearly touching the forest of pines behind the neighborhood, I gave Aspen a smile, watching him take in the gray sky brushed with thin clouds.

I was still reeling from my visit to the police department, but staying home meant more hours alone with Atlas and potentially letting the Moon Goddess and her *blessing* drive my decisions. The moonluck would give us some emotional distance and me a chance to talk to Lynx and find out the truth about why the APD had no missing person report filed for my sister.

"Here," Atlas said, placing a hand on the stroller's handlebar while simultaneously pushing on its brake with the ball of his loafer. "Why don't you get him situated while I go park this with the others?"

A row of about seven strollers—some covered in black lace, others with rose-gold embellishments, and a few doubles—all nestled side by side on the grass. I knelt down, grabbed my hip carrier from the storage basket, and wrapped it above my waist to clip it. I double checked the attached pouch, ensuring a few diapers and wipes were in there, along with an extra onesie, before standing.

Atlas stopped bouncing with Aspen and handed him over to me to prop him on the carrier's padded seat. His little body curled around my side, head resting where my shoulder met the top of my breast, and his tiny hand gripped my flowy backless halter dress.

Slipping my phone into its pocket, just in case Hazel or Fitz's private investigator contacted me, I began walking toward the moonluck—Atlas catching up after dropping the stroller with the others.

"Impressive." Atlas's eyes glinted at the modern opulence taking place inside and on the grounds belonging to 5 Blessed Crescent. Oversized thorny bushes plush with black roses led toward the gated backyard where twinkling lights floated in lazy circles overhead.

The gate was propped open, showcasing the busy yard full of witches. Small lounge areas were spread throughout the space, an ornate pergola situated at its center laced with vines and jet-black blooms. A large flower-embossed cauldron sat empty on top of a plush rug under its shelter, and witches huddled around it, mingling with cups and plates floating in front of them. A few peeked over their shoulders, murmuring when they saw us walk in. I wondered if they were chatting about their new neighbor, Hazel's missing status—which I had no doubts it'd made the street's gossip list at this point—or the fact that Archon Thorne from the capital had shown up at their soirée.

"Welcome," a familiar voice called over the throng of neighbors I hadn't met yet. Fitz walked through the crowd wearing a button-up shirt and charcoal slacks, a carnelian crystal attached to his wrist by a thick piece of twine. The bright-orange gem brought sexual energy and creativity to the wearer and could be enchanted to enhance its properties if cast on. Looking around, I realized he wasn't the only one with the talisman.

Seems to be some big full moon plans around here...

When he noticed my attention on his charm, I snapped my gaze back to Aspen, grabbing the pacifier that was hanging from him and popping it back in his mouth. Fitz waved behind him, shouting over the crowd. "Ah, Aurora, I wanted to introduce you. This is Oakley Brooks, Hazel's sister, and her son Aspen, and you already know Archon Thorne—"

"Atlas. Aspen's father," he corrected, slipping in smoothly while giving no indication that he wasn't thrilled there wasn't more to add. *Thank Goddess.* Always impeccable at keeping up the façade in public. "Thanks again for inviting us."

"Of course," Aurora replied, a silky huskiness dressing her tone. "I apologize I didn't make it over to introduce myself the other day."

Her blue eyes sparkled with intrigue, and I felt like I was being inspected. She wore a stunning lace maxi dress with strategic cutouts that showed off the curves of her muscular body. It gave me the impression she was perplexed at how Atlas and I ever fit as a couple. It didn't help that I'd worn a jersey knit high-neck dress that hung around my ankles like a flowy sack, hiding all my wobbly bits while making it easy enough to shift the fabric around to nurse.

"What a precious little witchling," she cooed at Aspen, giving him a tickle under his chin. He giggled, dropping his pacifier once again, which dangled from his clip. "I didn't get a chance to sneak a peek of him after Lynx's class. I needed to get home to get on top of some emails for the board of the Supernatural Arts Center. We've got a big fundraiser coming up in Seattle. Terribly boring stuff, but someone's got to do it."

"We'd love to put you down for a table if you can make it, Atlas," Fitz said, wrapping his arm around his wife. She leaned into the touch, running her gold-dipped nails along the panes of his chest.

"I'll have to check with my assistant. He handles my calendar."

"Of course," Aurora said, eye-fucking the shit out of him, though Fitz didn't seem to mind in the least. Heat flared in my chest a moment, then I remembered I had no claim to him.

Not anymore.

"Look who we have here." Her brilliant blues snagged on something behind Atlas, a smirk playing at her lips.

"Thanks for having us." I glanced over my shoulder, spotting Lynx heading right toward us. Anger knotted up my gut, and he stumbled, no doubt sensing it for himself.

"H-hey, Oakley," he croaked, straightening back up. He looked stupidly handsome tonight, dressed in a pair of dark-wash jeans and a black Henley that made all his muscles even more pronounced than usual. The heat that had flared in my chest shifted and shot up my neck into my cheeks.

"Atlas Thorne." He stuck out a hand before I could respond. "Pleasure to meet you."

Lynx tilted his head slightly in my direction before

returning his attention to the man currently shaking his hand.

"Nice to meet you too," he replied, confusion sweeping through his gaze, connecting the dots via the mini Atlas situated between us. "I'm a big fan of your family's work."

"Aren't we all?" added Fitz. "Grandson to one of the founders of our very government. Imagine my surprise when I ran into him right here in our little neighborhood at Ms. Brooks's place. I'm so glad you are here to celebrate the full moon with us."

Lynx's eyes refused to meet mine, lips clamping into a straight line.

Was he...upset?

"Ah, I was wondering when that handsome hubby of yours would arrive," Aurora said, glancing over her shoulder. "Bring any of those coffee grounds I requested?"

My eyes grew wide when a familiar pair of evergreen irises came into view.

Lynx and Saros?

Married?

Now that I thought about it, the coffee Lynx had brought over was from Luna's. It would make sense if he just visited with his husband and grabbed some coffees on his way to take pity on the new single-mom neighbor.

Holy Mother Goddess above, I almost kissed a married *man.*

Fury boiled through me, stamping out any steamy thoughts that had previously wafted in his direction.

"Nice to see you again, Oakley," Saros said with a curt nod, then turned his attention to the witch by my side. "Saros."

"Atlas." He didn't put out his hand as usual, instead giving him a curt nod in return.

Something thick clawed the air—or maybe it was just my

ribs constricting from the awkwardness. I felt like I might be sick if I stayed here much longer.

Aurora's gaze dropped to my chest, and I looked down to see Aspen rubbing with his mouth where my nipple hid beneath the black sack I was wearing. My face and neck heated in embarrassment.

"You're welcome to feed him anywhere you like. If you want privacy, Fitz's office should be empty." Aurora stroked his arm adoringly, gaze darting around the man buffet situated in front of her. I couldn't blame her. Unlike me, she wasn't covered in drool and spit-up, and they weren't out of her league.

"Thanks," I replied hastily, then turned to Atlas. "Why don't you grab some food, and I'll come find you?"

He nodded, and I quickly shuffled toward the house. I didn't care about privacy as much as I just needed a place to freak out in solitude.

((((●))))

THE INSIDE WAS BUSTLING WITH AT LEAST TWENTY WITCHES IN SMALL groups cluttering the dining room. Long tapered wine glasses were strewn across the table, thin candles dripping pale wax down their curved edges, some seeping onto the rich-purple runner overlaid with lace.

A large coffin-shaped display held various meats, cheeses, fruits, and vegetables, along with glossy jet-black caramel apples that reflected the dim candlelight. Aspen babbled and played with my dress as we passed assorted vials with different colored potions that were set on tiered trays with small tented labels. Some were marked to help with libido, others with calming, and a few give a witch enough energy to be able to stay up all night.

Witches were walking up to the display, taking vials and tucking them into their pockets. A few who seemed eager for the moon's arrival simply gulped the bright-blue liquid down and left the empty ones strewn about the table.

In another corner of the room, a floating ladle was serving dark-magenta drinks in stemless glasses, pale wisps of smoke billowing over their tops.

It was one of the most elaborate lunar celebrations I'd ever seen. Where I was from, our community threw subtle, small gatherings each month—other than official functions I attended with Atlas when we were together, which were never held on this sacred night.

I wondered if their rituals were any different too.

As if it could hear my thoughts, the leftover grains of Desire sifted under my skin. But I'd be abstaining from any of *that.* I just needed to buy time to keep Atlas distracted, then hide in my room tonight, away from the beautiful coppery orb and Goddess whose magic beckoned me.

I'm sorry. I grimaced on the off chance she or her acolytes could hear me somehow, not wanting to sound ungrateful for my gift. While I wasn't sure I wanted its return, I could never wish her blessings away. There were plenty of them that she'd brought into my life, including Aspen. I'd do an offering of some sort, an apology, once I was home and by myself.

I wandered down the lone narrow hallway, looking for the office.

"It's that one."

The familiar voice sent me jolting around.

"You're unbelievable," I gritted out at Lynx, not hiding my frustration since we were the only two in the hallway. "What are you doing here?"

He nodded toward the door his hand was on. "Bathroom."

Ugh. Of course I had to look like the asshole right now.

How could I have been so naïve? Maybe I had misread things, but I could have sworn we were about to kiss. There was a moment… I should have known it was all too good to be true.

"Look, Oakley. I wanted to talk to you—"

"There's nothing to talk about." Aspen's face bobbed into my dress again as he fussed.

"It's the second door to your left," he instructed in a gentle tone, looking at my witchling with a glint in his eye. "I'd just recommend aiming yourself away from the cameras. They are everywhere around here."

His gaze went up and I followed it, spotting a few cameras tucked out of view. That wasn't creepy at all.

"Thanks for the tip," I said, heading for the door he'd pointed out and twisting the knob, swinging it wide.

When I went to shut the door behind me, his hand stopped it, holding it open enough to peer through.

"So Archon Thorne is—"

"Aspen's father. Not that it's really any of your business." I put my hand on the wood, my voice lowering. "I stopped by the APD this morning after leaving them a few voice messages. They had no idea what I was talking about. Have something to say about that?" I arched a brow in challenge.

Lynx opened his mouth, eyes darting around the room quickly, the veins of his neck tense and raised.

When he didn't say more, I pushed on the door, sending him staggering back a step as I swung it shut.

CHAPTER 13

OAKLEY

The next twenty minutes I spent scrolling my phone, looking at photos and videos of Hazel, tears welling in my eyes at the memory of her holding my hand as I delivered Aspen. It was one of the few times I'd seen my sister cry, and I'd clutched her palm so tightly, she was probably in pain from my death grip, but all I could see was her overwhelming joy.

We'd made so many plans for sisterly shenanigans once Aspen and I moved in, like watching all our favorite classy witchy flicks. Mine being *Bell, Book and Candle*, hers, *The Craft*. We'd bring back our tradition of watching *Practical Magic* on All Hallows' Eve with margaritas in hand—the virgin variety when we were little, of course, the potent variety when we got older. Then we'd teach Aspen all about our magic and the Goddess that had blessed us.

That vision for our family felt like it was slipping away with each passing day she was gone. I'd tried to rationalize her absence, but if she were merely on a date, surely Atlas's people would have located her by now, or I'd at least have a reassuring text about what she was up to.

The not knowing if she was okay hung constantly over me like a blanket of exhaustion, on top of the exhaustion I already dealt with. Hopefully there'd be more news from Atlas's contact soon.

Aspen nestled into my shoulder perched back atop his cushioned seat after he'd finished feeding. I patted his back, shutting the office door behind us with a quivering hand. The crowd of witches in the kitchen and living area of the house seemed to have multiplied since I'd been tucked away, stewing over the revelation that Lynx was full of shit and conveniently left out the fact that he was married.

Unlike mortals, witches didn't traditionally wear bands to signify their committed partnerships. Instead, they had vow marks. Runes embedded with hex magic that punished those who broke their marital oaths.

Luckily, Lynx wasn't anywhere to be seen, but his lies were catching up with him tonight, and I deserved answers.

When I got back to the yard, Atlas was beaming, his voice carrying over the throng of witches, always a charmingly dominant presence. My neighbors congregated, waiting eagerly to sidle next to him for a selfie. I groaned. The last thing we needed was the gossip gremlins with their cameras and notepads showing up and disturbing the safe haven I'd made for us away from all *that*.

He waved me over once he spotted me, causing a few women to frown in my direction. Holding Aspen close to me, I smiled and nodded at Ivy and Jade, who were busy with their husbands and children in one corner of the yard. One toddler was spinning in circles, the other jumping and tugging on Jade's shirt. I could barely handle one, how did she manage three?

Probably with a heavy dose of magic and caffeine.

"You okay?" Atlas asked, taking Aspen from my arms.

"Just missing Hazel." It was true, but that was only one demon I was dealing with right now. The other came wrapped in a beautiful brawny package that had a window straight through my emotional walls.

"Of course." He nodded toward the yard's gate. "You want to get out of here? We can go back home and make a quiet night of it as the full moon finishes its ascent."

"No, it's okay." The last thing I wanted to do was go home during the full moon and have Atlas there with his...illusions. More like *delusions*.

I didn't know if I'd be able to resist him with my skittering Desire begging for replenishment.

The full moon recharged witches' individual gifts but it also made all supernaturals particularly insatiable. No one knew exactly why, but when the Moon Goddess rose high in the sky each month, it filled the air with wild energy and magic.

Steam wafted from the cauldron set on the pergola's dais. A small table and chair had been moved next to it with a deck of tarot cards spread across its top, a few floating midair. My next-door neighbor, an elderly woman with silver hair and maroon eyes, snatched one in her hand, showing it to the witch whose reading she was doing, pointing at the symbols. "I was actually thinking we could get our cards read by Ruby."

He huffed, unimpressed, but before I asked again, he put a hand on my spine, stepping behind me to follow. "Whatever you want."

We moved through the crowd, Atlas waving pleasantly to people that approached him. Suddenly everyone wanted to introduce themselves to the both of us, and my mom brain was finding it impossible to keep their names straight. After about ten introductions, we made it to the center of the moonluck.

"New faces for a full moon reading. How blessed am I?" Ruby said, lifting a finger toward the chair across from her. "Come. Sit."

Atlas nodded to me, so I sat down, scoping out the cards. The deck had a large bloated moon at its center, ornate swirls adorning the black background in coppery foiling. It had to have been the most beautiful design I'd ever seen. Not that I'd had a reading done many times, but my sister loved them when we were growing up, often dragging me along. Pairing it with her premonitions, she loved to draw out the true meanings behind the cards since they often were ambiguous.

"Go ahead and set your intention, dear."

With a wave of her hand she scooped up all the cards before dropping the deck into the cauldron in front of her. Pungent liquid swirled within, and I watched as they all disappeared into the bubbling, endless depths.

We sat there in silence for a few moments, Ruby dangling a clear quartz until its swinging motion came to an abrupt halt. Snapping the crystal into her palm, she tucked it into her pocket. "Now reach in, dear."

I wrinkled my nose at the unfamiliar smell coming from the cauldron. "What is it?"

"It's a blend of anise, arrowroot, and... liquefied entrails." A smile peeled up her lips. "Animals, of course."

Of course.

Atlas merely shrugged, still bouncing next to me with Aspen in his arms, who was giggling as his father tickled his belly. Taking a deep breath, I reached a hand in, trying not to grimace at the syrupy texture. "Okay. Now what?"

"You still haven't fully set your lunar intention. Once you do, and it's clear, the cards shall be within your grasp."

I'd never done a reading like this before. Usually no cauldron, or entrails, were involved.

"It's a ritual reserved only for high witches with proper certification to perform on the full moon," Ruby added, a mischievous lilt to her tone.

Could she read my thoughts?

"Yes. But only when you're touching my deck."

So that wasn't her gift. I didn't know much about high witches, other than they all had to serve the Council of Magical Welfare for six years in exchange for access to the advanced skills they learned in training. Only the most brilliant and promising witches were allowed into the program. Some of them were even blessed with more than one gift.

"The first card represents you, the second your life, and the third your love. Once you're ready, that is."

My mind cleared, finally focusing on the intention of wanting to figure out where my sister was. Five cards shot into my grasp.

"Go ahead and show us, dear." I lifted the cards out of the blackened ether. Flying out from my fingers, they floated midair above us, coated in the ichor that slowly dripped off, landing magically back in the cauldron.

"Hmm." Ruby wiggled her fingers, as if deciding which card to grab first.

"What is it?"

"Nothing," she replied, finally snatching one in her hand. "Just always interested to see what the cards will tell me about a person."

"What do they say?"

She flipped the card, revealing a beautiful woman dressed in black holding an iridescent crystal and ancient text, a large moon situated behind her, glinting in the dim light of the candles floating above us.

"The Empress." A nod to our Moon Goddess, the one who birthed magic to this world and changed the course of its history.

"Motherhood?" I held back the urge to roll my eyes. Maybe Ruby wasn't as legit as she claimed, though she couldn't lie about being a high witch. There would be runes, ones that couldn't be falsified. But it seemed a little too on the nose.

"Well, it also could mean fertility"—*better fucking not*—"or nature. Like tonight's full moon," Ruby said, waving her arms at the darkening sky. "It is the perfect time to go to the pines and recharge your magic."

Yes, real fucking perfect.

My gaze narrowed, darting up to Atlas whose brows lifted defensively as if to say *I didn't tell her to say that*. He continued to bounce with Aspen, grabbing a moon pie off a hovering tray and downing it in one bite.

"Death." My attention snapped back to Ruby, throat constricting.

What if that meant—

"Now don't get all doom and gloom on me. Death doesn't usually mean something so final. It could also mean a new beginning, letting go of things that don't serve you."

"But it could also mean *death*," I said, unable to stop clinging to the horrible word and the fear it drummed within my heart.

"It could..." Ruby furrowed her brow, not seeming to want to elaborate further. Just when I was about to get up and walk away, she spoke again. "Let's see the third."

She pulled down the third card, flipping it to face me.

"The Hermit." She merely shrugged. "You're searching for truth in love. Or maybe isolation..."

Well, those weren't totally opposing ideas.

She grimaced, handing me the card to look at. A man stood on a mountain, holding out a lantern, his face completely covered by the dark robes he wore. "Based on your dwindling magic...maybe a bad thing?"

"Excuse me?" I asked, eyes bugging wide before I remembered she could hear my thoughts when I held onto her deck.

"Apologies. It's hard for me to tune out sometimes."

I took a deep breath. "What about the other two?"

"Just extras."

"Extras?" Atlas asked with a frown.

She reached up to grab them, putting them back into the deck before I could see much of anything. I only saw bits for a moment, the letters *-cian* visible on the bottom card. The top had a woman clad in silver armor standing over a ferocious looking white beast that I couldn't make out clearly.

I'd have to pull out Hazel's deck later to look.

"Well, thanks for the *enlightening* reading," I said, standing quickly.

"You want a turn?" Ruby asked, looking up at Atlas. Her eyes glinted mischievously, and he bristled in response.

"I'm good, thanks."

"Afraid of the cards?"

"No. I just struggle to believe how useful vague predictions really are."

This was exactly why I could never tell him what Hazel had seen. He wouldn't believe me. In fact, he'd probably take it as a challenge. I swallowed hard, the image of him on the ground covered in blood as I held him on our wedding day, playing in my mind.

"Wishing you a Goddess-blessed full moon," I said, giving her a smile and a small nod.

"Same to you both," she replied, not taking her eyes off us as we strode away.

"You okay?" Atlas asked. "I think I'm near ready to head back." He ran his palm over Aspen's spine, getting a contented mid-sleep sigh in response. "What do you think? Get this little one down in his crib before the Moon Goddess sits on her throne?"

"Um, sure, but I'm really thirsty," I said quickly, trying to find a way to buy more time before we were alone and my Desire became a greedy slut. "Need me to grab you anything to take on the road?"

"Sure. If you're heading to the bar, I'll take a Dirty Devil."

Weaving through the crowd, I made sure to smile pleasantly at the neighbors I knew, and didn't know, hoping none of them came up to talk to me so I wouldn't have to try and remember their names right now. I had enough overwhelming my sleep-addled brain.

"I'll take two Dirty Devils, please, and make one of them a virgin," I said to the bartender, a lust demon with magenta flesh, large bat-like wings, and copper-colored irises. "And a glass of water."

He winked, pulling out a few dusky cups, then began to pour and blend the drink. "Coming right up."

I bet he'd make a lot of magical deals tonight when everyone seemed to be eager for a salacious evening.

"Saw you had one of Ruby's famous moonluck readings," a soft, familiar voice came from behind. I didn't turn my head, watching my three drinks float up from the bar before I slipped a few dollars on the counter as a tip.

"That the cause of your sudden thirst?" he continued, muttering over my shoulder. "Or is it that your ex is staying the night?"

"Nursing," I replied, tone clipped. "Must stay hydrated."

Lynx came up next to me and turned to the lust demon.

"I'll have two Headless Horsemen with an added shot of adrenaline elixir."

Of course. He'd be up all night with his *husband.* His equally handsome husband. Probably doing all sorts of things that—

My Desire fluttered to life in my belly like a butterfly bursting from its cocoon. *Nope.* No coochie flutters tonight.

None. At. All.

Lynx smiled at me, which only seemed to spur my gift on, prickling under my skin, begging me to invite him, his husband, and my ex over for a full moon get-your-freak-on. He eyed me curiously. Could he sense where my mind was going? *Fuck.* I pushed the image of the three forbidden witches out of my mind.

Why, Oakley?

But I already knew the reason. My Desire was rebelling against my intentional dry spell, the Moon Goddess coaxing me to not waste her blessing. A flurry of dusty magic swirled in my gut.

"I know you must be furious with me, but I promise I can explain." He reached for me, but I moved sideways, nodding to my drinks to move along with me. "Just not here. Not now."

"Did you or did you not contact your friend at the APD about Hazel?"

The usual stardust littering his irises vanished in an instant. "I did not."

"Tell me why," I pleaded.

He moved to speak but then clamped his mouth shut instead, a thick vein pulsing at his neck.

"If you're not going to tell me, then I really must be getting back to Aspen and Atlas." I whipped my head away from him. "Hope you and your *husband* have a Goddess-blessed full moon."

When the lust demon sent his two cocktails his way, I stormed off, heading toward Atlas. I refused to listen to any more lies, and there was really nothing for Lynx and I to discuss until he was willing to give me the truth.

"You okay?" Atlas asked when I got to him. He grabbed his floating Dirty Devil and took a sip. "You're pale."

"Yep. I'm fine." I chugged down my mocktail in one big gulp, then quickly grabbed the water, smacking my lips together when both cups were drained. They jetted off, weaving through the crowd on its way back toward the bar. "Let's get home. The Moon Goddess should reach her ascension soon."

Atlas guided us toward the yard's exit, and I loaded Aspen into the stroller. While I never glanced behind me, I couldn't help but feel a warm gaze heating my back as we left.

CHAPTER 14

OAKLEY

As soon as we got home, I readied Aspen for bed and fed him before settling him down for the night in his crib. I hovered over him a few extra minutes, watching his eyes drink in the constellations projected onto the ceiling. Being in here was probably distracting him from falling asleep, but the alternative was heading to the living room where I knew Atlas would be getting changed for bed.

A streak of spit-up smeared along the material of my dress caught my eye. That was enough to stop the flutters down under.

When did that happen?

Not that it mattered. Spit-up was basically an accessory for me at this point. A postpartum badge of honor.

Of survival.

I walked over to the bathroom and rinsed off the stain a bit before taking my time walking out to the living room. Atlas was already dressed in just dark-green pajama pants slung low at his hips, breaking up the divots that led straight toward—

"You look beautiful," he said, his full lips sliding into a rueful smile.

My Desire was still reacting to the moon and the lust running through me, ready to pin him down on the couch and ride him till first light.

Rude.

"Thanks," I said awkwardly. My gaze dragged over to the window, the coppery orb glittering down on the cul-de-sac below. Café au Luna's light was on, reminding me of Saros and his *husband*—who I refused to even think of by name.

"It's the full moon tonight," Atlas said, drawing my attention back to him and his stupidly perfect physique. *As if I didn't know.* He moved toward me, reaching out to clasp my hand. My skin crackled beneath his touch, starved for more of this. Of him. "I know you haven't replenished your magic and—"

"You're here to offer your services?" I pulled my hand back, brushing away the sensation beneath my skin. "We both know that would be a horrible idea."

"Would it?" he asked. "It wouldn't have to mean anything."

"You're living in one of your own illusions if you think that's possible." My mind flitted to our nights under the full moon together, and so many others. They were exquisite, ethereal, and I loved every moment of them. Part of me still loved him and probably always would. That was why I couldn't idly enjoy life by his side, knowing it would rip him away from me all too soon.

And it wasn't just us anymore.

I had Aspen to think about. If his father would brush off fate, I sure as fuck wouldn't.

A tear tracked down my cheek, cool against my skin.

"I'm worried about you," he said softly. "You ignore your

gift and in the next few moons it'll be gone completely. There's no going back after that."

There was nothing cruel or condescending about his words. He and I both knew what was coming if I didn't use my ability to recharge my magic.

"Maybe I don't want it back?" I said, keeping my tone hushed to not wake the baby.

Most witches avoided my Desire once they got close enough to experience it. Sure, a witch with my gift was alluring and the idea of experiencing it firsthand intrigued most, but the reality of it—the cost... Once that came into play, people usually felt very different.

Admittedly, there were beautiful things about my magic that I enjoyed, and I missed my business and bringing others more passion, love, and intimacy into their lives. But my Desire *took*...

And the fact that I loved how it felt when it did both thrilled and scared me.

Gifts weren't meant to be borrowed. They needed years to be fully mastered. My gift didn't discriminate, which had sometimes led to disastrous consequences. I'd been lucky with Atlas, but there were many other witches, other times, that hadn't worked out so well. Letting it wither away might be the best thing, even if I hated the idea of giving up my magic for good.

"Look, my offer still stands," he strode forward, and I backed up until I was pressed against the wall. He leaned over me, flattening his palm against the onyx paint. The other remained at his side, as if he knew I would run if he actually touched me. He nodded at the small patch of moonlight in the grass. "Let me help you through this full moon. Even if you want to do things *solo*, I could visualize some encourage-ment for you. We could recharge together right out back."

He looked pained, as if he was using every ounce of restraint to not cart me over his shoulder and seduce me with his salacious visions until I gave in and replenished my gifts in the moonlight. And I felt defenseless without my own gift to reflect back, to taunt him and drive him wild. I knew if I had my magic, it would work—Desire only worked on those who felt it already, and it was clear Atlas still felt it for me. "You'd love that, wouldn't you?"

He lowered his head until his warm breath tickled the crest of my ear, sending a shiver through me. "I think the answer to that is obvious."

You know you want to drop to your knees and take him in your mouth until he begs for more.

Goddess, the full moon, my gift, and my dirty mind were all driving me nuts tonight.

I swallowed thickly. "The answer is no, Atlas. For a multitude of reasons."

"I still don't understand." He crooked his finger, lifting my chin up to keep my eyes on his. "What did I do wrong?"

My gaze dropped to the point of contact, nervous he'd try to show me another illusion, one where we loved one another until our bodies were mapped in a constellation of wrinkles and scars. Beautiful evidence of a lifetime together.

But we couldn't have that, and I didn't have the courage to tell him why because if he fought me on it—if he fought for us—I didn't think I could walk away again.

I had to think about our son that would one day need his father even more than he did right now.

But the illusions never came. There was just his penetrating darkened gaze.

Absent-mindedly, I stroked his tanned cheek with my fingers, and his brows knit in confusion.

Shit.

I dropped my hand, gripping the thin jersey material of my dress before I did something stupid like kiss him or drag him outside under that perfect patch of buttery moonlight. "Look, I really appreciate that you came here to see Aspen, and I want to make co-parenting work, even with the distance. But I think it would be for the best if you didn't stay here tonight."

"Oak—"

"Please, Atlas?" I pleaded, clenching a fistful of fabric to ground myself from melting into his arms. "I can't have you here right now. It's too hard."

As much as I wanted to forget what I'd seen and writhe with him among the pines, I couldn't. He might think he could do this without any strings attached, but I knew better than that. He still loved me. Still wanted to build a life with me. And any hope I gave him of that being a possibility was selfish. I wouldn't do that to him. "One day you'll make some witch very happy. It just won't be me. Not in the way you want."

"Fine," he rubbed his chin, eyes narrowed in frustration. Slipping a black T-shirt over his head, he walked over and grabbed his duffel before gathering up his things. "I'll be at the Supernatural Suites down the road. If you change your mind, just send me a text. I'll keep it with me while I go out to charge up. Otherwise, I'll stop by in the morning to visit Aspen before I return to Salem."

"Thank you."

And with that, he headed out the garage. A few more tears streaked my cheeks, and I lifted my dress to wipe them away. Headlights flared through the window as he backed down the driveway and then swerved around the cul-de-sac, driving off in the darkness.

CHAPTER 15
OAKLEY

It was probably stupid to text my sister, but as I sat in my room, mind rippling with frustration over Atlas, I couldn't help myself. Sending it felt like I was still able to reach her somehow, even though I knew that wasn't really possible.

Going to the corner, I pulled out various crystals, setting the ones I wanted to use in their own pile before arranging eight of them into a circle, representing the full moon above. I looked out my window, making sure the slip of her illumination would cradle the stones. Then I took out the bowl, flower petals, and meteor dust for my offering.

Getting up from the floor, I walked to the night stand to grab my ceremonial knife. When I opened the drawer, my attention snagged on my *treasure box* of toys. All of them overwhelmed me.

The last thing I felt like doing right now was recharging. I grabbed the knife and snapped it shut, reaching a decision. There was still another month probably before I lost access to my magic completely. That gave me thirty more days to make a choice about what I wanted to do. Hopefully by then Hazel would be back so I could weigh the pros and cons with her, and I'd have a clearer idea of how to move forward.

"Moon Mother, take this offering in thanks." I began, pricking the tip of my thumb, letting a few drops of crimson hit the blackened stone mortar. Dropping the other ingredients into the mortar, I took the pestle and crushed it together until it became a thin paste. Then I scooped some in my fingertips and covered my palms. "I'm sorry I've hidden from your gaze all these moons. I'm sorry if it seems like I don't want what you've given. I just don't know how to move forward."

I held my hands up in supplication, the radiant glow of her essence bathing my palms with warmth. My Desire pricked beneath my skin, a small bit of magic sifting out of me with my plea. "And please, wherever she is, keep my sister safe under your light."

Slowly, the granules of paste vanished from my hands, disappearing with the slip of magic.

Knock, knock.

Knock, knock, knock, knock.

"Go away, Atlas," I groaned, glad I'd at least made it through my offering before he'd come back.

"Not Atlas..."

Fuck.

I got up and shuffled into the hallway before opening the front door. Lynx stood on the porch, a covered plate in his hands. The scent of crisp sugar and decadent chocolate wafted from the cracks in the foil, making my stomach grumble. "What are you doing here? Shouldn't you be home with your husband in the thralls of full moon rituals and...whatnot?"

"I had to see you," he said, attention flitting behind me. "Is now an okay time to talk?"

I crossed my arms. "If you're here to tell me what's going on, then feel free to come in." He ran a hand through his dark-blond waves, the other gripping the plate tightly. Stepping inside, his eyes darted around the space, as if he could find what he needed to say somewhere on the onyx walls. "Atlas isn't here, if that's where your mind is wandering."

His shoulders relaxed visibly at my words, though he didn't admit anything aloud.

"I don't like how things were left earlier." Walking over and placing the plate on the counter, he peeled back the foil. "And look, I brought desserts."

There were chocolate-covered strawberries, a slice of chocolate cake, and a piece of berry tart with a cup of dirt—a supernatural childhood staple—in a little plastic cup with a spoon set next to it. It all looked divine. I swiped my chin with my thumb, certain there'd be some drool there.

"Do you really think apology pudding makes everything go away? Like the fact that you never told the APD to look for my sister?"

His lips pressed into a thin line, the veins in his neck pulsing with tension. After a moment, and a deep inhale, he spoke. "I promise I'm searching for her. I just can't really say anything else."

I crossed my arms, taking inventory of the desserts again. Even though they had my mouth watering, I refused to take bribery treats from someone I couldn't trust. I wasn't some toddler that could be paid off with chocolate and sent on my merry way. "I'm sorry but that's not going to cut it when I don't know where my sister is or if she's safe."

"You're right." He placed his hand on the door, making sure it stayed quiet as he shut it. His eyes were glued to the nursery, and he lowered his voice to a whisper. "And I want to tell you the truth, but I really can't. Even if I did, I'm not sure you'd believe me."

This was true. It was hard to believe someone when they'd already been caught in a lie. Two, in fact. But there was something I had that could help. "You really want to tell me the truth?"

"I do," he replied, seemingly sincere.

"Hold on." I went into the bedroom, rifling through my old leftover potions with shaky hands.

Lynx had been the first witch to help me feel welcome here. Beyond that, he'd seemed to genuinely care about Aspen and me. Sure, we hadn't known each other long, but the comfort I felt when he was around was real and reassuring. At least it had been, before it'd been snatched away when I needed it most. With Hazel gone and things so precarious between Atlas and I, Lynx had been a lifeline. Now I didn't know what to trust. I thought there was something taking root between us, even if it was hard to understand why he'd be interested in me.

Maybe I'd just wanted to believe it...

Finally, I found what I'd been searching for, grabbing a vial filled with dark-green liquid, specks of golden dust floating within the tincture. I covered the lid and swirled the glass in my fingers, blending the settled bits as I walked back into the living room.

"Temporary truth elixir," I said, holding it up.

"I can't take that," he said, shaking his head.

"Why not?" Heat spread through my chest, but I willed down my frustration. That wouldn't get me answers. "You already said I won't believe you. Take this and I will."

"If I do this, you can't share anything I say."

"I don't care about sharing what you say. I care about knowing what the hell is going on with my sister."

"Fine." He grabbed the vial from me, twirling it around in his palm. "I'll take it if you take it with me."

"I can't."

He cocked his head at me. "Now who's the one with secrets?"

"I wish it were that simple, but I can't take any right now." I sighed, figuring I could offer him a small truth in exchange for him taking the potion. "My magic's almost depleted. That's my truth."

"Can I ask why?" He swigged the green liquid down in one gulp, smacking his lips together in disgust afterward.

"I just...haven't been under the full moon in a while."

"How long is a while?"

I answered with a grimace. "Long enough where it might be a permanent thing pretty soon."

"*Oh.*" He stood there a moment, leaning against the counter before cocking his head. "I guess that makes sense why you needed help with unpacking. Is that what you want?"

"I'm not sure." My chin dropped to look at my bare feet. They ached for the rich soil, the grass between my toes, the innate need to be outside under the swell of the moon, its golden light reinvigorating my magic. *Me.* "My gift tends to complicate things."

His expression didn't shift at all. Not even with an ounce of curiosity. My face heated. "You already know, don't you?"

His sienna eyes lit with amusement. "I could sense lust wafting off you from down the street. More than I'd usually be able to sense."

Wow. Let a witch play it cool, why don't you!

In college I'd been more bold about talking about my gift. Everyone was. Maybe because of the brews we drank or being off on our own on the East Coast and far from our families, but I'd quickly learned through a series of unfortunate accidents just how dangerous my Desire could be. Like the time I'd accidentally started a fire in my college dorm when a Pyro went down on me. The entire building had to be shut down the rest of the semester. Luckily, no one had been seriously hurt, but it was enough to slow my burgeoning sex life.

"Well, now that my truth is out there, it's only fair you tell me what is going on. Otherwise you can just go."

He took a deep breath and blurted, "Imnotmarried."

"What?" I was pretty sure my eyes had grown twice their usual size. "So you're not with Saros?"

"I am with Saros...sometimes." He chuckled darkly, and I had to admit my curiosity was piqued. "But he's not my husband. He's my...colleague."

He seemed to be choosing his words very carefully. The veins in his neck bulged, red-hot and angry. Whatever spelled him from saying more was extremely powerful.

"Then why does every witch in the neighborhood think you are married?"

"Because they need to," was all he managed to croak out, as if pained. "All I can say is that we are working to find your sister. She's not the only witch to go MIA on Starry Night."

Even if he hadn't told the police department, he was looking for her himself. With Saros. Doing a job for whoever they worked for.

While I still had more questions, I felt much more at ease that he'd come here to talk to me and tell me what he could.

"So you think my sister might be linked to these other disappearances?" I asked, trying to absorb his words.

He nodded, then picked up the spoon on the counter.

Scooping up some crushed Oreo and pudding mix, he shoved it into his mouth, letting out a hum that buzzed through me in all the right places. Desire skittered through my body in a series of desperate crackles.

"Hey!" I glared at him. "You can't eat my apology desserts."

"Well then, come here and enjoy them before I do," he challenged with a smirk.

Taking a few steps toward the plate, I swiped my finger through the cup of dirt, making sure to get all the layers of chocolate and crumbles. "This is mine."

I moaned as I licked it off my finger, unable to stifle the reaction. Goddess, it was divine.

Lynx stared at me, his pupils eclipsing the sienna of his irises.

Heat spread through my chest. "Sorry."

He looked... *I must be misreading things*. This was just the full moon's ascent playing tricks on me.

His Adam's apple bobbed in his throat before he cleared it. Then he mimicked me, scooping up some dirt cup with his fingers and licking them clean. "Oh yes, it's actually much better this way."

"Excuse you." I grabbed the cup, taking some more and holding it up to show him. But before I could bring it to my mouth, he snatched my wrist, gently guiding it toward his lips. Wriggling my wrist, I smeared the chocolate over the tip of his nose.

"Excuse me." He dipped his hand in the cup, and I backed up a few steps out of reach, coming around the other side of the kitchen island. I shifted on the balls of my feet, watching as he stalked toward me with his chocolate-striped nose. When he quickened his pace, I scampered to the cup, but instead of chasing after me, he managed to hop over the island and get me back, the cool, wet pudding with bits of Oreo streaked across my eyebrows and down my cheek.

I squeezed my eye shut, wanting to make sure no wayward dessert plopped into it. Taking my wrist, I wiped off my lid until it felt okay to open. Lynx was standing in front of me, smiling, irises softened into amber pools.

He brushed his thumb across my brow line. The crackle beneath my skin skittered to where he touched, craving it. His eyes dropped to my cheek, and he swept his finger along it, before his palm came up to cradle my jaw.

My Desire followed the caress, flitting to the spot where his skin met mine. His brows lifted a bit, as if he could sense the shift as well. Pressing onto the balls of my feet, I gripped his shirt, my gift prickling beneath my lips as I pined for his.

A small halfhearted cry came from the nursery, inflating my breasts into full-on balloon mode, luckily well hidden beneath my drapey dress. I breathed through the tightness in my chest.

"If you're more comfortable, I can wait out here while you feed him," Lynx said.

"How did you—"

He merely raised his brows.

Empath. Duh.

"Could you sense him or me?" I had to ask. If he could sense my boob alerts, I didn't know if that was highly considerate or extra creepy.

"A bit of both." His lips pressed into a thin line, as if he hadn't meant to say all that. "I try not to share too much of what I read from people since I know it can bother them."

"So you could sense my..." My gaze dropped to my breasts, crossing my arms over them as I started walking toward the nursery. A sliver of light spilled into it, not quite reaching the rocking chair. I grabbed Aspen out of the crib, then sat back in the rocker, tossing a burp cloth over my shoulder. Then I pulled the top of my dress to the side to give Aspen access to eat. His eyes were still shut, fluttering every few seconds until he latched and began suckling. "You're welcome to hang in the doorway, Lynx."

At least that wouldn't be so up close, and I was still mostly covered in darkness anyway.

"Who do you work for?" I asked, rocking in the chair, more to get out my nerves than to soothe my already mostly asleep witchling.

His jaw screwed tight. "I. Can't. Say," he gritted out.

"You're here on some secret investigation?" I supplied. "Undercover?"

He gave one slow nod, veins pronounced. "Looking into the missing witches."

"Like Hazel?"

"Yes, like Hazel."

"So all of this is just a front? To get to know the neighbors, like me?" My voice cracked a bit as my eyes darted in the direction of the kitchen.

Aspen had already fallen back asleep, apparently sated by a light snack, so I rearranged my dress.

"I thought maybe you were— I don't know, it's probably silly," I tittered, shoulders hunching forward.

Aspen settled against my shoulder and I drew firm circles over his back in case he needed to burp.

"I admit, I came by to introduce myself so I could meet you, like I do with everyone in the neighborhood when they move in, given my gifts. I can't say much, but I promise everything we're doing is to help. We're on your side." He came closer. "But ever since I met you, I haven't been able to stop thinking about you."

My watch said it'd been about ten minutes since he'd

taken the potion. It would still be working for another twenty or so.

Which meant he wasn't lying.

Which meant I hadn't been misreading things.

"But why?" Placing Aspen back in the crib, I watched him a few moments before guiding Lynx out of the room.

"Why are you so surprised?"

"Well, you've got that whole everyone-in-the-neighbor-hood-would-want-to-spend-a-full-moon-with-me vibe."

He stopped walking, grasping my hand and pulling me into him. "Yet, here I am. With you."

"Look, I don't fully understand what is going on with you and Saros...romantically, but I'm not going to be some side fling. I may be months into a dry spell and covered in spit-up half the time, but I'm not desperate."

I did have some standards, even if my gift didn't.

"There you go making assumptions." He swept back my hair, leaving his hand at the nape of my neck, fingers tangling in the strands. When I tried to back up a step, he held me in place, speaking in a hushed whisper. "You assume I'm not interested or that I think you're desperate."

His breath was a warm caress, flitting across my skin and igniting things in me I'd tried to push down deep. To forget about. "And you assume Saros doesn't know I'm here."

He waved to the window. My gaze darted to the coffee truck, its light silhouetting Saros. He was fumbling around within, and though I couldn't see exactly what he was doing, I did see his hand lift to us.

"If Saros wasn't okay with my interest in you, he'd try to stop me from doing this, wouldn't he?"

"Doing wh—"

His kiss crashed into me like a storm, brutal enough to make my knees buckle but calm at its center. My Desire crackled under my skin, spreading low past my belly and making my thighs clench. A wave of it surged upward, tingling up my chest, my neck, my lips.

When Lynx pulled back, he trailed a finger along my bottom lip, as if he could sense my gift kindling below. A familiar sensation coated us in its decadent lather, so sweet and thick it seeped down to my bones, and all I wanted to do was become submerged in it.

It wasn't mine, though. It was *his*.

A thousand tiny particles ignited in my belly, shooting in every direction. I wanted to be saturated by the feelings he poured into me through his kiss. Meanwhile, my Desire sensed the full moon above, nudging me to follow through on my feelings for him and take him directly under its light.

To throw off this dress and do more than just kiss.

To have those hands pull me closer, stroking every inch of my skin.

To sink him deep within me, nothing between us, letting his magic and pleasure rush through me like an explosive wave.

"You can't just—be kissing—me—by an open—window," was all I managed to heave out, catching my breath and clamping my thighs together. "What would—the neighbors—say?"

My eyes darted around the street, which was empty aside from Saros, who remained silhouetted in Luna's window, attention glued to us. I couldn't really see his expression, but the fact that his focus still hadn't budged sent a bolt of *fuck yeah* between my thighs.

"You haven't experienced a full moon in our pines if you're seriously asking me that."

I'd put that part of the pamphlet out of my mind, but now I was wishing I'd saved it to look over again. When we'd moved here, Hazel had raved about the pine forest that all the supernatural communities shared. Every neighborhood touched them, and they served a sacred purpose for each. For witches, our covens used the pines both for rituals and to replenish our gifts in semiprivate. It helped deter nudity in the streets, which the HOA had determined was not a suitable place for such activities.

"You're curious," he said, mirth rippling over each word as he arched a brow at me.

I crossed my arms, shifting from one foot to the other, still trying to dispel the naughty thoughts I had around this witch. "What do you want, Lynx?"

"Well, the list is long, considering it's the full moon and I can sense all that lust you're trying to stuff down."

I swallowed thickly. "You can't be serious."

His nose traced along mine, and he pressed a lingering kiss to my forehead before lifting my chin to look up at him. He leaned in to kiss me again—

I jerked my head back, retreating a few steps. "We can't do this."

"Is it because of Aspen's father? The Archon?" he asked, his hands tucking into the pockets of his dark jeans. "I thought you weren't together?"

"We aren't together like *that*." I shuffled over to the plate of desserts, grabbing a brownie and shoving it in my mouth, chewing slowly to buy myself time to think of more reasons why I should deny myself. "But you and Saros—"

"I would never betray him in such a way. As a lover or... business partner. He knows of my intentions with you."

"And you're sure he's okay with it?" I asked between chews, finding the silhouette gone and the light out when I looked back at Luna's.

"Yes. Of course." A few veins pulsed at his words. He

reached into his back pocket, pulling out his cell phone and swiping at the screen a few times. "If you don't believe me, I can call him to come over and watch. Or join."

I choked on my piece of brownie. After I managed to swallow it down, my voice came out in a squeak. "That won't be necessary."

"You sure? Your Desire seemed to perk up at the idea." He gave me a smug grin.

"Umm...no that's okay." My attention dropped to my body hidden by the flowy fabric draped around my feet.

When I trailed it back up, Lynx shook his head, running his palm over the lower half of his face. Then he tucked it back into his pocket. "You really have no idea how incredible you are, do you?"

"Oh yes, as I wander around half asleep, looking a mess. I am sure the first thought that men have is wow—"

"She's not only beautiful, she's strong," he cut in, gaze locked with mine, tone blanketed with sincerity.

"You can't say things like that."

"Why not?" He shifted toward me, but when I retreated again, he slowly backed up until he sat on the couch. "Look, *you* asked for the truth. Had me drink that elixir too."

"I know." I exhaled aloud, cradling my elbows in my hands. My eyes snapped over to the window, the Moon Goddess beamed in all her glory through the pane. Had she heard my apology? Was Lynx being here now, somehow her way of guiding me forward?

"I still don't fully understand what you have with Saros and how your *work* could involve my missing sister. But besides that, I also don't know how much longer I'll even be in Celestial Haven."

"What do you mean?" Concern threaded his words. He

leaned back, his hands gripping the thighs of his jeans, as if he was pinning them in place.

"Well, my sister is still missing. No word on her. And my magic is dwindling with each passing moon."

His elbows dropped to his knees, and he wrung his hands together, tilting his head to the side. "Is there a reason why you don't want to recharge it?"

"Once I decided I wasn't staying with Aspen's father, I stopped *replenishing* on the full moons. And I haven't since..."

His brows lifted in surprise.

"I just... I feel like I don't even know my body anymore," I admitted, my voice barely above a whisper, not believing I'd actually said it aloud.

"Well get to know it." Lynx's eyes raked over me before he clasped his hands together. Then he brought them to his knees once again, knuckles pale from how hard he was holding onto them.

"Oh, like it's that easy." I laughed. "I used to have a bustling business and could wear lingerie and sell people a better love life."

"Fuck, Oakley. You can still wear lingerie. Just the thought of you..." He ran a hand through his hair, as if weighing something. "It does wicked things to me, when I know it'd be better to stay away."

"Then stay away if you have to, but first help my sister," I said, deflecting from acknowledging the words he said and the feelings blooming inside me in response. "Please. I need to find her."

"Oh shit, I meant to ask about that." He stood, eyes flitting over to my room and then Hazel's. "You don't happen to have any communal magic tied to any jewelry, clothing, objects you shared?"

Communal magic usually involved a blood oath and

incantation where the blended liquid was embedded into something. Many witches did them with best friends or loved ones to commemorate special occasions. Hazel and I had only done it once. "Our back tattoos."

We each had gotten a large tree representing each other etched onto our backs as sisterly bonding. I pointed over my shoulder to where my hazel tree was displayed above the back of my dress.

"Now, there's no pressure to get your magic flowing again, but it would take some to be able to cast on it and trace her."

"Would I need mine back for it to work? Couldn't I just let you use your magic with my tattoo to do the spell?"

"Since we'd be utilizing your communal magic with Hazel, it would pull more heavily on you, even if we helped. Saros would probably be the best one to cast." He ran his palms along my arms, then dragged me to him and kissed me again, stroking my spine and spinning circles at its valley.

My body warmed, starved to take him to bathe in the moonlight. But before I could drag him outside, his pocket buzzed. He brushed a hand to my cheek and broke the kiss, then withdrew his phone, swiping a few times, looking serious. "We can work with whatever you have but I won't risk putting you in any danger. Meet me at Luna's tomorrow. Text me what time is convenient for you and Aspen."

"Tomorrow?" I repeated, voice dropping low in disappointment. "I thought... Never mind."

"Oh, I haven't changed my mind about wanting this." He tutted, drifting his hand to just below my clavicle. "Looks like you need a reminder before I go, though."

He winked, and a surge of his own desire shot between my thighs, warmth spreading deliciously all the way to my toes, making them curl. His eyes were pinned to the movement, a smirk playing at his lips. "See you tomorrow, Wicked."

He strode out the door, shutting it quietly behind him.

I leaned against the wall, chest heaving, legs clenched together, the full moon beating on me, as if the Goddess herself wanted to know: was I really ready to let my magic fizzle out?

CHAPTER 16
OAKLEY

*B*uzz.

Buzz.

Buzz.

I craned open one eyelid, then the other, gaze settling on Aspen asleep in my arms in the plush rocking chair, curled around one exposed breast. Light pulsed from the ground as my phone continued to vibrate.

Buzz.

Buzz.

Slowly standing, careful not to wake Aspen, I lifted him to the crook of my neck, rocking him a few moments before pressing a kiss to his forehead and placing him back in his crib.

The buzzing stopped and the illumination vanished. I lowered to the ground, crawling around in the pitch, running my hand along the carpet, feeling for my phone. My fingers hit the plastic of my case, and I gripped it just as Aspen released a big yawn. I tapped on the screen.

Two missed calls and a text message asking me to call him.

Fuck. Does he have news on Hazel?

I scrambled on my hands and knees, as quietly as possible, out of the nursery and into my room. Then I slowly closed the door, waiting until I felt it click shut before sitting against it and pulling my phone back out. I took a deep breath, tapping it to dial Lynx. My nerves catapulted in my fingertips, nearly making me hang up just as his smooth voice dripped like honey through the speaker. "Hey. You okay? I got worried."

Concern wove through his tone.

I kept my voice just above a whisper. "Sorry. I had my phone on silent. Aspen was hungry and I couldn't answer."

"He sleeping now?"

"Yeah." I yawned, moving away from the door until I was leaning against the foot of the bed. "Did you learn something about Hazel?"

"No. I'm sorry. Didn't mean to get your hopes up."

My heart sank a bit. But if he wasn't calling about Hazel... "Why did you call, then?"

"I was thinking about you, Wicked," he said, leaving a long pause after. When I didn't respond, rendered speechless by his admission, he continued, "I know I left things a bit unsettled earlier."

If by *unsettled* he meant horny as fuck on a full moon... It had taken me a full ten minutes and a quick cold splash to my face to clear away the desperate ache. "Yes."

The phone remained silent, and I wondered if I was supposed to say more. It had been so long since I'd dated, if that even was what this was or where it was headed. That seemed like such a distant concept, especially with having Aspen. "What did you have to do?"

"I had to go before I dragged you out under the stars."

Silence filled both ends of the line.

My chest warmed, and my Desire crackled under my skin, perking up at that idea. When I realized he wasn't going to say anymore until I broke through the quiet, I stirred up every ounce of courage I could, summoning a sultry lilt to my tone. "Why didn't you?"

The words came out raspy and rough, like those spoken just after waking in the morning. My lilt was rusty. Maybe rustier than my Desire.

I winced at my own awkwardness.

"We both know you weren't ready."

Oof. I didn't know whether to swoon at his perceptiveness or be resentful of it. My Desire was definitely feeling the latter.

"If you want your magic, that is your choice. Not one I will influence."

My small crest of ecstasy was eclipsed by a surge, knocking the wind out of me and drenching me in molten heat. It seeped into every part of me, liquid magma coursing through my veins and into my core. I clenched my thighs tightly together.

Lynx chuckled on the other line.

This witch.

"You are doing a pretty poor job of *not* influencing me right now." My voice was breathy as I gulped back the sensations rippling through me. Some decadently familiar, others dangerously new. This wasn't just my own lust or Desire coursing through my veins, this was *his.* "I thought you could only manipulate emotions if you are touching?"

"Sometimes I get a little temporary linger time afterward to share my own feelings. It just depends." He paused for a moment, then added, "Just because I want you to have the space to decide for yourself doesn't mean I didn't want more tonight."

He wanted more tonight.

He wanted... me.

"What did you have in mind?" My voice must have cracked at least twice to get the words out. I shook my head to make sure I wasn't still asleep in the rocking chair in some sort of hormone-induced daydream.

"Come to the window," he instructed. "Leave the phone next to you."

Yes, sir. His voice was firm like the way he'd set up a circuit in his bootcamp, only my body was much more eager to listen to these commands.

"Okay."

I pushed to stand, padding over to the window. A thin sliver of coppery moonlight caressed the pane, beckoning me to its glow. I hesitated, staying a few steps back from its illumination, unsure how much claim I wanted to give my magic yet, if at all. Moonlight could still recharge our gifts through the enchanted glass that'd been installed with all the houses in Celestial Haven, lunar paneling constructed into the molding.

My gaze dropped to the light popping on diagonal from me and the silhouette caressed by it. I could see enough to tell he was only in a pair of pants, his muscles defined by the glow around him.

"N-now what?" I stumbled over my words, throat suddenly dry. Every part of me felt parched.

"Show me how you like to be touched."

Great Goddess.

Now not only was my throat dry, all the air had been sucked out of my lungs. My chest heated, my gift prickling beneath its flush. "I-I don't even know anymore."

And I really didn't. It'd been so long since I'd had the urge to act on a *craving*.

"Put those fingers to use and find out."

Being so sleep deprived, so starved of even an iota of self-care navigating life as a single mom, my sex life felt like a luxury I couldn't afford. Besides, up until now, the only person who'd conjured those feelings in me had been Atlas. It almost seemed easier to chip away that facet of myself—the one that used to fuck unashamed in the moonlight.

When was the last time I'd even felt like that witch?

"You still there, Wicked? Need me to send some encouragement?"

"Please don't!" I said much too quickly, not ready for another punishing pleasure wave to smack my witchy bits. "Just give me a moment. I'm very out of practice with this."

"You think this is something I practice often?"

"Probably." I laughed, shaking my head. "Have you seen yourself?"

"I have." He chuckled in response, running a hand through his hair. "But this isn't something I make a habit of."

"What are you going to do?" I asked, awkwardly. Was he going to stand there while I did this? How would I even look him in the eye tomorrow, or Saros for that matter?

"I'm going to enjoy the show, Wicked."

"But you can't even see." My gaze dropped to my drapey dress that left much to the imagination.

"I don't need to. I can feel you."

Empath vibes. "All the way from there?"

"What do you think?" he taunted. A tsunami of want washed through me, and I clenched my thighs tighter.

This was going to take some getting used to. Not that there would necessarily be more after tonight. Maybe there wouldn't be. I didn't know, and that was both scary and part of the allure.

Be brave, Oakley.

He was all the way across the cul-de-sac and could sense if I needed to stop. I knew he wouldn't push me to do anything if I said no, even if my insides—my Desire—was shouting at me to take him into the pines.

He unbuckled the belt of his jeans, pulling down at the waist until a long, thick outline bobbed in the window. I suddenly wished there wasn't a cul-de-sac or these stupid walls between us. "Now fuck that pretty pussy and tell me how soaked you are."

His words, his desire, were like a bolt of adrenaline striking me deep. Silently, I obeyed, gripping the skirt of my maxi and bunching the fabric in one hand until it was at my thigh. My free hand trailed the skin there, body aching for it to go higher. I lifted the dress a few more inches, gaze dropping when my fingers came to a halt at the crop of curls settled at my center.

I probably could do with a shave. Or wax. My core winced at the thought.

"Eyes on me, Wicked."

And just like that, my attention snapped back up to Lynx's illuminated perfection in the window. Somehow, he looked even larger than he had a moment ago, his body shifting so I could see the full length of him. He gripped himself, giving a long, mouth-watering stroke.

Scraps of lust floated giddily up my tummy, warming my chest, cheering at the sight. My gift wanted him.

But more importantly, *I* wanted him.

Dipping tentatively into my folds, I steadied my leg on the windowseat, my other hand holding my dress high enough to reach without putting myself on display.

But he was.

He twisted up and down his shaft in rough, commanding movements that made me slick. I brushed along my seam, sinking two fingers inside of myself. My thumb strummed experimentally at my clit, playing with the pressure while I curled my fingers in time with his strokes. His upper arm flexed, muscles taut in the coppery moonlight, and I could hear his breath quicken through the phone.

"You like it, don't you?" he teased, tone flooded with mirth. "Seeing what you do to me."

My exhales came out in ragged spurts, intensity building deliciously under my touch. "I do."

Pulsing against my clit in quick succession, my breath caught, legs starting to quiver. I was getting close.

"That feels good, doesn't it, Wicked?"

My voice dropped a husky octave. "You would know."

There was no pretending possible with his gift, every wave of pleasure that crashed into me crashed into him. And the knowledge of that only spurred me on.

I strummed myself into a heady crescendo, becoming bolder with each stroke. "Why don't you come here and find out for yourself?"

What the hell am I saying? And whose voice is this?

"Don't tempt me, Wicked," he gritted out through the line. "It's taking everything not to come just watching you like this."

"I'm not stopping you," I rasped, head rolling back uncontrollably until the urge to watch him, to see his reaction to me, tugged my chin down.

"Ladies first." His arm moved faster, and my pulse raced as I envisioned my own hand stroking him, my lips wrapped around his cock. Wondering what he would taste like. How deep he could reach inside me.

Imagination running wild, my legs shook uncontrollably. I braced myself on the windowsill, not giving a fuck about anything other than enjoying every sensation jolting through me and the instinct to shred away every wall and path that stood between us.

"Just like that, Wicked," Lynx demanded, his breath more ragged than before. He was close. "Keep going and I'll give you a reward."

I gritted my teeth. All I wanted was to never stop feeling this. Droplets of Desire rose up through me. Sensations I missed that, I realized in this moment, were just as much a part of myself as everything else.

My body and its cravings still belonged to me.

An intense crest of his lust surged through my veins, spinning my own waves of ecstasy into a tsunami.

"Goddess!" I shouted, every part of me pulled deliciously taut before I went slack against the glass pane.

"Yes, you are." Lynx chuckled darkly. "Glad you enjoyed my gift."

"I did." The dress's material pooled at my feet, legs still quivering.

Lynx was slowing his strokes, twisting up and down, up and down. I could only make out its thick outline, but I was more than ready to hop on for a moonlit ride.

"Did you...finish?" I asked, worry suddenly floating to the surface.

"Oh, Wicked." His silhouette shook its head in the darkness. "You did this to me, so I'm saving every last drop for you."

Goddess, this witch.

"Okay," was all I managed to croak out, making him chuckle more. My throat was dry, but every other part of me felt wet, wet, wet—including some of my formerly dusty crumbs of Desire. While I wasn't replenished by any means, maybe it would be enough to help find Hazel.

And for the first time since I'd let my magic begin to slip away, I was certain that I wanted it all back.

CHAPTER 17

LYNX

I wrapped the towel around myself, still shivering from my cold shower. While my libido had calmed down, my body felt like a live wire, drenched in the lust I'd channeled from Oakley and the rest of our coven and their full moon activities.

When I walked into the bedroom Saros was still fully dressed, legs crossed with case files strewn around him in a messy circle. His version of organized chaos. I knew better than to question it.

Brow furrowed, he squinted at the holographic board situated in front of the bed.

"Someone looks sour."

He pointed at the hologram, shifting a string and repositioning an orb into another spot. He was looking at the timeline again—which disappearances had happened and after which new moons. "Not all of us have time to think with our dicks when there are people missing or potentially murdered out there."

"Ah." I picked up a few of the case files, making room for myself to sit across from him on the bed. "I see."

"What?" He finally looked up at me before snatching the files from my hand. The air slithered around us, telling me there was more to him just being annoyed with work. "I'm not jealous, if that's what you're thinking," he continued, much too quickly. Envy pulsed through him, laced with a thick ribbon of sugar. Lust.

"Your lips might be saying one thing but that *other* sensation I'm getting from you disagrees." I knew better than to mention the other one, though I'm sure he already knew he couldn't hide anything from me. We'd been friends and colleagues—occasionally more—for over a decade now.

He closed his eyes, pinching the bridge of his nose. "Can't you turn that off?"

"No more than you can," I stated, arching a brow at him.

"Fair enough."

I knew that would shut him up. Not that it was what I wanted, but he wouldn't tell me what was really going on tonight, not even when I'd let him use his gift on me to replenish his magic. It was rare Saros ever said exactly what was on his mind. Fortunately, we'd known each other so long that between my empath status and that foundation, I could usually piece it together myself.

My attention drifted to the board, trying to note if anything else on it had changed before I walked in. There were still a few key suspects on the list when it came to the disappearances: a rebellious group of shifters whose favorite full moon spot had been encroached on when this street was built; the Vivaldi Syndicate, a vampire mob with their fingers in many of the supernatural and mortal communities; and finally, a rival coven. There were three others in Celestial Haven housed on Sable Sky Street, Meridian Manor, and Astral Plains Place, not to mention the twenty-seven others spread throughout the globe, though their distance made it less likely with the power they would need to cast from so far.

As agents of SNO-OPS, Supernatural Neighborhood Order Operations, it was our job to handle intersupernatural community conflict. We'd been here a year and were no closer to narrowing down our list of suspects. The only thing we did know was that the disappearances always coincided with the new moon, when the sky was empty, as if the perpetrator wanted to make sure the Moon Goddess couldn't see them casting from her midnight perch.

"Learn anything new?" I asked, changing the subject.

"You mean while you were off seducing the neighbor?"

Guess the subject wasn't going to change.

"Oakley," I replied with a frown, though I knew better than to let him get to me. "She has a name, Saros."

"Look, I just don't want you getting attached. What happens when we solve all this and the boss tells us it's time to leave?"

"I don't know." Realistically, we weren't any closer than we were a year ago, but he had a point. I couldn't help how I felt when I was around her, and the way all her jumbled emotions both perplexed and intrigued me. "But I'm interested enough to see what's possible."

He let out an exasperated sigh. "Just be careful."

The slight sweet dust of desire flavored the air despite the bristle in his tone.

"Are you warning me or reminding yourself?" I asked, pursing my lips.

His eyes snapped to mine as he began collecting up the files into a stack. "What is that supposed to mean?"

"I've seen the way you watch her." *And the way you feel, though if I said it, you'd only retreat more.*

"And?"

"And you're interested."

He collected the folders, sliding them into the hidden panel of his nightstand before clicking it into place. Then he waved his hands, spelling the board into hiding beneath the floorboard.

"I'm interested because she could have *clues* to help us solve this case," he lied, the air becoming acrid. Taking off his pants and shirt, he headed into the bathroom and began brushing his teeth.

"Oh, I think you want to solve more than this case when it comes to her." He bristled at my accusation but continued brushing. Spitting into the sink, he rinsed his mouth, then wiped it on the towel before coming back into the room. His glasses were on, right before bed was one of the few times he wore them.

They were sexy as hell.

I tipped my head at him. "When are you going to stop hiding behind the job?"

"When I'm not literally *hiding*." He climbed into the bed, grabbed his e-reader from the night table, and rolled to his side to face me before spelling the lights to turn off. His eyes darted back and forth between me and the screen. "We are undercover, Lynx. You've already told her more than you should, Goddess only knows how with the runes we've got." He pointed to the one hidden within the constellations that traveled up his arm and across his chest. "What happens if headquarters finds out? That could tank our careers. Everything we've worked toward."

"Like you said, she could have clues to help us solve the case. We've never had someone left in the house when the others disappeared. That makes her an asset."

He raised a brow. "You sure you're not focused more on her other *assets*?"

"Oh, so you're admitting you've noticed them?" I replied with a grin.

"You are a right pain in my ass, you know that?" His eyes went back to the screen, but the way he shifted in the bed told me just as much as the syrupy air curling thick around me. I'd also bet anything he was engrossed in some spicy fantasy book that he usually claimed he read for the *well-done magic systems* and *unique worlds.*

"Look, she needs to be able to trust us. I told her as much as I could so she would. And now she's coming to work with us willingly tomorrow. She and Hazel have communal tattoos."

"Is she going to be able to handle the spellwork needed to use it?" The air shook a bit, his nerves creeping through his words. "And please don't tell me your little window display was just to help her recharge so she has power to draw on for the locator spell. I know we want to catch this perp, but that would be fifty shades of fucked up, Lynx."

"Are you suggesting I'm trying to screw our neighbor just to gain the advantage in our case?"

"I would hope not, especially since you are *interested* in her. But if on some level you're doing this to further the case and not out of genuine feelings, I'm asking you to stop. Now. Before you do any damage. She deserves better than that."

I smirked, glad he was paying attention to his book boyfriends and girlfriends more than me at the moment. It was better he didn't know I was on to the real reason behind his protectiveness.

"The sooner we close this case, the better," he grumbled, tapping another page on his tablet.

"Tired of being married to me already?" I taunted, gripping my chest with my hand dramatically. "It's only been a year."

"Unfortunately, the newlywed stage really is only a thing for actual newlyweds, Lynx. Those temporary vow marks we have will be erased just as quickly as they were installed before our assignment."

"Ouch," I said, biting back the sting of his words.

"You know what I mean." He let his tablet fall on his chest, giving me his full attention. "I want a real life. One where I don't have to pretend constantly. Once we are finished with this case, I'm requesting out of undercover. It was better than the alternative for me, but now— I'm just getting too old for this."

"Forty-four isn't old." I'd be there soon enough in about six years. Other than the crinkles around his eyes and the silver scattered through his stubble when he let it grow, he'd barely aged in my mind. Still the handsome man I met at twenty-five, just a little less broken and a little more jaded.

"Oh, I know it's not. But it's too old to not be building my own life." He tapped the side of his reader, blotting out its light before returning it to the nightstand. Then he took off his glasses, placing them next to it. "Don't you want to be able to go *home* and have a *real family*?"

"I know what you're saying," I conceded. "But you are my real family."

"And you're mine." His eyes softened, realizing the harshness of his words, and he reached for my cheek, resting his palm there. "But I'd like to have more than just a set of posed wedding photos in a house that we'll never own, on a street where I have to vet every witch I meet to see if they are a suspect for a case I'm working."

Valid.

"Well, hopefully things will go well with Oakley tomorrow," I said, grabbing his wrist and pressing a kiss to it.

"At this point any clue we can get would be useful." He

sighed, orange wisps of frustration rolling off him as he turned away from me. "Guess we will see how it goes."

"I have a good feeling about her, Saros."

"Of course you do." He chuckled before muttering low, "I just wish it wasn't in a way that might compromise our case."

WHAT HAD OCCURRED IN THE WINDOWS OF NUMBERS 13 AND 16 HAD BEEN A SURPRISE, NOT THAT THERE WERE MANY SHOCKING THINGS THAT HAPPENED ON STARRY NIGHT LANE.

In fact, it had probably been the most shocking sighting since the Larks had gotten *flocked* by a teenage pack of wolves from two streets over.

Sixty-two plastic ravens spanned the lawn, sixty-two stakes driven deep into the grass.

Disturbing its hallowed ground.

Then the offensive display had been left there. The Larks had the audacity to believe it was *funny*.

After several strongly worded emails from the HOA—all ignored—the absolute flocking disaster remained. When prospective tenants drove down the lane, they gawked through their windows. A few even spun around the cul-de-sac, skipping their real estate appointments, leaving Hazel Brooks, Celestial Haven's exclusive realtor, in a lurch yet again.

Luckily, that had been a while ago, and this new shocking window display hadn't elicited nearly as much gaping. It hadn't gone unnoticed, though. As Jade and Jacob Fisher returned to number 12 in the wee hours of the morning, she shot her husband a grin, then pulled the glowing yellow vial from her pocket. Popping the lid, he drank it down before following her inside.

When the light blinked on in their upstairs bedroom and their two silhouettes formed into one, the sounds filtered out into the quiet street. But they weren't the only ones who had seen it, and while more magic was brewed that night for Starry Night's coven, so had a heavy dose of envy.

CHAPTER 18

OAKLEY

I tossed in the last few rattles and grabbed the baby seat, throwing it into the stroller's basket before heading down the drive. Usually the afternoons were quiet, everyone having already dispersed from their Sunday morning coffee and chitchat outside of the Coven Community Center.

My mind raced, tripping over last night's moonlit exhibition. The small streak of luminescence absorbed through the windowsill's lunar panels had supplied me with a small amount of magical juice, which was good since the tracking spell would draw from my energy.

Energy.

Ha. That seemed like a foreign concept ever since I'd become a mother. Honestly, even months prior, when my growing belly and anxious thoughts made it near impossible to sleep.

While I had planned to wait another month, never expecting last night to play out how it did, it felt good to reconnect with myself, even if only a smidge. I didn't have nearly the amount my body could be blessed with, but hopefully it was enough to help find my sister—it had to be. If the spell took every speck of magic I had in me, I'd give it up in a heartbeat for her.

My phone buzzed in the cupholder and I picked it up, hoping for an update on Hazel.

ATLAS

Miss you both already.

My chest ached, holding back the urge to text back. To say I missed him too, even though I had no right to. I'd find a way to summon the courage to reply later—when I could formulate what I'd say.

When Atlas visited this morning, I'd hidden the small amount of magic I'd replenished, keeping my distance as he said goodbye to Aspen. There was a part of me that felt a twinge of remorse about making him leave last night, but my willpower was much too weak around him. If he'd stayed, it would have ended up with us both wrapped up in the moonlight, giving him the opening I knew he hungered for to confirm why we should be together.

The fallout would have been disastrous.

Meanwhile, I didn't have any regrets about what I'd done with Lynx. Did that make me a horrible witch or was it a sign that things were truly over between Atlas and I?

The only thing that nagged at me was if Saros knew. They lived together, so I assumed he did. But what if he *didn't*? Lynx had said Saros was aware of his feelings for me, he'd witnessed our less-than-timid kiss, but I didn't want to do anything to come between them—especially with them working together to find my sister. I needed her back.

Two strollers wheeled side by side in my direction. I stopped, not wanting to draw more attention to the fact that I was heading to Luna's after the morning rush. It would look especially odd when I went *inside* the coffee truck to meet with them.

"Did you have a blessed full moon?" Ivy called out, a brilliant smile gracing her lips. She had a little pep in her step, probably from replenishing her magic among enjoying *other* full moon activities.

I returned the smile in full. "I did. Thanks for asking."

"Goddess, I'm still recovering from last night. Jacob was insatiable after we'd recharged. I shouldn't have let him take that extra adrenaline shot." Jade chuckled, shaking her head.

I couldn't say anything in response. As far as the neighborhood was concerned, Lynx and Saros were married, devoted solely to each other. While supernaturals were no strangers to sharing or opening up their sex lives within the coven, it wasn't something they talked about. Marriages were sacred, more so than in the mortal world.

In fact, our Goddess-blessed wedding runes held them to any vows they made to each other. Any deviation from them was punishable via the mark they wore. There was no room for secrets in a marriage, something our community took seriously.

"I'm so glad you came to the moonluck. Aren't they amazing?" Jade asked, pushing down the brake on her stroller alongside Ivy. "I swear, only Starry Night Lane does it like that, but even the other Celestial Haven covens have similar things."

"Just not nearly as spectacular," Ivy said as she brushed back her platinum tresses, a few streaks of silver intermixed.

A whine came from in front of Jade, and she rolled her violet eyes, grabbing her toddler out of the back seat of her double stroller and setting him down to waddle barefoot around the sidewalk. "Well, we do pride ourselves on being the model street and coven."

"We haven't won the HOA Stellar Street award all these years for nothing. Every year since the houses went up on Starry Night Lane. This one will be no different." Ivy reached a hand into her stroller, and I could hear the contented giggles of Parker filter through the air. I looked down, spotting Aspen staring at me, his chestnut eyes so intensely focused I wished I knew what he was thinking.

"Thanks to Aurora and Fitz—" Jade sprinted after her little witch, black hair whipping behind her, managing to snatch him up before he ran out into the middle of the cul-de-sac. "This one. Always a runner. I should have known."

Goddess help me once Aspen was mobile.

"Did I just hear my name?"

Aurora was dressed in a black workout ensemble, her zip-up sports bra only halfway done, showing off her ample cleavage. How were her breasts so perky? I was certain mine would be a set of sad flapjacks once Aspen was through with them.

She sipped from her water bottle, the dusky shade muting the bubbling, bright-green elixir within.

"What's that?" Ivy asked, eagerly, looking at her drink.

"My usual energy elixir, just added some electrolytes to restore all the full moon activities." She gave a languid sigh then brought her attention from Ivy to me. "Highly recommend them to help maximize the moon's replenishment. I have a monthly subscription for Madame Mercer's Potions."

"I'll have to do that." Ivy already had her phone out, looking at her site on the dark web. When her attention came back up, she stared at Aurora like a groupie about to drop to her knees at a Winter's Revenge concert. "We were just raving about the moonluck."

"As always, you sure know how to throw a party." While

Jade didn't give the same devout, awe-induced stare, her compliment felt no less overdone.

A self-impressed smile played at Aurora's lips. Somehow, despite being maybe an inch taller or the same height as all of us, she always appeared to be looking down. I held back my urge to eye roll or make a gagging sound. "Oakley, you must come to the blackout bash."

"I'd love to"—*there's nothing I'd rather do less right now*—"but there's no one to watch Aspen."

Sometimes having a little witchling *keeping* you from social events had its advantages.

"So no word on Hazel yet?" Ivy asked.

"No. Not yet." As if on cue, my phone buzzed in my palm. "How did you know?"

My eyes dropped to the screen, swiping to see what it was.

LYNX

Last-minute training session. Be there as soon as I can.

"Oh, there are no secrets in Starry Night's coven," Aurora stated.

Of course there weren't.

This type of coven, one where everyone did everything together all the time, was very different from what I was used to in Salem. There, Atlas and I had mainly kept to ourselves, sometimes having parties or gatherings to attend, but usually he was the guest of honor and I was tagging along as his date. I didn't understand the appeal of hanging out in large groups where half the niceties were forced.

That was Hazel's thing. She would love going to a blackout bash. Maybe she'd even been to one here before I had moved in. I never asked. I really should have. Maybe if I'd not been so preoccupied with adjusting to motherhood—

"Come anyway. You're welcome to bring the little witchling," the Queen of Blessed Crescent continued, pulling me from my thoughts. She smiled but it didn't reach her eyes.

Dammit.

"Are you sure?" I asked, hoping to give her another way to let me out of this. "It didn't sound like these were really meant to be witchling friendly."

"Not a problem." The way Aurora said it like a challenge made it seem like she knew all too well what I was trying to do. "We don't cast until midnight anyway. And we'll have plenty of magic to pull from with everyone else in attendance. I do hope you'll join us."

Was that a dig that she knew I didn't have enough magic to cast with them?

"I'll try my best," I replied with a forced smile.

Maybe I was reading into it, my anxiety over my waning power taking root. If this had been a month ago, I wouldn't have given a fuck. But now that my magic dwindled to near extinction, it made me more sensitive about it. Letting a little of it come out to play during the full moon had been incredible, and I wanted the rest of it back.

"You really should come," Jade insisted.

Ivy nodded. "It would be a blast."

"Well, I better run. Lots to do." Aurora gave a halfhearted wave before speed walking toward Blessed Crescent.

"We better head toward the bus stop before the kids arrive," Jade said to Ivy, looking my way. "We'll catch you later."

"Sounds good!"

I watched them continue down the sidewalk a bit, playing with Aspen in his stroller. Then I parked behind Luna's and looped my diaper bag over my shoulder. Grabbing Aspen in one arm, I knelt and picked up the portable baby seat with my free hand, the strap of my diaper bag sliding down. I quickly caught it and tried again, holding Aspen tightly while I scooped it up, hair falling in my face.

I took a deep breath before knocking on the truck's door. The clinking of glass and rustling came from inside, steady footsteps growing louder before the door opened. Saros's brow furrowed, then his eyes darted around behind me.

"It's just me," I said with a shrug, the motion sending my diaper bag off my shoulder again. Saros reached down and grabbed it, along with the baby seat. Setting them on the truck's floor, he held the door open for me as I squeezed in, Aspen snuggled up against my chest.

"Aurora must have called another last-minute personal training session." His lips pressed into a thin line.

His reaction set me on edge. Was Lynx not actually training her? I knew he had said that Saros was fine with Lynx's interest in me. Could the same be true of Aurora? I hadn't asked if he was with anyone else. Maybe I didn't have a right to, but unease swirled in my gut, regardless. "He trains her a lot?"

"He does."

Saros was a man of few words. Not that I usually minded, but right now my insecurities were creeping in and poking through my ribs, leaving my heart all too vulnerable.

He set the baby seat down on the ground, placing a cushion on the floor next to it. "It's nothing more than training, though, if that's what you're wondering."

Could everyone in this damned neighborhood read minds?

"I mean, it's not really my business," I replied, trying to play it cool and sounding completely not cool.

His voice deepened and his spine went rigid. "It might not be your business...but it's *mine*. And I would know."

Well, fine then, Mr. Bristles.

I put Aspen in the seat and reached into the diaper bag to set out some toys. Saros picked up the rattle in the shape of a quartz and knelt, shaking it a few times. Aspen giggled, and he did it again, the hard crinkles edging his eyes softening a bit. When the witchling wrapped his fingers around one of Saros's, he froze. It was as if he'd turned into marble, brows lifting in surprise the only movement. Then he continued playing, as if nothing had happened, keeping his attention turned away from me.

"Do you mind me asking what your relationship is exactly? Lynx said you're not married, but he also said you were involved outside of working together."

"Yes." The vein in his forehead popped out, and he swallowed audibly. "Let me just say that I have to be careful how I answer because of certain oaths."

I tickled Aspen, picking up toys and placing them in his hands to shake around. "So what are you to each other?"

"I can't imagine my life without Lynx."

A wayward faux crystal flew into the air, smacking him right in the face. He grimaced, opening one eye at Aspen. Then Saros shook his head and handed the plush toy back to him. "He's my family. The only one I've got."

"I understand." I kept my gaze on Aspen, afraid to look Saros in the eye, still unsure how much he knew about last night. "I don't want to interfere with anything."

"You won't. You aren't." He stood up, grabbing a bottle of water and handing it to me. "I would never stop him from pursuing someone he really wanted, and he'd do the same."

"So you've been with other people since you've been together?"

"Yes."

I unscrewed the cap, taking a swig, all the questions swirling in my mind. "And it hasn't worked out?"

"We move often for work." The same vein ticked again, pulsing in his forehead. It looked painful but he didn't show any signs if it did bother him.

"I see."

This was just their normal thing: have flings while they were investigating something and then move on. My chest zinged at how not special this all made me feel. But at the same time, I didn't know if I was ready for anything serious.

"What happens once you guys find my sister and who's been causing these disappearances? Will you have to leave?" I tried not to sound too attached to the outcome of his answer.

"Most likely." This time it was Saros who refused to look at me, his eyes on Aspen, who'd managed to wrangle his giant finger into his palm again, squeezing tight.

I guess that was good to know. To set the expectation. This could be a short fling. Right now, the only man I'd commit fully to was the tiny witchling in front of me.

I could do simple. Unattached. It would probably be easier that way, especially with all the leftover baggage with Atlas I was still navigating...or avoiding, depending how you looked at it.

"I honestly don't see what he sees in me." My hand came to my mouth at my own admission. Did he have a truth-telling gift? Why would I just confide something like that to a stranger? To Saros no less. I always managed to spew enough verbal diarrhea for the both of us when he was around.

"I've found most people don't see themselves as they truly are," Saros said, nothing but pure sincerity infusing his words.

I brushed them off, not wanting to reflect on them too

long. He was probably right, but it was hard for me to see myself as the sexy woman Lynx seemed to view me as when all I saw was a sloppier, wigglier, and more discombobulated version of my former self.

It was probably better to stay focused on the task at hand right now anyway. "So, should we go ahead and get started?"

CHAPTER 19

OAKLEY

"**D**id you replenish enough of your magical stores for this last night? Lynx briefed me on your situation." Saros held eye contact, all business, like he wasn't asking if I got my freak on under the full moon. My cheeks heated. "I know it's an awkward question, but I need to know before I cast the spell, otherwise you could be putting yourself in danger."

My gaze dropped to my lap. "I replenished some... I still don't have much, but I'll use whatever I have to find Hazel."

He cleared his throat. "Okay. Good."

"And are you sure you're okay with Lynx and me?" I clenched my pants, not sure what to do with the nervous energy thrumming through me. "You don't feel...I don't know, left out?"

His evergreen eyes snapped to mine. "Was that an invitation, Midnight?"

Damn.

I tittered nervously, afraid of what that answer was. I wouldn't ever want him to feel obligated to be interested just because Lynx was. Meanwhile, my chest heated, spreading up through my neck, and my throat dried at the thought of the two of them together...with me. Desire thrummed under the surface, curious to see if I'd send any his way with the little magic that I had. There was part of me that was curious if he wanted that invitation. If I did release some Desire, it would only work on him if it existed there already. But if it didn't, I wasn't going to look like a fool in front of Saros more than I already did.

Cutting into the silence, he continued, as if he hadn't just sent a smolder to my witchy bits.

"I'll need to see your tattoo."

I turned around, pointing over my shoulder at the center of my upper back.

"You'll need to shift your top so I can access the whole thing."

A wail came from the seat next to us, and my chest tightened, tingling as my breasts filled in response.

Just perfect.

"Well, this should make it easier." I laughed awkwardly, leaning over to pick up Aspen. Saros went and shut Luna's service window. Holding Aspen in the crook of one arm, I reached behind me to fumble with the clasp of my halter top, thumbing over it a few times and missing the latch.

"Allow me," Saros offered. I nodded, and a moment later it was undone. He moved so deftly, his fingers didn't even brush my skin. "Do you need me to grab anything else for you?"

"A burp cloth would be great." I shimmied the top down until my front was uncovered, pulling Aspen to me.

I stayed quiet, listening to the rustle of him combing through my diaper bag. A moment later, a Luna's-branded towel had been draped over my shoulder. "I didn't see what you were looking for, but you can just use this."

"That's fine," I said, massaging the breast Aspen was currently latched to, stroking in downward motions to hopefully speed this up and ease the discomfort. "You can go ahead and do whatever you need to, unless the spellwork is going to do anything to him while he feeds?"

"Not at all. I just need to put some balm on it to establish the connection with you and your sister's communal magic before I do the incantation."

The scent of pine and eucalyptus filled the truck, wiping out any previous coffee smells that had accumulated there. I wrinkled my nose.

"Sorry, I know it's strong stuff." It was cool against my skin, tracing my tattoo, outlining every leaf and stroke of ink it was composed of. He did a few coats, all using magic, never actually touching me with his hands. Goosebumps flitted down my arms. "Cold too," he added.

Yeah…it was the cold doing that. Not the fact that I was half naked being ghost-touched by this rugged and unattainable witch.

"I'm going to cast the spell now." I felt the energy from his palms hovering over either side of the tattoo, as if an electric thrum pulsed within the small gap between the pads of his hands and my skin. I wanted to erase that distance. To feel those strong hands, his calloused fingers trailing down my spine, gripping me tightly—

Aspen smacked my chest, halting my wayward libido. He was still hungry and had managed to drain me on that side, leaving me lopsided. "Hold on. Let me switch him."

"No problem."

Flicking my pinky against his lips to get him to unlatch, I switched him, trying to stay as covered as possible, not wanting to make Saros uncomfortable.

When I finished adjusting, I nodded for him to continue.

The magic from his hands moved slowly up and down either side of my spine. My Desire perked in response, surging with what little magical juice it had to the spot. The lines where he'd etched burned a bit, and he mumbled the spell so low in his rich timbre that I only caught every few words as he summoned the connection to Hazel.

It felt almost like getting tattooed all over again, only less painful. My magic pulsed through the outline, then scraped up and down along the shading until my back arched and I hissed out in pain.

"Sorry," Saros rasped. "The connection is established now but tell me if this gets to be too much. I'm going to start the locator spell."

I peered over my shoulder at the now pulsating lines of my tattoo. Crackling sounds flickered from my body, the ink's magic feeding into Saros's palm. With each passing second, I felt weaker, like my chest might cave right in, but I pushed through.

I needed to find my sister.

The searing spread through my back until it wrapped around my front. I must have flinched because a second later he'd taken Aspen from my arms.

"I told you to stop me if it got to be too much," Saros said through gritted teeth, fury rolling off him in waves. Only a small slip of evergreen shone in his narrowed gaze. "You didn't have as much magic to use as you let on. You should have told me."

Was he *mad*?

A twinge of guilt bounced off my ribs. He was right, but we were just so close to finding Hazel. I would push that limit as far as it could go if it meant locating her.

When I reached my shaking hands out, Saros refused to give Aspen to me, keeping him seated in his lap, arms crossing his small frame. "Not until you've at least had some water."

His tone was gruff but gentleness and worry blended in. I nodded in agreement, touched by his concern. Something about it made the space between my ribs shudder.

He shifted Aspen to his hip and stood up, bouncing to the fridge. Just as I went to warn him, a *blech* echoed within the confined space and projectile milk burst all over Saros and the side of the countertop.

"Shit. I'm sorry," I said, using the counter to pull myself up and grab Aspen. Saros let out a choking sound, only it wasn't aimed at the tiny spewing spawn in his arms. His eyes were wide at *me*.

My gaze dropped to my boobs still out to party.

Shit.

A little too delayed, Saros cleared his throat and took off his shirt, diverting his focus to wiping up the spewed leftovers of Aspen's meal from around the interior. A map of constellations and swirling stars were scattered across his upper back and chest, wrapping their way down one arm.

I suddenly had the urge to know what each one was and trace the swirls with my tongue—

"Looks like I missed out on all the fun." A smooth drawl filtered in from the open door, Lynx staring at us both half dressed, Aspen the only thing strategically blocking my nipples. He chuckled with amusement at our mutual mortification, stepping inside while Saros continued to clean up the truck.

"Spit-up," I said with a shrug and a matching awkward smile.

"I see."

I held the top of my halter up, positioning Aspen in front of me to keep it pinned in place.

"Hazel is alive," Saros said, drawing both our attention. "And not far."

"Thank Goddess." I let out a loud sigh, a few tears tracking down my cheeks. "Could you see anything else?"

"Not without hurting you." His jaw ticked.

I swayed back and forth with Aspen who'd begun babbling in my arms. "This is all my fault. If I didn't have such a hang up about my gift, I could have fully recharged last night. Then I would have had more for you to use for the locator spell."

Both of their brows shot to the tops of their foreheads, but before they could say anything more about what that would've involved, I cut in. "We would know more right now if I had. We could have a lead."

"You can't think like that." Saros shook his head. "She wouldn't want you to either. She'd want you to get your magic back on your own terms. Your choice, not a forced decision out of fear."

This was true. But it had never felt more selfish of a choice than it did right now.

Lynx came behind me and rested his hands on my shoulders, playing with Aspen, who was peeking over my left one. Calm washed through me, and I knew he was directing it. "We will figure it out."

I took a deep breath. "What are the chances we find her?"

"Honestly? Exponentially lower than if this were within the forty-eight hours of her disappearing," Saros replied, and Lynx cut him a glare.

"Great—"

"But statistically she wouldn't likely be alive at this point. The fact that she is says something," Lynx offered.

"Can we try again?"

Saros shook his head. "That's not a good idea, Midnight."

"Just try." I picked up a cup and went and got the water Saros hadn't managed to pour before Aspen had decorated his shirt. I chugged it down in a few gulps, then refilled and did it again, shaking the empty glass in their faces. "Please. Maybe we can get a clearer location on her."

Saros's fingers massaged his temples. "I need to assess how much magic I can pull without potentially harming you."

"I need to do this," I said, tone swathed in resolve.

"Here." Lynx held his hands out. "Why don't I take him if you're going to try again? We'll go on a little walk around the cul-de-sac."

"That's a good idea," agreed Saros. I wasn't about to fight them, considering I wanted to see if we could learn anything more about Hazel's whereabouts. I rummaged through the diaper bag and grabbed the burp cloth, throwing it over Lynx's shoulder.

After he stepped out of the truck, Saros turned toward me. "How much magic do you feel like you have left?"

"Not much." My eyes dropped, then trailed back up to him.

He pointed to the cushion on the floor. After I sat down, he undid the halter clasp once again. I held the cups in front of me, suddenly all too aware of our proximity and the fact that we were alone now.

He hovered his hands on either side of my spine and my heart raced, waiting for him to pull on the communal magic again. Silence hung between us, like a delicate spiderweb. Then his baritone slipped between its threads, tone low. "Believe me. I understand having a gift that can also seem like a curse."

I craned my neck around. "You do?"

"My gift is Recollection." His throat bobbed a few times. "Seeing and unearthing memories, to be more exact."

"That's really helpful for your work, I'm sure." His gift seemed to almost be the opposite of Hazel's, and I had witnessed the issue with hers firsthand when people felt it was an intrusion on their privacy.

"It is. I can pull anything I want if I have a timeframe to work from. A focal point." His voice became a hush. "If I touch someone, I can see the moments that subconsciously weigh on them."

"That must be hard," I said, realizing why he'd been avoiding coming in contact with me, understanding how it felt to avoid having your gift take something from another whether you wanted it to or not.

"Yeah, most people don't enjoy their past being invaded like that." He reached for more of the balm he'd used earlier, and I let out another hiss as he established the connection. Luckily, it seemed to happen quicker this time, my magic more willing to cooperate with his spellwork. "Lynx is an exception, but we also don't have any secrets from each other."

"Well, between his Empathy and your Recollection, I'd guess that'd be impossible."

"Now you can see why I don't hold it against you opting to let your magic dwindle." He made a few small circles, like he was trying to relax me before casting the spell again. "I almost did when I was younger."

"Really?"

"Yes. Until our boss found me. Talked to me about it. I realized there was a lot of good that could be done with it."

"I'm glad you had someone to show you that. I'm still trying to find what the benefits are that outweigh the burdens."

I shrugged, clutching my halter tightly to me, pushing away the tingling chill streaking my spine where his spell grazed. "With my Desire, it can sometimes be hard to know what's been influenced by my gift. Sure, it has to play on feelings the person has already within them, but it still nags at me."

"I can assure you, I think your appeal has little to do with your ability. It just enhances what's already there."

"Maybe." My chest flushed, heat rushing through me at his compliment. "Then there's the bigger problem that comes with it…"

I trailed off, entranced by him as he whispered the spell. It breezed against my skin, only a slight sting of magic pricking me, taking from what little I had.

When my eyes fluttered, he stopped, grabbing me another glass of water. "That's enough."

I blinked, snapping out of my daze. "Were you able to get anything else?"

"Her presence is strong," he said, looking pleased. His smirk instantly lifting my spirits.

"What does that even mean?"

"She's here in Celestial Haven."

(((●)))

A FEW MINUTES LATER, A TAP ON MY SHOULDER HAD ME WAKING TO Lynx and Aspen's smiles.

Saros whispered from above me and I propped myself up to sit. "Lynx is going to take you home. I'll come by after I close up."

"I can get back on my own," I insisted, but when I went to stand, my legs shook, about to give out. My limbs were heavy, as if I'd just run a marathon—not that I would ever do that, but it seemed like that's how it would feel if I were ever crazy enough to run that far on purpose.

"I'm free for the rest of the day, Wicked," Lynx said, grabbing Aspen's things and throwing them into the diaper bag. Saros picked up the baby seat and helped me down from the truck as Lynx loaded everything into the stroller. "You're stuck with me until Saros comes over later."

I nodded lazily, too exhausted to pick a fight. Saros handed me water in a to-go cup. "Stay hydrated and get some rest. I'll see you both soon."

And with that, Lynx and I strolled toward the house, my mind swirling despite the exhaustion, feeling both dread and hope that Hazel was so close.

CHAPTER 20

OAKLEY

"You really didn't have to walk me home," I said, staggering a bit and using the stroller to support and guide me instead of the other way around.

"You could barely stand after that spell, Wicked. There's no way I'd let you handle this little witchling alone right now." Aspen sat in Lynx's arms, facing out toward the neighborhood, his eyes growing wide taking in the orange and yellow leaves spilling from the trees, a stark contrast to the jet-black houses stacked like near carbon copies lining the sides of the road.

"Well technically, I'd be pushing him back in the stroller."

"You seem barely able to push yourself back with the stroller." He chuckled, and Aspen broke into a gummy grin in front of him. "Anyway, I couldn't miss out on this cute company."

"He is cute," I agreed with a lazy sigh. "I only wish he'd let me have one outfit he didn't have to embellish with spit-up." I looked down, spotting a few slightly yellowed stains on the side of my top that we'd missed when he'd gotten Saros earlier.

"You sure you're okay?" Lynx asked, stopping our stroll.

"Yeah, why?"

"You walked right past your house."

I turned, finding a pumpkin-hued door. The Hendrix's house. "Oops. Guess I was just enjoying our stroll."

"I'd suggest we continue with it, but I think you need a nap."

"A nap. What is that?" I gave a half-assed chuckle—I didn't have enough energy to put my full ass behind it. "I'm okay. A little exhausted, but that is also my general vibe nowadays. Plus, Aspen will need another feed soon since most of his meal was left in Luna's."

I wobbled a bit going up the drive, and Lynx quickly shifted Aspen to his shoulder, grabbing the stroller from me to push it the rest of the way. I pressed my hand to the garage panel, waiting for it to take in my data and let me in, its red light still blinking. Turning to Lynx, I held out my arms to take Aspen inside. "Well, here we are safe and sound."

He made no move to give him to me. "Why don't I get some snacks together? You can feed the little witch and we'll eat. Then I'll watch him for a bit so you get a nap and shower in?"

It was a question that felt nothing like a question with the concern diffusing over his tone.

I touched the door, letting it slip open, then cocked my head at him. "Are you implying I smell?"

He moved in front of me, Aspen still in his arms as he held it open. Shaking a bit, I stepped into the laundry nook, a firm palm coming to the low part of my spine to steady me. "No. I just figure you don't get many uninterrupted showers these days."

"You're right. I don't." I brushed Aspen's cheek with my thumb, getting another sweet smile from him.

"Then let me keep him entertained and help you out." He sniffed himself, then laughed. "I can be the stinky one, since I just got done working out. How does that sound?"

He definitely had that post-workout musk, but for whatever reason getting farther away from it didn't appeal to me.

"Not being the stinky one sounds wonderful." I clutched his shirt to not fall over and pressed a quick kiss to his cheek. "Thank you."

Before I moved out of his arms, he cradled my chin, kissing me in a way that told me he hadn't forgotten about last night's moonlit show. Then he *booped* his nose with mine, giving me a salacious grin. "Get this witchling fed. I've got this."

He walked me to the nursery and waited for me to sit down in the rocking chair before handing me Aspen. A minute later he was in the kitchen, the sounds of cabinets and drawers and the fridge opening and closing. Undoing the clasp of my halter, I latched Aspen to me, stroking his cheek softly as he relaxed into his meal.

(((●)))

"Hey."

The whisper made my eyelids flutter open, finding Aspen passed out over Lynx's shoulder. He swayed back and forth, continuing to speak in hushed tones, not wanting to startle the sleeping witchling. "Sorry to wake you, but I got worried when you were in here awhile and he was starting to make noise. I didn't want to disturb you."

The only thing that disturbed me right now was the trail of drool hanging from my chin. I wiped it away, then rubbed my eyes, noticing that my halter had been redone. Probably better than just being conked out with my boobs showing, like usual. "Guess I was more tired than I thought."

"Understandable." Lynx moved with Aspen toward the crib. "That was no low-level magic spell and you don't have much to pull from right now."

He hesitated a moment, so I slowly stood up to help him. "It's okay. He shouldn't wake when you lay him down."

Setting him on the mattress, Lynx let his hand linger on the side of the crib, watching Aspen sleep. "I envy that peace."

"You and me both." I chuckled.

"I'm sorry the locator spell took so much from you," he whispered, laying a hand on my shoulder.

"I'm not. It got us more answers. I know that she's alive." I took his hand, sliding it down to the base of my spine as I wrapped myself closer to him. "So I guess it's a good thing last night happened."

Saros had said he knew about us and that he was okay with it. This would be temporary. Casual. If I didn't test the waters now, it might never happen. Sure, I hadn't done that in years, but maybe it would be easier this way.

"I'd say it was a good thing for many reasons, but yes." He kissed me, then interlaced his fingers with mine, leading me out to the kitchen. Pulling out a small plate from the fridge, he set it on the counter, along with a few other ones that were already filled. "I conjured up some cheese, crackers, and grapes."

"Thanks." I grabbed a grape, popping it in my mouth and savoring its burst of sweetness.

Within the next ten minutes, I'd eaten about two-thirds of what he'd set out. Goddess, nursing and using my magical stores made me ravenous. It also probably didn't help that I'd skipped a handful of meals since Hazel hadn't come back from her date.

Lynx smiled, seemingly pleased that I'd demolished what he'd put together for me. Leaning on the counter, he nodded toward the nursery. "If you want to go nap longer, you can. I can keep an eye on him and watch him when he wakes."

"When did he fall asleep?" I asked.

"Just before I woke you."

"I think I'll shower, then." I nodded toward my room, taking a few steps in that direction. I paused. Maybe it was the warmth of his gaze on my back that made me bold. Maybe I just didn't want to give myself time to overthink it. But I took a deep breath before turning back around to face him. "Join me?"

He choked on the cracker he was eating, little bits falling onto his shirt and the floor. Quickly grabbing a napkin, he cleaned them up, the look of surprise never leaving his face. I had to admit, I was enjoying sending him off his axis. It was only fair.

"Why don't we get cleaned up together?" I offered with a shrug. "You said it yourself that you're stinky."

"I did say that, didn't I?" He smirked, the sienna hue of his irises darkening into molten amber. "Still worked up after spending time with a certain sexy brewista?"

I clenched my thighs together, my chest heating, flush with embarrassment.

"Oh, Wicked, even in silence I can read you loud and clear." He moved away from the counter, prowling a few steps toward me. Then he gripped my chin to meet his gaze. "But I do want to make sure you're certain about this. I need to *hear* it."

"Yes," I managed to rasp out. My body leaned toward him like a blade of grass reaching for the sun, and I clutched his shirt, feeling the strong panes of his chest. "We'll have to keep an ear out for Aspen in case he wakes, but we should have twenty to forty minutes."

Lynx's smile grew as he took off his shirt at the speed of light. "Then what are we waiting for?"

CHAPTER 21

OAKLEY

Goddess, I knew his body was amazing from the silhouetted preview I'd had last night, but being this close to him made my wicked heart giddy with all the things I wanted to do.

My gift was practically prancing.

My eyes zoomed to the ink spanning his side, a large, intricate tree trunk with constellations stretched over its bark and branches that reached out toward his shoulder blade and climbed his chest.

Beautiful.

Lynx's attention drifted to where mine was pinned. "It's—"

"An oak tree," I said, voice breaking at the realization but not wanting to examine it much further.

Casual, Oakley.

This is casual.

And he just likes trees so much he wanted a tattoo.

Who doesn't like trees?

With every step my heart sped faster, my body flushing

with heat. I could do this. I'd already made myself come in front of him, for Goddess's sake.

I unclasped the halter of my top, pausing before I let it fall past my breasts.

"What is it?" he asked.

"I just want to forewarn you..." I stared down at myself, the balls of my feet digging into the carpet, as if my nerves were shooting straight through the floorboards. "I don't know if you've ever been with someone who's had kids."

What would he think of my body?

What if he only said kind things to make me feel better?

"I haven't." He stepped out of his sweats, his briefs hugging around the thickening bulge beneath. Eyes hooded, he looked at me and gave himself a stroke, the tip of him poking out through the bottom of his boxers, deep crimson with want. "If you think anything is going to change how much I want you, then you're dead wrong."

I gulped audibly, shimmying out of my halter. When my hands moved to my high-waisted leggings, I paused again, every insecurity rising to the surface over the softness of my body. The stretch marks. The scars.

Lynx stepped to me, all hard panes of muscle, and placed his hands over mine. "May I?"

"Sure," I croaked out, my breath catching when he began to pull my leggings down past my hips, taking my underwear with them. Cold air rushed between my thighs.

I didn't exhale until I'd shed them completely, fighting the urge to bring my hands in front of me.

I'd never been this way before. Afraid. But I wasn't the same witch I was a year ago. I was still figuring out who this one was, wobbly bits and all.

"Goddess, you're beautiful." His eyes traced over me, twin

pools shimmering with desire. My legs clenched, wetness building at their apex.

"You are," I said, my brain devoid of any intelligible thought other than 'is this real life?' and 'how will it feel to have him deep inside of me?' Would sex even *feel* the same? I was desperate to know, but the idea of finding out terrified me. I quickly turned, walking robotically into the wall-length walk-in shower and twisting the valve. Water rained from above and from the showerhead in front of me, and I let the droplets cover me, hoping it would stifle the way my body shook under Lynx's gaze.

The rustle of clothing came from behind me—

"Shit. I forgot the monitor."

"Witchy monitor at your service," Lynx said, stepping into the shower behind me. "I will be able to sense when he wakes. Right now, though, let's get you lathered up."

A muscled arm reached past my head, grabbing the soap and pumping it a few times into his palm. He massaged gentle circles along my shoulder, passing the nape of my neck before doing the same on the other side. Then he moved up and down my spine, adding more pressure where my tattoo was to clean off the balm's remains. He slowly placed his hands on my shoulders. "I'm going to turn you around now."

I nodded, shifting my weight and facing him. His hands swept along my collarbone, my body tingling in response.

When he grazed the side of my breast, I nudged his hand away, snapping my arms across me like a protective shield.

Shit. I wasn't expecting that.

He retreated, dropping his hands by his sides. "Are you okay? Did I do something wrong?"

"Not at all." I grimaced. "Sorry. Normally I'd be all for you touching me there, but right now it's kind of a no-go zone. Property of Aspen, if you will."

"Ah. I understand." He took a tentative step toward me again.

I glanced down. Bright purple and blue veins mapped my pale breasts, their angry streaks heading straight for my nipples. *Oh great.* "And sorry in advance if there's...leakage."

"Leakage?"

"It's a nursing thing," I replied with a shrug, arms still wrapped around me. I hadn't experienced it myself, but I'd read enough mommy blogs to have an idea of what to expect.

He cocked his head. "Should I be concerned if it happens?"

"No. I just don't know if it will. I haven't done any of *this* since before," I said, waving my hand over his sculpted body and too-tempting length.

"I see."

"I just know it can happen when I'm turned on," I said, figuring it was better to be upfront at this point instead of smacking him again if he got too close to making my balloon twins burst.

He looked up at me, arching a brow. "So you're saying I should try to make you leak?"

"Goddess no." I breathed out an awkward laugh. "I was just warning you."

"By telling me that I might be able to see how much I turn you on?" He made a face like my words were some sort of intriguing challenge. Then he stood and grabbed more soap, lathering himself up. "Noted, Wicked. And not in the least worried if it happens."

Instead of going back to washing my upper body, he grabbed more soap and knelt, painting circles over the softness of my belly. I clenched it in response, not that it did much since my abs had disappeared right along with my perfectly palmed-sized breasts. His hands ventured lower, parting my thighs as he gently lathered between them, moving down my legs until he'd made it to my toes.

He stood up, reaching over me again and grabbing for the shampoo before spinning me away from the water's spray. Tugging back the ends of my hair so I lifted my chin to the sky, he massaged my scalp, working my tresses into a sparkling foam that smelled of lavender, stardust, and bad decisions. "Why don't we take it one step at a time, starting with this shower?"

I nodded, my head still angled back, arching into him until the base of my spine met his hard length. Lifting his arm up, he grabbed the showerhead, taking it out of its holder and releasing some magic. It floated just above me while he combed through the strands of my wet hair. Then he waved his hands, drawing the sprayer across my shoulders, the suds trickling to the ground as he rinsed off every last bubble. With a snap of his fingers, its pulse quickened with my own, and he nudged my legs apart, splaying a hand across my waist, drifting its pressure to the sensitive nerves there.

I nearly slipped, and his grip tightened around me, then he walked me backward until I could sit down on the shower seat. He braced one arm on the tile, the other remained held out spelling the showerhead to aim between my legs, strumming my clit with its pelting water.

I arched back, savoring the sensation but also wanting to do one more thing before the little bit of my Desire possibly stole away the magic of this moment.

"You made a promise last night," I said, looking up at him. His cock was mere inches away, its crimson tip begging for my lips to wrap around it.

Which is exactly what I did.

"*Fuck*, Wicked," he growled, threading the fingers of one hand through my hair, pulling himself deeper into my mouth.

It stole my breath in the best way, until he edged out of me a few inches. Gripping around him, I stroked up and down his shaft, twisting as I did.

I lapped up every salty drop of precum, licking up the slit at his tip, feeling more powerful than I had in months. He tugged my hair, thrusting into me, the water from the rain shower above beating down on his back. My eyes were glued to him with each drive of his hips as he fucked my mouth.

I continued stroking him, my head popping off his cock and snapping to the doorway when I could have sworn I heard Aspen's cry. *Fuck. Of course this would happen.*

"He's still asleep," Lynx rasped, brushing back the soaking strands of my hair. "As good as you feel, I couldn't forget about him."

I sighed in relief, and he chuckled—until my eyes locked with his and I pulled him deep enough that he punched the back of my throat. "*Shit.* Just like that, Wicked."

A flood of molten heat spread through my body, making me shudder around him.

"See how incredible you make me feel?"

I nodded, his desire spurring me to take him deeper, faster, wanting to taste

Every.

Last.

Drop.

Pressure built low in my belly, and a second later, when another pulsing stream of water from the shower head struck my clit, I screamed as he jerked between my lips. Waves of pleasure washed through my body, a rippling blend of his own and mine. I couldn't tell who the sensations belonged to and I didn't care.

I just never wanted it to end.

"Tongue out, Wicked," Lynx commanded, his finger

crooking under my chin while the other hand continued to attack my clit with the water's spray. My whole body shook, becoming a fluid jumble of nerves. I opened my mouth, sticking my tongue out for him, giving him a few more strokes. Panting through my orgasm, my eyes locked with his, then trailed down to watch the veins strain in his neck. I loved how I could experience his release *with him* through his Empathy. White-hot lust shot in delicious spurts across my taste buds, and I held back the urge to close my mouth and swallow him down until I knew he'd finished.

Pride shimmered in my chest.

"So fucking beautiful." His upper body went slack, bracing himself against the tile on either side of me, catching his breath. "Never doubt how incredible you are."

I couldn't completely erase the doubts, the insecurities, but what he'd shown me with his Empathy had truly been a gift for me. That sinful satisfaction coming off him, golden and syrupy, was mine to claim. To own. I had made him feel that good.

Me.

He was right. I didn't see myself how he did. Maybe I never would. But he'd shown me in a way only he could. He'd given me a front-row seat—his captivated audience of one— and there was no way to deny how he felt about me.

After he finished rinsing us both off, we stepped out of the shower, and I grabbed us towels. Now that I could really look at his tattoo, the large tree crawled across near half the width of his back, climbing over his shoulder, the roots burrowing past his hip. As soon as I'd dried off, he scooped me over his shoulder and tossed me onto the bed climbing in after me. He shimmied down to the bottom of the comforter and lifted my hips, placing a pillow beneath them.

"What are you doing?" I asked, thighs glued together, gulping back my nerves of having him right *there*.

He sat on his knees in front of me, running his palms up my legs, he tilted his head at me with a mischievous grin. "Seeing how many times you can come before nap time is over."

Goddess above.

My eyes darted to the doorway.

"Still sleeping, I promise," Lynx reminded me. "Now, spread that pretty pussy for me, Wicked."

I took a deep breath, then pushed my thighs to the side with my hands, letting them fall toward the bed.

He licked his bottom lip and *stared*.

All the air in the room had been vacuumed away, and I held my breath. *Does something look wrong there?* I'd gotten a few stitches post-delivery, but they should be healed by now. *Did they disfigure my lady cave?*

Lynx squeezed my ankles, his brows knitting before his gaze came up to mine. "I can feel your anxiety prickling at me and I haven't even touched you. Do you want me to stop?"

"No."

"Then what is it?"

"I'm nervous." I let the words bubble over, spilling out of me like an overbrewed potion. "Things might not be the same...down there...after—"

"Wicked, I'm just a starved witch staring at my next meal." He kissed up my thigh, then mimicked his worship on the other side. I could still sense every ounce of his want, and it breathed belief into me, despite the nerves. "You're perfect."

I sighed in relief, dropping my head back to the pillow.

"Now keep those beautiful thighs open wide."

Before I could take another deep breath, he dove straight

for my center, parting me with his tongue. The sensation jolted me, but I arched into his face, ready for more after the showergasm. His skin was outlined in golden warmth, like the shimmer of the first morning sun, his self-satisfaction and joy rippling through me, intensifying the sensations his tongue struck within me. "Great Goddess!"

"How's that?" he asked between strokes, licking at every part of me until I was sopping between my thighs.

"So good." I used what little of his gift I could control to show him firsthand, wisps of fuchsia curling around him.

He stilled a moment when they touched him, realizing I now had access to his Empathy. I held my breath, nerves sparking through me. Just when I began to worry he was going to be angry over the transference, he let out a groan, seemingly spurred on. "You want more, Wicked?"

"Yes," I rasped.

He slipped his fingers inside, curling toward that sweet spot, making my hips jolt erratically.

"Holy shit," I panted, writhing against his palm, my body melting into the bedding.

"That's a good witch," he whispered, his words brushing my clit, sending my body into another frenzied wave as pleasure coiled in the deepest parts of me.

His fingers, his tongue, Goddess it all felt *incredible…*

But I wanted more.

My core clenched, wishing his fingers were *him*, hips bucking with abandon. The tension spun up and exploded out. It was as if I'd left my body, becoming a burst of red-hot passion, searing away every part of me until I floated down like ash on the wind and reclaimed my form.

I whimpered, numb with satisfaction, but ready to take things further. "Lynx, I need you. More."

He smiled, his body radiating, making him all the more

handsome. *How beautiful it must be to see this every day.*

"You have no idea how much I want that right now, Wicked, but your plus-one has other plans." He climbed forward to give me a quick kiss on the cheek and then moved back, his eyes darting a minute to the wet spot next to me on the sheets.

My eyes widened. "Shit."

"*Damn,*" he had a smug grin on his face as he thumbed his jaw. "You weren't lying."

I pulled the covers over myself, and he quickly grabbed them, pulling them back down. "Don't you dare cover yourself up, Wicked," he said, climbing back on top of me, his cock wedged against my leg, thick with want. He ran his hand over the wet spot, giving himself another self-impressed smirk that matched the not-so-angelic glow radiating from him. "There is no part of you that I adore less than the rest."

"Even the leaky bits?" I shrugged with a small grimace.

The tip of his nose pressed against mine, giving me nowhere to look but into his breathtaking brown eyes. "Oh, Wicked, now that I know about that, I'll be wildly offended if you aren't a sopping mess when I finally get to fuck you."

My whole body warmed and just as quickly chilled as he climbed off me and threw on a pair of gym shorts from his bag.

"Do you mind bringing him in here to me?" I pulled the pillow out from beneath my hips and tossed it to the ground, turning to my side. "I'd rather lay down. Someone tired me out."

"Of course," he said, pride filling his tone. "But only if you promise to take another nap afterward."

"I promise," I replied, sighing to myself, knowing full well if the opportunity presented itself I'd swap the nap out in a heartbeat for something much more *wicked.*

CHAPTER 22

OAKLEY

A disgusted hiss followed by a few coughs came from the other room. "Something lethal happened in that diaper."

I cackled at Lynx's expense, unable to stop myself.

The sound of their laughs, along with the attaching and reattaching of Velcro, filtered from the other room, followed by the *swoosh* of the diaper being disposed of.

It was nice he was trying. Amazing, actually.

I could get used to this.

And that scared me most of all.

Temporary, I reminded myself. *Casual.*

Slipping out from under the sheets, I shuffled to the dresser, pulling on a nursing bra and stuffing it with a pair of cloth pads. Then I threw on an oversized Winter's Revenge concert tee and boy shorts. When I turned around, Lynx was bopping along with Aspen, holding his hand between his fingers and swaying him back and forth. Wrangling my hair into a messy bun and securing it with a scrunchie, I grabbed my eye pencil and mascara, applying it quickly so I looked a little more alert. Then I walked over and took Aspen, kissing his button nose before resting him on my side. "Thanks. But you didn't have to do that."

"I know that," Lynx said, lips pressing into a line as he eyed me curiously.

"How long was I out for?"

"After he fed last?" He tickled Aspen's belly. "About two hours."

Great Goddess, when was the last time I got this much sleep?

My body felt much more energized, better than it had even before Saros had cast the locator spell.

I shifted back and forth, rocking Aspen. He let me know very quickly with his fussing that was not going to cut it, opening his mouth above my breast. Putting him in a football hold, I walked back a few steps and sat on the edge of the bed, maneuvering my shirt and nursing bra, settling him to feed.

As much as everything about this moment filled me with joy, I also knew better than to want to hold on to it. That would only end in disappointment. I needed to set some boundaries. "Look, I know what this is. Saros and I talked earlier, and I get it. I'm not expecting anything more from you."

"What do you think *this* is?" Lynx leaned against the doorframe, arms crossed, gaze narrowed.

"You won't be here long. This is temporary for you. I just want you to know I understand that once you solve the case you're leaving." I shrugged to show my nonchalance, while my heel tapped against the floor, giving my nerves some-where to go. "No strings attached."

Suddenly the room went cold, the ember of warmth thieved away, and the glow cradling Lynx extinguished.

"I don't want you thinking I'm reading more into this than it is, Lynx," I said, trying to stay relaxed and as cool-looking as possible with a baby half hidden beneath my shirt.

"I see."

Reaching under, I massaged my breast a bit to let down more milk, but the power of it sent spray right into Aspen's mouth and he sputtered. I quickly lifted him to my shoulder, wiping his face with my sleeve. Rubbing his back a few times, I uncrossed and recrossed my legs before situating him on the other side. Lynx remained silent, not commenting on the fact that I'd already managed to end up with drool on my shirt in less than five minutes or the fact that he'd seen me projectile spray breastmilk onto the carpet.

He walked into the room, the previous chill subsiding, and knelt in front of me so our eyes were level. Gripping my chin with his fingers, he made certain I couldn't look away. "I guess you haven't accepted it yet, Wicked, but I want you. This isn't some little *no strings attached,* temporary bullshit."

"But I'm—"

"The most sexy, strong, and stubborn witch I've ever met. To the point that you're currently pissing me off," he said, pinning me with the gravity of his words. He brushed his lips against my cheek, drifting up over the crest of my ear. "And just so you know, I adore this little witchling." He stroked Aspen's cheek a few times while he fed. "Even when he wakes up smelling like death and stops me from being inside his beautiful mom."

I sucked in a breath. Trying to piece together what he was saying. We hadn't known each other that long but I couldn't deny wanting this. Him. *Us.* "You really don't mind?"

"Not in the fucking least," he whispered before sitting back on his heels. "What I mind is you selling yourself short. If you didn't have that precious little witchling attached to you right now I'd make it my mission to make you scream until you realized it as well."

My throat dried, my voice becoming raspy. "You can't say things like that."

"Why the hell not?"

"Because what happens when—"

"If or when that happens, we can talk about what we want to do. Don't just diminish these feelings"—he waved his arms around, as if indicating something only he could see —"because we don't know what the future holds."

"Okay." My gaze dropped to Aspen who was still nursing happily. "Keep me company until he's done?"

"I'd love nothing more, Wicked." He sat down on the bed next to me, putting an arm around my shoulder, letting his head settle against mine. I relaxed into the strong panes of his hold.

Was this what it was like to allow someone else to give you their support and unwavering devotion?

If so, then why was I always so hell-bent on pushing this away?

(((●)))

SAROS ARRIVED ABOUT AN HOUR LATER, CARTING A DRINK CARRIER with three black cups sporting Luna's logo.

"Figured we might need some extra caffeine."

"You would be correct." I reached my arms up, Aspen passed out in my lap after playing with Lynx's keys the last fifteen minutes.

Something acrid bubbled from his aura before he even got to the door. Hesitation? Frustration? It was strange to still have access to Lynx's power, and I wondered when it would fizzle out. Usually the effects of the magical transference ended anywhere from two to twenty-four hours afterward.

"Here you go, Midnight." He handed me a cup, our fingers

accidentally brushing. His brows lifted a moment, surprised, then he cleared his throat, not saying another word. When he made extra care not to touch Lynx, floating the cup into his palm, it confirmed what I'd wondered.

He had seen something when he touched me.

Somehow, he'd managed to pull a memory of mine. My guess was something from the hours since we'd last seen him due to the strange blend of hues and flavors coming off him. It felt like a flare of jealousy mixed in with...something else? I should have asked Lynx more about how people's emotions presented themselves instead of just fumbling through it.

I brought the coffee cup to my lips and took a sip, savoring the sweet raspberry with its tart undercurrent as it hit my tongue. How did he always manage to have the drink at the perfect temperature?

There probably was a spell for that.

He joined us on the floor, leaning against the love seat.

"So Hazel is in Celestial Haven?" I asked, eager to find my sister.

"Yes." Saros picked up his coffee, taking a sip and releasing a sigh. A heaviness settled over him, like a blanket of exhaustion hovering over his aura, but he had worked a full day at the truck and now had his second job, well really his first, to contend with. I suspected his work didn't end until he found who or what he was looking for. "Her presence is near. I'm wondering if she could even be somewhere on Starry Night Lane."

"This close?" Lynx asked, brow furrowed in confusion. "Wouldn't any of the neighbors be acting stranger than usual if she were here somewhere?"

"The connection I got from Oakley's tattoo was very strong. That makes me think the tether between them isn't extended too far."

"Do you want to try again?" I asked, feeling better than I had prior to him doing the spell this morning.

"No," Saros and Lynx said in unison.

Well then.

"But we can't exactly go house to house without arousing suspicion. It would have been ideal to do it when we'd had the moonluck and everyone was out at the Wellses' place."

"I might have an idea," I volunteered, and their attention snapped to me. "I was invited to the blackout bash."

"You were?" Lynx asked. "How did you manage that?"

I shrugged, then placed my cup on the coffee table before standing up with Aspen and taking him to his room to put him down for the night. "Aurora came over to Ivy and Jade and invited me along."

When I returned from the nursery, the two were whispering to each other, bickering over something from the feel of it, though even that was starting to get fuzzy, the effects of the transference already beginning to wane.

"That could be perfect," Lynx agreed, cutting off whatever he and Saros were talking about when he noticed me standing there.

"That's what I'm thinking." I picked up my coffee cup, taking another sip and humming with satisfaction. Ribbons of fuchsia curled around me, the smell of freshly baked brownies wafting through the air.

I looked them both over. Lynx was all smiles while Saros's jaw was pulled taut, lips pressed together.

"How so?" Saros asked, not seeming to be on board with this idea.

"We've been wanting to get a better idea of what goes on at the blackout bash, especially since every disappearance has coincided with the new moon."

I shook my head. "That can't just be a coincidence."

"If it's not, you really want to put her in danger?" Saros replied with a glare in Lynx's direction.

"Isn't there some sort of spell you could do or a listening device, camera, something you could strap to me?"

"A magic one would be ideal, but that could take too much from you, considering your current state. We have other options, though," Saros said, tapping his fingers as if listing them off in his head.

I took a deep breath, steeling my resolve. "Then let's do it."

"Perfect." Lynx clapped his hands together before Saros could continue on, his pleasant way of cutting the conversation off. The air hung thick between them. I was pretty sure they were going to have a fun conversation when they left.

Glad I was missing out on that.

"One of us can do some recon while the other stays in the truck nearby in case Oakley needs back up," Lynx suggested.

"Fine," Saros conceded. "I'm not thrilled by the idea, but it's the most we've had to work with since we got here. We will still keep a discreet eye on the neighbors in the meantime."

"Sounds like that's settled, then." I chugged down the rest of my coffee in a few big gulps. "Now, walk me through what I'll need to do."

CHAPTER 23

OAKLEY

Static crackled, searing into my ear. *"Can you hear us, Midnight?"*

"Yep," I replied, brushing along the thick braid trailing down to the nape of my neck where my hair was tied in a wavy ponytail. The coven's blackout bash started at nine. I peered down at my watch. 8:55 p.m. I'd make sure to not arrive less than ten minutes after its start, not wanting to awkwardly be the first person there or stand out like a sore thumb—more so than I already would between being new and the only one wearing a baby strapped to me.

Lynx's comforting voice cut through the line. *"You ready for this?"*

"Stop asking me that. I already told you I was the last four times you asked when we were getting ready." I chuckled, thinking back to his mother-henning as he'd gotten me wired up. Luckily, I wasn't staying for the spell casting, which was usually done in little-to-no clothing. It was meant to expose as much skin and energy to the Moon Goddess's glittering acolytes peeking from the stars. They would be the only ones out to answer any magical intentions tonight. It was said that the acolytes were those who devoted themselves to the Goddess in life and were blessed with ascension by her side in death.

Not one of the worst ways to live out your afterlife, though I always wondered what it was like up there. Could they merely watch us from above, or did they have their own shimmering society tucked away in the sky?

I stumbled over the heel of my booties climbing up the long driveway leading to 5 Blessed Crescent, mentally flipping through all the notes Lynx and Saros had given me before I'd come here.

My phone buzzed and I slipped it out of my pocket, not surprised in the least when it was a text from Atlas.

ATLAS

Just wanted to check in and see how you and Aspen are doing. Still no word on Hazel but my contacts are still looking into it.

Thanks. I appreciate it.

There was no way I'd tell him that I was working with Lynx and Saros, trying to find her myself. That would just send him into a panic, the last thing I needed right now.

ATLAS

I'll let you know if I hear anything. Miss you.

Same.

I stared down at the impulsive message, my palm meeting my forehead when I realized the implication—not that it wasn't true—but I didn't have time to worry about that. Tonight was about getting answers about my sister. I pocketed my phone before I continued to overthink it.

Aspen was nestled in, asleep in his ring sling, shades of

sparkling midnight painted across the fabric with coppery flecks. Saros had fed a wire through the lining of it, in case the one under my clothes was too muffled with him attached to me.

Since he'd most likely just sleep and we'd be gone before any rituals took place, it was the perfect way for Lynx and Saros to listen in and help if needed. Not that I anticipated needing them, but it did bolster me as I continued to climb up the long paved driveway. I felt both oddly naked and free having my hands available and no stroller to push.

As I stepped on the black welcome mat donning the word *blessed* with all the phases of the moon spanning its width, the door creaked open slowly. No one welcomed me on the other side. I looked around the porch, spotting a few cameras blinking down at me, a silver star painted on its side.

Fitz served on Pierce Protection's board, the tech security company Wade Pierce from next door had started up. It made sense that his home would be tricked out. I guess I just hadn't noticed when I'd been here for the moonluck, though I'd mainly stayed in the yard, other than coming inside briefly to nurse in Fitz's office.

"Look who actually made it!" Aurora called down the stairs. She and the other *Blessed Bitches* were fully made up, living perfection in attire that was definitely not spit-up friendly.

"And look at you all fashion momma'd out," Cordelia crooned. Since I didn't really know her, I couldn't tell if it was genuine or put on.

As I climbed the staircase, Heather nodded at my outfit in approval. "Those black rose-embellished leggings and blouse are perfection. And those shoes! Which bootique did you go to?"

She seemed like the nicest of the group, but I still was

leery of their entire inner-coven clique. "Sally's Bootique that she runs out of her house on Sable Sky."

"I'll have to follow her socials so I know where to shop next," Laurel said, tapping her phone.

Here, I could make a fresh start with *real* friends. Not groupies that clung to me because of Atlas's position back in Salem. Of course, now everyone here knew he was Aspen's father, but he wouldn't be around much, and this wasn't his jurisdiction anyway.

The problem was, who wanted to make friends with a hot mess mom that was doused in dribble and had an erratic sleep and feeding schedule? Maybe other hot mess moms, but even Ivy and Jade, who were currently scampering over from the bar, seemed to have it more together than me. Maybe because they were veterans. Maybe because they hadn't lost most of their magic along with every identity they'd ever known when they'd had kids.

"Speaking of, don't you have a little shop?" Aurora asked, pulling out her phone, tapping and swiping at it a few times. "I could have sworn I already followed it, but I haven't seen any updates in a while."

"Oh! What kind of shop?" Jade piped in, grabbing her phone as well. "I'd love to place an order."

Ivy reached into her bra, where she'd apparently stored hers. "Me too!"

I couldn't imagine fitting a phone alongside my milk makers, no matter how stretchy my nursing bra was.

It felt as if all eyes were on me, and my hands became clammy, sweat beading my brow. I was pretty sure when I took Aspen out of his ring sling later I'd have damp prints from where the fabric cradled him against me.

"It's a romance and lingerie shop." I gave a small smile, gulping back my nerves. "Full Moon Emporium."

"Following," a few witches shouted.

Jade beamed. "Same!"

My chest heated, insecurity boiling me from the inside out as the witches shouted that they were now following along. "Hopefully I'll be getting the shop up and running here soon."

"Oh really?" Aurora asked, seemingly not convinced I'd be doing that. "How exciting."

She somehow had a way of saying things that scraped you down to nothing, all with a brilliant smile on her face. The worst part was that it was as if no one else could sense it but me.

But maybe it was in my head, my insecurity running away with me. She could just be trying to be nice?

Why did I instantly think the worst?

"Yeah. Adjusting to motherhood and then moving delayed things a bit, but I think I'll start putting together some elixirs and enchanted goodies soon."

"Is it true you model the lingerie yourself?" Jade asked, a mischievous smile playing at her lips.

"Oh really, Wicked?" Lynx's voice made me jerk, not expecting him to still be listening in. *"Pulling up the website now."*

I figured he'd already started checking out the empty houses while the guys were hanging at Forest Delta's to watch the supernatural football finals taking place in Romania.

"Can you stay focused? We're working." Saros's stern voice rang out in the background, followed by a muffled, *"Damn, that's Midnight?"*

"Yes, it's true. I model them." A different sort of heat spread through me, but I tried to keep a straight face, playing off any blushing from the guys' commentary. I'd taken such pride in showing the sexy silks, satins, leather, and lace on a real body.

Mine.

My body was still just as real. Yes, it was different than before, but why did the idea of doing what I'd advocated for and shouted from the rooftops months ago terrify me more than anything now?

"Hell yes," Jade said, holding her hand up for a high five.

Ivy's eyes kept going from her phone back up to me. "You look incredible."

"I could never." Heather grimaced, looking down at herself with a frown. She was overdue by almost two weeks with her sixth baby. All of them moon-blessed, meaning they'd been conceived on the full moon, like most of the coven's children.

"You totally could. You're stunning," I reminded her. Every witch here was. Something I apparently needed to remind myself too. "Once I get up and running, I'd love to have you witches model some of the new stock. You all would make incredible models for the line. Hopefully Hazel will be back by then. She's a great photographer."

Hopefully tonight would get us more answers as to where she was.

Heather's eyes went wide, aglitter with excitement. "Really?"

"Look at you go, Wicked. Does that mean there's a private fashion show coming? Maybe for the full moon." Lynx's voice melted into my ear, the last word gasped out, and I guessed Saros had smacked him. The prospect of full moon activities perked me and my Desire right up.

"Yes," I said confidently, answering both my secret and in-person questions.

I couldn't hear what came through the line next because

everyone was talking over each other, giving ideas or volunteering themselves to be models. For the first time since I had opened the shop seven years ago, I felt that fire and excitement that had made me want to create it in the first place. It was like a thread had been strung to a part of myself I'd let float away when I'd let the politics and limelight in Salem overtake me and then even more so when I'd been focused on my pregnancy and being in postpartum survival mode.

Maybe the witch I was still existed underneath, I just needed to yank that tether a little harder to get her back.

Realistically, I was forever changed now. But that didn't mean I couldn't evolve into something better—a sexier, stronger, more badass version of the woman I'd been. And what could be more badass than literally keeping another small witch thriving? Maybe I hadn't felt sexy—and Goddess knew that was valid, considering the bodily fluids I dealt with on a daily basis—but that didn't mean I wasn't.

Why was I so hard on myself when I could see the beauty in everyone else around me?

"Witches," Aurora raised her voice, commanding the space. All chatter ceased, and she stepped up on the bench to look over the crowd. "Thank you all for being here tonight on this auspicious new moon. I have loved our tradition of these little get-togethers since they started and look forward to many more to come. Bountiful blessings, Witches!"

"Bountiful blessings!" everyone shouted, clinking their glasses together if they had them.

"Please, indulge with some refreshments. As you can see, there are various stations set up around the house for you to enjoy. At the bar there are a handful of elixirs available: beauty serum, stress eliminating elixir, and full moon formula for those of you looking to continue the celebration at home," she said with a wink.

I looked over at the fully stocked bar and the baskets of herbs hanging from the ceiling, along with ones filled with various fruits and garnishes. "Casting will begin just after midnight for those joining in."

My attention darted around the room. Ruby was situated at a table doing readings, a small cauldron set beside her, probably filled with more intestine purée. Another table was set with little plates holding sage, rosemary, thyme, roses, and pine needles. A large spool of twine and a pair of scissors were laying on a tray, along with framed instructions. Jade and Ivy started in that direction, so I followed, sitting on the long bench opposite them.

Grabbing a handful of pine needles, I added some blue sage, rosemary, and thyme before I tied it up with the cotton twine, securing it at the base with a knot. Then I moved up the bundle, crisscrossing the string as I did, going back down once I'd made it all the way to the top.

Next to us a few of the coven jotted down notes on pieces of seed paper. And out on the patio witches clustered around a large soaking tub. Cordelia Blossom stood within in only her underwear while a few of the coven brushed her in glittering opalescent paint in honor of the Moon Goddess who hid this night. A reminder that we served her from below, just as her acolytes did above us, regardless of whether she hung within reach.

"The runes you all use for the new moon are different from the ones we used in Salem," I said to Ivy and Jade, tying off the end of my smudge stick. While they were all half naked and casting tonight, making up for the moon's glow, I'd be at home cleansing myself of the last four weeks since Hazel disappeared. "I didn't realize covens adopted different ones."

"It's unique to each coven and their values," Jade replied,

starting on a second smudging stick. "Usually set by the coveness."

"So Aurora?"

Ivy nodded, then reached for my smudge stick, taking a few sniffs before adding some extra blue sage to hers. "It should be Ruby, but she didn't want the position. She prefers to be behind the scenes."

I could hear my neighbor talking to someone about their fortune. She was trying to comfort them from her tone.

Jade finished her smudge stick, then got up and moved to the seed paper farther down the table. "Aurora was nice enough to volunteer to take on the position."

Well, wasn't she the perfect little witch? I withheld the urge to mock hurl, instead scooting down the bench toward the seed paper, making sure not to wake Aspen. He let out a yawn and gripped my shirt but remained asleep.

Phew.

"I don't know how she does it along with everything else on her plate," Jade continued.

I grabbed a small block of paper, thumbing over the texture and scanning for the bits of seedlings. Then I took a pen and sat there staring at the paper, thinking exactly how I wanted to set my intention for this moon cycle. The wording had to be just right. "She's quite the multitasker."

"Luckily, Laurel, Cordelia, and Heather help her out," Jade said, looking deep in thought as she scribbled on the page.

I began writing down my new moon intention, then crumpled my piece of paper. "The perfect little circle of Blessed Crescent."

"Well, yeah, minus Acacia," Ivy grumbled, quickly jotting something down on the sheet and then handing it to Jade to carry for her like it was covered in rodent crap.

I still had yet to formally meet the woman from 1 Blessed

Crescent Jade and Ivy had warned me so much about. "Why doesn't she go to anything?"

"I don't know. Probably too busy for us with her research."

Too busy, or is there something else to it?

I clutched the seed paper in my hand. "What kind of research does she do?"

"No clue," Jade said, getting up. "I'd love to know, but she's never around to ask. Anyway, looks like we can just go right out back to plant these in the pines."

"Sounds good." I followed, wondering if Lynx and Saros had heard or found anything tonight that would bring us closer to Hazel.

CHAPTER 24

OAKLEY

Passing the witches decorating themselves in glittering paint, we descended the staircase, following the floating fairy lights out of the yard. They lined the paths reaching toward the pines, beckoning us forth. After planting their intentions and chanting low until they rooted themselves into the ground, a few witches wandered back toward us.

My magic flared in my chest, no closer to replenishing but still feeling the enchanting essence of this night. The small amount I had would suffice, enough to nurture the paper held in my grasp. This was one tradition we all held, whether alone on our garden path, from our kitchen in a small pot nestled in the windowsill, or within the forest's dark embrace. Even those still hidden away, living on the outside, did this. It was easy enough to keep disguised.

And it was the first magic tradition I'd really taken part in since I'd moved to Starry Night Lane.

"You okay?" Ivy asked, her voice quiet with concern. "Any word from Hazel?"

I blinked away the tears that had begun trailing down my cheeks. "Not yet."

"We're going to find her," Lynx said, reassuring me, and I wished he could siphon some of his calm to me.

I came up next to Ivy and Jade, pines surrounding us in their comforting embrace and fresh scent. "This the spot?"

Ivy looked over at her friend. "She'd be the one to know it. Always finds the best soil."

Jade held out her hands. It was too dark to see what she was doing, but as we all knelt to the ground, there were little green saplings sprouting from the dirt.

"Harvesting," she whispered. An answer to a question I knew better than to ask.

We all held our hands to the dirt and with a nod from Jade, began chanting in unison. *"Moon Mother, hear our plea. Bless our sacred intention. Be our light in the darkness."* Once we'd repeated it eight times, one for each phase of the lunar cycle, we dug our fingers into the velvety earth.

I savored the dirt scraping beneath my nails, the crumble against my fingers, manipulating it until I'd made the perfect spot to plant my intention. It was unlucky to plant any deeper than six inches. Too close to potentially disturbing the dead.

When Jade put Ivy's paper into the hole she'd dug, I gave a questioning look. Ivy's fingers flared to life. "Pyro. I always get nervous I'll burn my intention up and that just feels unlucky."

Chuckling, I pushed away the memory of the last Pyro I'd met, pressing my crumpled paper into the ground. Aspen continued snoozing happily against my chest.

Gathering dirt to fill in the hole, I realized they'd both shared with me their specialties, but they weren't sitting there waiting for me to tell them mine. They were already chatting about the next moonluck and upcoming Hallowed festivities. Nothing suggested they expected me to share in return. But I would anyway.

"Desire," I whispered, looking at them both and getting wide eyes from Ivy and a smirk from Jade.

"Wow," was all Ivy could manage to get out. "That's got to be—"

"Hot as fuck," said Jade, releasing a breath.

"She has no idea," Lynx crooned through the line.

"I was going to say, interesting..." Ivy offered with a small smile. "I bet the full moon is especially *intense* for you."

"How intense can it get for you, Wicked?"

My cheeks flushed with heat, luckily hidden by darkness, but my lips pulled into a salacious grin. "You have no idea."

"I'd love to have a better idea. Firsthand." The heat from my cheeks traveled down my chest, coiling in knots below my belly. Then, after a long pause, Lynx added, *"Bet I'm not the only one."*

The only sounds traveling through the wire were two audible gulps, that was until Lynx filled the line with his smooth chuckle.

After chatting a bit more and finishing up with our new moon intentions under the fairy lights, we stood up, brushing the dirt off our hands and knees. I gave my intention one last glance before my gaze drifted to the acolytes above. I hoped beyond hope that they would carry my plea to their mistress, blessing it to take root.

Found.

(((●)))

We headed back toward the house, rinsing our hands in the small basin at the bottom of the deck's staircase. When I got inside, I realized I'd lost Jade and Ivy behind me. They'd been scooped up by the other witches of the coven, who were now helping them out of their clothes and grabbing paint.

Cordelia came up to me before remembering I was wearing Aspen.

"I'm not participating in the rites tonight, but I'd be happy to help anoint them," I offered, gaining an enthusiastic nod in exchange. Glowing tubes floated over from the bar, and witches summoned them to their palms before chugging them down in a gulp. Ivy and Jade each grabbed neon-blue ones, their lips smacking from whatever potent elixir swirled within.

"None for you?" Aurora asked smoothly, striding to stand next to me.

"I prefer not to imbibe while nursing. Personal choice," I added, not wanting to offend her or anyone else who might be listening. It was easier than explaining I didn't want it pulling the little magic I had. I'd already given some over when we'd planted our intentions, I didn't want to overdo things. At least not until I'd replenished my magic supply at the full moon.

That decision now felt less like a burden and more exciting.

"What is it anyway?" I asked, nodding to the neon-blue tubes.

"Full moon formula. Have you ever had any?"

"I actually used to brew it all the time, but mine normally turned out more bright teal. What's in yours?"

"No clue," she said with a small shrug, "I get my elixir cups in the mail by a renowned potions mistress and bubble them up in my Brewrig."

Atlas had a Brewrig too, though he had rarely used it when we were together. It had a personal-sized cauldron situated in the middle of it, filling into two-ounce tubes, depending on how big of a batch you wanted. I preferred to brew from scratch, knowing everything that was going into the potions I was making, but I understood the convenience of having one.

It didn't surprise me that the Wellses used and loved theirs. Everything in their house screamed luxury and top-of-the-line. Even the temperature started to feel warmer on its own as more people disrobed to get skyclad, either through something Aurora was controlling on her phone or whatever gadgets had been created with their elaborate home system.

"I'm sorry you won't be staying for the new moon rites tonight. We will do an extra blessing for Hazel's safe return."

I half believed her.

"Another time," I said, graciously. "In fact, I should probably get this little one to bed since things look like they are going to be getting wild here soon enough." Jade and Ivy were dancing along with about seven other witches, twirling around themselves in the moonlight.

"Yes, she's gonna walk me back," Ruby said, looping her arm in mine. "I prefer to pay homage to the acolytes from my own backyard. So many sisters up there."

Sisters. The word seared into my chest.

Once we'd said our goodbyes and had headed down the driveway, my gaze darted directly to Luna's. The lights were dimmed to the point of looking nearly off through the darkened service window. But I knew better.

"Go on," she said, nodding toward the truck. "He's waiting for you."

She winked, and I stared at her, dumbfounded. Did she know I was with Lynx? Had she seen us under the full moon at our windows?

There was no freaking way I'd ask for clarification.

"I'd like to walk you home first," I insisted.

"Fine, but I'll be watching you til you get to the truck. Even the safest haven can house the deadliest presence."

"There's no arguing with you on that," I continued, escorting her to the edge of the cul-de-sac, waiting until she'd gotten to the top of the drive and made it into her house before turning and heading toward Luna's.

My breasts tingled, getting fuller but not to the point of discomfort. Adjusting my bra, I situated them back into place.

"Everything okay, Midnight?" Saros's stern yet concerned voice filtered into my ear. I'd nearly forgotten they were listening in.

"Yeah, it's fine."

"The line was cutting in and out."

I grimaced. I'd probably messed with the wire cord. "My boulder holder needed a little adjustment."

Silence. Radio fucking silence.

Lynx would have laughed at that, and when I opened the coffee truck door, I instantly knew why he hadn't. Only Saros was there with his lips clenched together in a stern line. Was that what kept his skin so tight and steely? Despite the harshness of his jaw, the crinkles at the corners of his eyes were soft. "You had me worried for a second."

"Sorry. I know you don't need to hear or understand this but these"—I nodded down to my breasts—"don't stay in one place for me anymore. I'm just hoping Aspen remains asleep before you have to get flashed unnecessarily or pistoled with some Oakley original."

Please stop talking.

The ball in his throat bobbed, swallowing down whatever retort that'd come to mind.

"Where's Lynx?" I asked, trying to change the subject. "Did he find anything?"

"Out patrolling," was all Saros said, but his temple throbbed. He was looking at a small screen hidden underneath the counter, cords plugged into a series of inputs. A panel had been pulled to the side that matched the rest of the interior. He set it back into place before turning to me. "He's combed through the houses on the lane. Now he's working around the cul-de-sac. Hasn't spotted anything yet."

He grabbed a cushion, helping me get Aspen out of the ring sling. When the witchling nuzzled his shoulder, Saros stiffened at first, as if stunned. Then he slowly made little circles on Aspen's back before laying him on the cushion next to me.

"So what do we do?" I asked, unfastening the ring sling and handing it over to him. He worked through the material, meticulously removing the wires without ruining the fabric. "Just sit around and wait?"

"Well, you will go home once I undo your wire and get this little witch to bed." Clearing his throat, he nodded at my top. I unbuttoned the black lacy blouse I'd dared to wear for the blackout bash, knowing I was willing to part with it if needed. Then I unsnapped the fasteners of my nursing bra, pulling it down enough so he could start disconnecting the wires.

Lynx had placed the ones across my chest earlier, my skin flushing beneath his touch. Now as Saros got past unweaving the ones connected to my bra, he paused, hovering where the wires had been taped to my breasts. You would have thought they were two explosives he was worried would detonate at any moment—which I guess in some way he wasn't completely wrong.

Then I remembered why: his gift worked via touch. "Do you have gloves or something? Does that help?"

"Unfortunately not."

So his Recollection was more like my Desire. Only within our control to a certain point.

"Sorry there wasn't much useful stuff I got tonight. But maybe you'll see something I didn't?" I offered, trying to help him find a time to focus on since he said he could pinpoint and see memories that way, otherwise he'd have a free-for-all with my past. Not that I was worried he'd see something bad, but I also still couldn't get a clear sense of him. There was always something brewing in his eyes, but it fizzled out before I could look closer.

"I wouldn't say it wasn't useful." He finally skimmed the corner of one of the pieces of tape, avoiding scratching me as he used his nail to peel it off. If he was seeing a memory, he didn't show it. "People are always more interesting when they don't realize who's listening."

"What do you mean?" I asked, wanting to keep his attention on my face so he wouldn't notice the swell of me beneath his touch or the veins that were starting to look angry and purple. I'd need to feed Aspen or pump soon.

"Take Aurora for instance." He removed the last few pieces of tape, not saying a word, then untangled me from the wires. "She's always sweet as pie to Lynx, batting her lashes and showing off her kindness."

"And?"

"She is quite threatened by you." He chuckled, seemingly pleased with that thought. I guess he wasn't a fan of her either.

"You think she knows about Lynx and I?" I grimaced. What if she had seen or heard something? Jade and Ivy had indicated she knew everything that happened in the neighborhood. If she was interested in Lynx, that would definitely put me high up on her hex list. "Wouldn't that be bad for you guys and your cover story?"

"I doubt she knows anything, but she has eyes." His gaze darted away, like looking at me as he spoke right now would be too painful. "A beautiful woman who's self-sufficient, building things for herself...that's a threat to her delicately crafted ecosystem."

I cocked my head, enjoying his discomfort a little too much. "Did you just call me beautiful?"

His eyes were still averted, but he gave a nonchalant shrug. "I may have."

"I think you did." Reaching out, I lifted his chin to face me, stilling when he jolted at my touch. I dropped my hand quickly, realizing my error. "Fuck. I'm sorry, Saros. I wasn't thinking. I just—"

"Relax, Midnight." He brushed it off as if it'd never happened. "We're cool."

We're cool?

"Okay," I said, trying to will back the tinge of disappointed confusion threatening to coat my words. "I should probably get Aspen home."

Just then, the coffee machine kicked on, as if on its own, sending Saros to his feet. He sprang over to the panel, ripping it off its hinges and scanning the screen. Concern etched his brow, eyes searching for something. When he found whatever he was looking for, he popped his earbud back in. I could just make out Lynx's shape in the neon green-and-black night vision video playing for us.

Saros's face fell before his lips pressed back into their usual line. The expression ripped the air clear from my lungs, my mind racing with all the worst-case scenarios.

"He thinks he found something." He reached into the cabinets where he stocked extra syrups and coffees, pressing something to release a set of leather cuffs.

I'd seen the contraptions before on the supernatural cop

shows I used to throw on. They were imbued with physical powers, ones that had been donated by those with gifts useful to the government. It made it possible for them to lift heavy objects, subdue criminals, and—worst case—execute on site.

He strapped one around each wrist, clenching and unclenching his fists a few times. "You head home. I need to go meet him."

"I'm coming with you."

"No, Oakley."

His use of my name told me that whatever it was, it was serious. "I promise one or both of us will come as soon as we can and give you an update."

"Is it Hazel?"

"No. It's not." His tone was firm. There was no discussing this further with him, and I didn't know whether to be relieved by that or not. On the one hand, I was glad if it was as urgent and dangerous as it seemed that it didn't involve her. On the other, I felt no closer to finding Hazel and didn't like the idea of them heading into harm's way—even if it was their job.

I picked up Aspen, fastening him against me in the ring sling, then Saros swung the door open, ushering me toward the cul-de-sac.

"Promise me you'll come by later?"

He nodded without another word, then took off past the coven's community center, headed toward Blessed Crescent.

What the hell had happened?

CHAPTER 25

OAKLEY

As curious as I was about what had Saros rushing out of Luna's, and as worried as I was about Lynx, I knew heading after him would not only put them in more danger but also endangered Aspen. And at the end of the day there was one life I would protect above all others.

My son's.

However, I stood in the center of the cul-de-sac paralyzed, unable to make my feet move. Which house was he going to? Was he back in the pines? Had I missed something when I'd been out there planting with Jade and Ivy earlier? The pines spanned miles, how far away was Lynx?

What if he was hurt?

A bubbling sound came from just above my stomach, and I looked down to see Aspen smiling, his eyes still shut, a pungent smell unleashing into the air. Wetness crept up my blouse. I peeled back a bit of the ring sling to inspect the damage. Yellow had seeped through the back of his sleeper, spreading past where I could see.

Fuck.

I winced, trying to block out the smell as I sped home, not

wanting to think about the wetness pressed against my stomach or that one of my nicer blouses had made it into the *desecrated by Aspen* pile. The one saving grace was that it was black, so I could possibly wash it and wear it again.

Possibly.

I carefully removed the ring sling, weighing which mess to clean up first: the sling, Aspen, or myself. I put a towel on the floor, laying Aspen on it while I peeled off my shirt, inspecting my bra for any poo residue. *Phew.* Seemed that it had survived outside of the booty bomb radius.

Small blessings.

Taking off the rest of my clothes, I spotted Aspen staring up at me, half dazed.

"Let's get you cleaned up, little demon," I teased, unzipping his sleeper and finding a non-yellowed spot of fabric to carry it over between two fingers to the washer. Grabbing the stain spray, I quickly doused the clothes we'd worn, along with the ring sling, then popped them into the machine. I disposed of the useless diaper, then carted both our naked butts to my shower, juggling him around while I rinsed us off.

It wasn't until both of us were under the shower's cleansing spray, that I was finally able to focus back on Lynx and Saros. What if they had already tried to come by and give an update and I was in the shower? Quickly turning off the spigot, I threw a robe on, taking Aspen into his room to get a diaper on him.

"All clean," I whispered, tickling under his chin to make him laugh, grateful for his fresh baby smell in return. Once he was dressed and I finished feeding him, I got him settled in his crib. The whole time, I listened for the doorbell, but it remained silent.

Each tick of the clock nagged at my sanity. My imagination running wild with possibilities of what they discovered, what sort of danger they might be in. My hope dwindled like flour through a sieve, leaving behind only chunks of concern.

They could both be seriously hurt.

Or *worse*.

My breaths became shallow at the thought of something happening to them on top of my sister being missing. Maybe I'd tried to tell myself I could do things on my own, and maybe that was true, but I didn't want to find out. They meant so much more to me beyond helping with my sister's case and they both cared about me, even if Saros was much more grumbly about it. The realization of that startled me.

Tears streaked my cheeks, my chest tight with anxiety, cutting off my air supply. Shuffling into my room, I grabbed the blue-green smithsonite and clutched it in my palm before going into my sister's room and snatched up her dark-teal throw. I pulled it around myself, heading back toward the couch. Curling up under Hazel's favorite blanket, I repeated the incantation from earlier, both to steady my breath and ground myself.

"Moon Mother, hear our plea. Bless our sacred intention. Be our light in the darkness."

Over and over I chanted the words, the crystal squeezed in one palm, my phone in the other. As the tears began to slow and my inhales and exhales returned to their usual rhythm, my eyes fluttered shut until sleep claimed me.

Buzz.

Buzz.

Buzz.

I wiped my crusted eyes, looking at the phone.

UNKNOWN

Peering at the time on the kitchen clock, I saw that I'd been asleep for over four hours. I picked up, my heart beating wildly in my chest, wondering who and what would be awaiting me on the other end of the line.

"I know I said it didn't have anything to do with Hazel..." Saros's deep timbre drifted through the phone.

"What is it?" My heart dropped like a heavy stone in my gut.

There was a long pause. "We found her."

Found.

"Is she okay?" I asked, part of me too afraid to know the answer.

"Yes. But we wanted to make sure to get her monitored and gather any evidence before it could become compromised."

What evidence? "What happened to her? Where are you?"

I peeked my head out the window, looking around the neighborhood. From what I could see of it, everything still looked quiet.

"We are at Devereux Hospital with her right now. We still need her account of what happened but—"

"Can I see her?"

"Not just yet, but she should be done here soon. You are welcome to wait for her at the hospital while we finish up. Hopefully not much longer."

If he said anything else, I didn't hear it.

Hazel has been found, and she's okay.

I hung up the phone, throwing random things into the diaper bag. Rummaging through Hazel's clothes, I grabbed a few things in case they had taken hers for evidence, trying to recall any procedural shows I'd seen and what kinds of items they might collect.

Scooping Aspen out of the crib, I snapped him into the car seat, hands shaking the entire time. Tapping the steering wheel with my fingers, nerves in overdrive, I sped to the hospital, cursing like a wrath demon each time a stop sign or red light got in my way. All the while, I begged the Moon Goddess that once I got to my sister everything would be okay.

((《●》))

Hazel sat in the bed, wrapped in a fleece blanket. Her brunette hair fell in matted strings around her face and there was a vacantness about her eyes as Lynx, Saros, and another witch in a gray suit stood in the room, talking to her. I bounced on my heels, Aspen feeding beneath my shirt while I watched, ready to get her home.

To see for myself if she was *actually* okay.

The gray-suit man had his arms crossed, eyes narrowed at Hazel while Lynx seemed to ask her a few questions. She shook her head, and I could read her lips saying *I don't know*, but otherwise it was hard to see what was going on. The unfamiliar witch said something to Saros that made him frown, replying sternly with his brows knit before stalking out the door.

The man in the gray suit followed him out. "Now is not the time to pull back when we are this close to answers."

"Not like this," Saros fumed. "Give her a few more days to see if anything else comes to her. To regain her strength."

"It's your ass on the line, Agent Holt," the man warned. A buzzing sound had him reaching into his back pocket and pulling out his phone. "I need to take this." He stormed off down a hallway and out of eyeshot.

"What happened?" I asked Saros.

"I still can't say much," he whispered, eyes darting around. The vein on his head was raised and angry-looking, but he gritted out what he could. "Lynx had me meet him at Acacia's house. He'd gone there after listening in to Jade and Ivy mention her at the blackout bash. As soon as I got there, we could make out Acacia through a window. Something was wrong with her."

"What happened?"

"She's dead." The vein in Saros's temple throbbed.

"Dead?" I asked. "How?"

"When we finally worked through her wards and got closer to her, we spotted a handful of empty vials scattered around," Saros said quietly. "We've sent them off to the lab for testing."

Lynx opened the door, waving us into the room. "She insisted on seeing you, so let's sneak you in quickly before the boss gets back. I'll hang out with him."

Securing Aspen in his stroller, I swapped places with Lynx, running into the room.

"Haze!" My voice cracked, feet carrying me to her bed in a few long strides. I wrapped my arms around her, tears streaming down my cheeks.

"I'm so glad to see you, sis." Hazel's arms slid to my back, holding me tighter than she ever had, so tight I almost felt like she'd squeeze the air straight from my lungs. But I didn't care, I needed the reminder that she was really here.

Maybe she did too.

Goddess above.

My arms shook, still clamped around Hazel, and her body sank into mine. The woman that never needed anyone was leaning on me right now. What had been done to her?

I pulled back enough to see her face, arms braced at her sides. "How did they find you?"

She didn't reply, breath catching as if it was too much to utter the words.

"After we found Acacia's body and called for backup, we checked the house in case the assailant was still there. We are waiting to see if there was foul play involved. That's when we heard a muffled sound coming from behind the bookcase and discovered a small hidden room with Hazel handcuffed to a pipe," explained Saros.

Icy dread slithered down my throat. How horrible must it have been being locked away all that time?

I wanted to crumple right there with her. Instead, I willed away the tears, keeping my shoulders pressed back, chin raised. She needed me to be strong for the both of us.

"Can I take her home yet? Or at least bring her something *real* to eat?" I asked, looking at the sad tray of barely picked at hospital food.

"Not just yet," Saros said, eyes sorrowful. "We need to wait for headquarters to give us the okay. Our boss is insisting we interview her further. Speaking of, he will be back soon. Best to get back in the hallway."

Before I could protest, Hazel nudged me to get up. "Go ahead, sis. We'll be heading home together before you know it."

I followed him out to the hallway reluctantly, attention still focused on my sister. Lynx flashed her his usual charming smile from the doorway.

"I'm so glad you found her," I said to the guys, still captivated by the fact that my sister was on the other side of the wall.

"Just doing our job," Saros said, giving me a crooked smile with his lips clamped together. Was it even possible for him to show teeth?

Lynx nodded before heading back in to be with Hazel. He

reached out a hand, and she took it, instantly seeming to calm at his presence.

Saros swallowed hard. "I don't know what would have happened if she'd been left much longer without access to food or water. We don't know when Acacia died, and Hazel doesn't seem to recall much, at least not yet."

"Couldn't you touch her to see?" I asked, wondering if that wouldn't be the easiest thing, especially since he had the ability to.

"I could," he said, face contorting a bit, as if pained. "But I would prefer to do that once she's rested and I have her consent to use my Recollection. My boss...would prefer otherwise."

"Is that what he was pissed off about when he followed you out here?"

"Yes, but he'll just have to get over it." His face dropped to the ground, hands folding into his pockets.

I took a tentative step toward him. "Now that Hazel has been found...does that mean the case is closed?"

"No."

I released a sigh, cutting it off midway when I realized how it sounded.

"Sorry," I winced. Of course I wanted Hazel's case solved. I wanted answers for all the disappearances. I wanted to know why Hazel's case had been different and if we were still in any sort of danger.

"Don't be." He leaned closer, his whisper caressing my ear. "We still have to go through everything we found at the crime scene. Acacia was keeping quite a lot of research hidden away. Some of it was encrypted, though. Some even locked up with complex wards. They are all being sent back to headquarters. We'll have to see if it is enough to give us details on the other disappearances and if there are any bodies at her place or buried within the pines."

"Wouldn't it be hard to search for them?"

"Hard but not impossible. I'm sure we'd piss the community off around the full moon." He shifted, taking his hand out of his pocket and letting it fall at his side between us. "Anything we do won't be until after the next one. These things usually take a while."

"Would it be bad if I said I didn't mind that?" I reached for his hand instinctively, wanting to hold it. To feel his calloused palm in mine and be assured everything would be okay. For some reason, those words from Saros seemed like they would hold a different weight.

He lifted his hand a bit closer but was careful not to touch me. Somehow, I still felt the distance lessen between us. "Not unless it's bad if I say I don't mind either."

The sound of a throat clearing had us spinning to find the man in the gray suit scanning over us with a frown. Seeing him up close, I noticed he had orange eyes with peeks of blue bursting from his irises. "Sorry to interrupt, but we need to finish up our report, Miss Brooks."

"Of course," I said, finding it interesting that the witch didn't introduce himself but addressed me by name.

"Thanks again for finding her and bringing her home," I said to Saros, taking a more appropriate step back.

His hands retreated to his pockets. "It was nothing."

"No." I shook my head, tucking a few strands of hair behind my ear. "It was *everything*."

Silence hung in the air, thick with whatever *this* was. All I wanted to do was throw my arms around him. Thank him. But there was the issue of how he felt about touching me and what that would bring with his gifts. Not to mention the grumpy-looking boss ushering him into my sister's hospital room.

"We'll make sure to finish up with her shortly, Miss Brooks. Then your sister should be able to go home," the man in the gray suit called out from the door before shutting it swiftly behind him.

My eyes darted up to the sky outside the window. The acolytes had heard my plea, and the Moon Goddess had answered it. Hope brewed in my chest, my heart feeling lighter than it had in weeks.

My sister was safe, and soon I'd get to take her *home*.

CHAPTER 26

OAKLEY

The next week flew by in a blur, the days and nights blending into each other between taking care of Aspen and hovering over Hazel. The coven came together, scheduling food deliveries from Hedley Haycox every other day, along with a grocery drop. Knowing they had come together to help us only solidified my desire to stay.

To build a life for us here.

"How are you doing?"

"I'm fine," Hazel said with an exasperated exhale. "Like I said the last *ten times* you've asked me in the four hours I've been awake."

"Sorry." I winced. While I didn't want to pry—I wanted her to come to me in her own time—I knew she wasn't fine. How could she be? She was kidnapped and held in a tiny room hidden behind Acacia's bookcase for weeks.

"Invite your boyfriends, Agent Carver and Holt, over. There are a few things I've remembered that should be added to my statement."

"Th-they're not..." I stammered, unable to finish my sentence, realizing she also knew their real last names. Their real identities. We both would need to keep that secret together. I swept Aspen up to my shoulder, patting his back until he let out a burp, then dropped his chubby cheek back to my shoulder.

"Maybe not yet," she groaned in annoyance, the corner of her lip quirking a bit.

"Wait." I stilled, letting the silence take a beat as I thought about her words. "Did you *see* something?"

"I'm not answering that." She shook her head, bringing her hands up by her shoulders. "We both know how it went last time you got a vision out of me."

Sipping water from the straw of her *100% that witch* tumbler I'd gotten her for her thirtieth birthday, she took her time before speaking again. My curiosity was brimming over. "I've learned my lesson and I'm keeping them to myself from now on."

I glared. "So you would have just never told me about it?"

The vision that had led me here... Me in that plum wedding dress, streaks of black crawling down my cheeks. Broken shards scattered across cobblestone. Atlas laying in a pool of blood.

Dead.

"Did knowing bring you any peace?" Hazel asked, all humor stripped from her tone so only concern remained. She didn't need to be concerned for me. If anything, that was my job to do for her.

"No." I swallowed the lump of anxiety conjured at the back of my throat. "But it gave me the ability to maybe alter it."

I could only hope. Hazel could have another premonition —not that Atlas had been around since her return for her to get a reading from him. He'd offered to come out a few times, relieved when I'd called to tell him we'd found her and that he could notify his contacts to stop searching.

The fact that he wanted to be here for us meant everything, but I knew it would just make things harder. He still didn't understand why I'd left. Why I kept my distance. But what was the point of telling him something so horrible? Removing myself from the equation made the outcome impossible... I just didn't know if it had been enough to veer fate off its course.

Hazel wouldn't tell me now anyway.

"Call them and let's get this over with," she groaned, cutting into my spiral before I could ask her any more about her premonitions. "Then you have to promise me to only ask about my well-being once every twenty-four-hour period. Think you can do that?"

"I suppose."

"Good." She reached out both hands. "Now let me have that yummy little nephew of mine."

I passed Aspen over to her, and she sat him in her lap, his little hands wrapped around her fingers as she made his upper body dance to "Hexed For You" by Winter's Revenge in the background. Taking out my phone, I sent a text to Lynx and Saros, not sure who would be quicker to respond.

> Hazel said she would like to add to her statement. Either of you free today?

LYNX

> We can be there in thirty.

> Perfect. Thanks.

SAROS

> See you then.

I hadn't heard from either of them since the hospital and figured they were busy with their case. Maybe they hadn't been. Maybe this was their way of distancing themselves before the case closed and they left.

Lynx had said he wanted to explore a relationship with me, but was that still true if he'd be done here soon? Saros said it might take a while. Knowing how much he wanted to be finished with the case and the fact that I still wasn't fully sure how he saw me had me unsteady.

"Ugh. I missed you buddy," Hazel said, leaning to nuzzle his cheek with hers. His eyes went wide, catching on the aspen tree tattoo descending the inside of her forearm that matched mine. He swatted at it playfully, a long strip of drool hanging from his mouth.

I grabbed the burp cloth on my shoulder and wiped his chin just in time to catch the infantile ooze before it dribbled onto her pants. Knowing Hazel, they were probably designer. "He missed you too."

"Obviously." She rolled her eyes. Her fingers dove for his belly, making him giggle as she tickled his tiny body. "Your cool auntie is back to wreak havoc with you. Now to figure out where to start..."

My heart filled seeing the two of them together. Our little family reunited.

I really couldn't ask for more.

((((●))))

"THANKS FOR COMING," I SAID TO THE GUYS WHEN THEY ARRIVED. I was bouncing Aspen on my hip, trying to keep him content. He reached his stubby fingers toward Saros, whose brows bolted up in surprise. I didn't get the impression that he was used to being around kids. I moved to let them both in, wanting Hazel to be able to give her statement while she was up to it, considering it had taken a week for her to get to this point.

"Hey, Hazel. I know you met us briefly the other day but my name is Agent Carver and that's Agent Holt, but you can call us Lynx and Saros if you prefer," Lynx said with a smile.

"I remember," she said before standing and walking over to us, holding her hand out to shake theirs. Lynx took it quickly, moving in front of Saros, obviously not wanting to tell my sister about his abilities or invade her memories without invitation. She gave him an odd look, noticing it despite Lynx's effort.

He guided her back toward the couch, taking the other end of it while Saros sat in the loveseat.

"Why don't I take Aspen on a stroll and you guys can chat?" I offered, not wanting to make things awkward as to whether or not I should be in the room with them. I was guessing I shouldn't stay. Plus, leaving would be easier than letting curiosity over what my sister had been through get to me.

"That's a great idea," Lynx replied with a smile. I returned it halfheartedly, still unsure where we stood.

"Be back soon, sis." I walked over and pressed a kiss to her forehead. Then I nodded curtly to the guys before heading out the garage to get Aspen situated in the stroller.

⟨⟨⟨●⟩⟩⟩

THE STREET WAS QUIETER SINCE WORD HAD SPREAD ABOUT ACACIA'S death and my sister's return. The only times I usually saw folks out were for Lynx's workouts or to grab their coffee or smoothies from Luna's. Not that I'd looked out there often to see if I could catch a glimpse of two handsome witches...

The pounding of footsteps hitting the pavement behind me brought me to a halt. I turned around, spotting Lynx sprinting toward me.

"What are you doing here?"

"Hazel gave Saros the go-ahead to...*do his thing*. So I figured I'd keep you company," he replied, only a little breathless as he started walking next to me. I continued down the street with the stroller. "How's she been doing the last week?"

I kept my gaze forward, inhaling the fresh fall breeze. Leaves trickled down from the branches in beautiful shades of fiery reds and mustard yellows. "She's been doing pretty well, considering. She seems to be most at ease when she's watching Aspen, and I can't lie, I'm enjoying the extra set of hands. But I know there's no way to be as *fine* as she says after all she's been through." I finally looked over at Lynx, giving him a resigned shrug. "I'm not sure what to do."

"Give her time. She will come around when she's ready. Just being there for her right now is huge." He placed his hand on top of mine on the stroller bar. "Sometimes that's all you can do."

"I'll try to remember that." I stared down at where our hands touched, then my attention darted to the street, wondering if anyone was out and what they would think. As far as they all knew, Lynx was happily married and helped run the coffee truck with his husband when he wasn't training clients. How would this look to them?

I nudged his hand away, not wanting to do anything that could put his undercover status in jeopardy. "I was surprised I didn't hear from you sooner."

He frowned, running a hand through his sandy-blond waves. "We wanted to check in, but between being swamped with filing reports, waiting on evidence, and keeping up the training and coffee shop—it's been nuts. Plus, Saros thought Hazel might need some time without our presence in case it triggered anything before she was ready."

"I get that." Of course it didn't have to do with me. It was about the case. "Honestly, I barely believe a whole week has already passed. Anything new on the case front?"

"We did get the autopsy report. I can't say much more until we hear from toxicology, but...Acacia was murdered. We still aren't sure how your sister's disappearance fits into the picture. They seem related, but usually it was the whole household taken, not just one person from it, and we've never found anyone else who disappeared."

Shit. That would mean there could be even more to my sister's kidnapping than I'd thought. Hopefully whatever was happening with Saros right now gave them some clues. If someone else was out there, did that put Hazel in more danger? "Maybe they didn't realize Aspen and I would be there since she moved in first?"

"I'm not sure. Ideally between your sister's report and the evidence we sent in, something will shake out. We'll be going through our notes again at home tonight after he's done talking to Hazel."

Home. Did he even really think of it as his home? How could he when he spent most of his time undercover traveling wherever the case took him?

"Wicked, there wasn't a day that I didn't think about you," he admitted, coming around in front of the stroller so I'd be forced to stop. He knelt, making silly faces at Aspen, who giggled wildly in response. "Both of you."

"Really?" I bent down next to him, whispering low. "And here I was thinking you were trying to speed up this investigation so you could be rid of Celestial Haven."

"I'd love to have the case solved, but I'm not complaining

about getting to stick around while we wait to hear from headquarters."

"What happens once you do?" I asked, not sure I wanted the answer.

"I don't know, Wicked." He put his hand on my knee, making my heart race. "All I know is that I can't stop myself when it comes to you."

"I don't want you to." My mind flitted back to when he'd held that knee and devoured me... The way his Empathy flowed through me and the hours afterward. Desire swam in my veins, eager to reach the source. For more. "But I have to ask...do you know what's going on with Saros?"

"I promised him I wouldn't interfere." His lips pulled into a line, reminding me of his grouchy faux hubby. "He has his own way of handling his emotions—"

"Or lack thereof." I chuckled, eliciting a frown from Lynx that quickly had me shutting myself up.

"As someone who has a front-row seat to how much he keeps bottled up, I've learned not to always read into his stoicism."

I shrugged. "It's hard not to."

"I know." He stood, coming back around the stroller and pushing it himself as I walked next to them. "But look at Hazel. You know she's not okay, even if she says she is."

"She's the strongest person I know."

"People are only strong because of the traumatic shit that made them that way." He kept his face forward. "Don't write him off just yet."

What didn't I know?

A lot, considering how little Saros seemed to want to let me in.

If he even wanted to let me in.

A buzz came from Lynx's pocket, and he grabbed his

phone, swiping to see whatever message had come through. "They're done. Wanna head back?"

"Sounds good," I replied, ready to check if Hazel was okay, especially if whoever had killed Acacia was still out there.

(((●)))

"How'd it go?" I asked after the guys left, unsure if I should or if Hazel would jump on me for being nosey. With Acacia's murder, I couldn't help but wonder what she'd witnessed.

"Good, I think." She stood from the couch, heading toward the fridge and pulling out a few charcuterie boards that had been sent from a local shop. "I like him."

"You do?" My response came off more stunned than it probably should have.

"Yeah." She laughed, then added more seriously, "He doesn't treat me with kid gloves."

Point taken. "I'm glad it went well."

"Me too. And that this part is done at least."

She seemed genuinely relieved, and I was grateful she'd let Saros look at her memories. It was probably easier than having to recount it all, though I understood why some people would be against it.

Stuffing a few pieces of cheese in her mouth, she wandered over and stuck out her hands. "Now, give me my bestie and tell me more about what I've missed. Not the few things you've said since I've been back between asking me how I am and hovering over me."

I passed Aspen to her, then headed over to the tray of food, grabbing some olives and popping them in my mouth, unsure of what to say or where to even begin. "I don't know. Not much."

"Bullshit, Oaks," she said, covering Aspen's ears as she

swore. "You are not the woman that was hiding away before —I saw you unpacked everything. Your supplies are starting to take up space in the garage, and the ring light is put together, along with your other gear."

Pride bloomed in my chest but also stuttered a bit with nerves. Nerves that she'd think I was trying to do too much; that I should wait until Aspen was older. Nerves that I'd fail and everyone would know. What if I tried and couldn't build back the brand that once had hundreds of witches and supernaturals ordering daily?

"I'm going to get the shop up and running again. Figured I'd start with some of the potions and talismans. I'm also thinking of incorporating a new nursing-friendly lingerie line…"

I held my breath, waiting for the business-minded big sister to come out. Instead, Hazel broke into a wide smile. "Nursing-friendly lingerie? I am here for this!"

Exhaling audibly, I grabbed a few pieces of prosciutto and shoved them in my mouth.

"Does that mean your magic is back?" Hazel asked.

I nearly choked.

She obviously knew about my Desire—we weren't secretive about our sexuality or romantic life, and we'd grown up knowing about each other's gifts. Still, I wasn't expecting that question. She hadn't even asked me about my gift once since I'd allowed it to dwindle.

"Only a little bit. Which is why I'm just doing little things for now so I don't burn out. But I have decided to recharge this full moon."

"Get it, sis," she said, shimmying her shoulders and giving her hips a subtle seductive twist. "I can watch Aspen for you."

"What about recharging yourself? You already missed the

last one." I didn't want her to feel obligated to watch Aspen when she could probably use the magical boost. "Plus, you normally go out on full moon nights…all night."

"I love a full moon fuckfest as much as the next single witch, but there will be plenty more. Honestly, I'd rather get in the extra baby snuggles I've missed out on. I can go out earlier in the evening for a quick bit, see if any witches are up for a reading, then come back to watch him for the night. The magic I have will tide me over until the next one. I can always test-drive the lunar panels on the windows."

"They work," I said quickly, before realizing the implication.

"Oh really?" She waggled her eyebrows but, *thank Goddess*, didn't ask anything more. "Then see? It'll be perfect."

"You sure?" I cocked my head, searching for any hidden sign that she might not really want to do this. "I'll make it up to you."

She wrapped an arm around me, Aspen balancing on her opposite hip. "You can make it up to me by treating me to a Seattle family date once you get your business up and running. I need a weekend away in the city with you and our little guy."

"It's a deal." I gave her a squeeze, resting my head on her shoulder.

She went to the counter, munching more food before taking out the pitcher of sparkling raspberry lemonade from the fridge and pouring it into a set of wine glasses. She held one up in the air, and I clutched around mine, clinking it with hers and taking a refreshing sip. It felt so gloriously normal, the three of us together. Almost like the last month hadn't happened.

Maybe one day I'd ask her more about what she'd been

through. But at least she was talking, and I'd keep showing her that I was here whenever she was ready.

A smirk spanned her lips, and she set her drink down. "Now, tell me more about these new designs you're working on."

CHAPTER 27

OAKLEY

The possessed cups suctioned my nipples, elongating them into odd, unappealing shapes, making me frown. I was short on time and needed a quick way to exorcise some milk for Hazel to watch Aspen. I'd been stockpiling since she'd offered to stay with him, and while there was plenty, I was also nervous about my own discomfort tonight.

Just one final round with the demonic contraption and I would be ready to go.

Well, as ready as I could be.

The coppery full moon hung high above, glowing like a beacon. But instead of feeling the heavy weight of its arrival, it reminded me that I'd have my magic back soon.

We'd skipped the moonluck at the Wellses' house, opting for a quiet night at home. Neither of us wanted to deal with the crowd, the inevitable stares and questions. Hazel was still uneasy with Acacia's case unsolved. From the few things she'd opened up to me about, the strange woman had taken her and locked her away, muttering things that didn't make sense and jotting down lots of notes, probably the ones the guys had sent back for evidence.

She had also heard someone else there, but she didn't know when, since there had been no way for her to keep track of time where she was being held. According to the autopsy report, Acacia had been dead for almost forty-eight hours before Lynx and Saros had found her.

I was quickly learning that investigations took time. A lot of it. Especially when things were being sent out to a head-quarters lab to avoid any tampering. Apparently there wasn't much trust in the police department here, which didn't shock me in the least. No wonder Lynx hadn't wanted them handling Hazel's case.

They had gone to the moonluck tonight, both to keep up appearances within the neighborhood and to scope it out for potential suspects while they continued combing through the evidence for their case. The pair would probably be heading to the pines afterward, along with most of the coven.

Would they be together? Where would they go? In the patch of trees behind their house or deeper into the woods?

I clenched my thighs together, Desire fidgeting through me, feeling the full moon's effects and eager for magical replenishment. The small amount I'd toyed with this month was already nearly depleted.

While there were aspects of having my gift that made me nervous, I knew I could figure it out. And I couldn't lie, I hadn't minded borrowing Lynx's power for the short stint I'd been bestowed his blessing. Especially when I experienced deep in the marrow of my bones how he felt when he looked at me.

Touched me.

Tasted me.

I could only imagine how intense it would be when he was *inside* of me.

My magical tank needed filling...along with other things.

Goddess only knew when that would be. I'd been too embarrassed to ask Lynx to join me tonight. I mean, how do you even lead in to invite someone out to the pines with you? Especially when that person needed to keep up appearances of being married to someone else...who also might want to join you?

Or not.

I still wasn't fully sure on Saros, but my mind and Desire had its own ideas when it came to imaginative ways to spend a full moon with the two handsome witches.

There was a spot right at the edge of the forest where I'd be within the Moon Goddess's glowing embrace but also not too far from home. I glanced over at it before heading into the living room. Capping the two freshly pumped bottles of milk, I stuck them on the countertop. "Start with these for his next feeding since they are fresh and room temp and then move to the stuff in the freezer. There's also some formula in the pantry that can be brewed up if he somehow needs more."

That would be nearly impossible since I'd pumped enough milk to feed him for at least three nights, but it was one thing I could do to feel less nervous about leaving him to go recharge my magic.

"You ready for tonight?" Hazel asked, bopping along with Aspen on her hip. "You look..." she swallowed, "comfortable."

Her eyes dropped to the fuzzy black robe and pumpkin gourd slippers on my feet. "Figured it's easy access, and who am I trying to impress? Just need to be able to, you know..."

"Reach down and recharge your battery?" She winked, making my cheeks and chest heat. "Speaking of, I have a little —or not so little—gift for you."

"What did you do?"

"What?" she asked with mock innocence, handing me a satin-trimmed box. When I opened it, there was a black rose-shaped toy with a matching remote. "Figured this might come in handy."

I had to admit, it looked...*intriguing*. My Desire agreed, bursting like tiny firecrackers in my belly.

"I packed a few extra goodies in your bag, along with lube. Can never have enough. I hear your witchy bits are drier when you're nursing."

I cut her a glare. "Oh my Goddess, Hazel."

"What?" she said, bringing a hand up in halfhearted surrender. "I'm just looking out for my little sister and her gift."

I shook my head, waving off my embarrassment. She wasn't wrong, though I hadn't remembered any desert issues with Lynx.

But solo? And with these nerves jolting through me right now? Give me all the naughty tricks for my treats.

"Thanks, Haze."

"No need for any of that. I'm excited to have a night to hang with this cutie." She peppered Aspen's cheeks and nose with kisses before taking his hand and waving at me. "Stay out late, Momma."

I'd probably need to in order to get enough time under the moon's light. "If you need anything, I'll have my phone on me."

"Don't worry," she reassured me, giving me another wave off. "I've got this."

"I know you do." And I did. There was no one I trusted more with Aspen than Hazel, outside of myself and his father. "Thanks again."

"Now get going." She nudged me with her free hand. I put

the satin box into my bag, wondering what other items I'd find in there.

When I got out to the porch, there was a black candle floating midair, my name carved into its side, cream wax peeking through the etchings. Other runes for luck spanned its exterior, and once I touched the candle, it floated away, heading out toward the pines.

This had Hazel written all over it.

Turning back to the house, I caught her staring out the window, a big grin on her face, waving me on.

I followed her illuminated token, pausing only a moment when I realized I'd gone farther into the woods than I'd planned. *She can text me if she needs me,* I reminded myself, patting the phone in the pocket of my fluffy robe.

Pleasured moans echoed through the pine canopy. Bodies were pressed up against trees in the distance, some spread blankets. Jade nodded at me as I passed, skyclad, her body bathing directly in the night's luminescence. Emerald green vines began twisting up the pines and sweeping across to connect with other trunks under the canopy. I watched in awe as she replenished her gift.

Most supernaturals found spots within the pines' shelter on the full moon. Not all needed it to recharge their magic, but the intensity of its coppery radiance called to the entire community. Shifters would be running deeper in the forest, taking up with each other in caves or out in the open. Vampires would welcome their new bloods, guiding them through their first feedings. Demons would be bargaining, competing within their hellish hierarchy for dominance.

Anything was fair game when it came to the full moon.

Especially from what I'd heard about Celestial Haven. I'd never experienced something like this. We'd had a private wooded area behind Atlas's home that we would go to.

The grunts and groans were beckoning me to touch the damp spot building between my bare legs. I tried to keep my focus on the candle, curious where it led. Trekking up a hill, closer to the Moon Goddess's embrace, my thighs began to burn, until the candle came to a halt, extinguishing itself.

Fairy lights flicked on, rising from the ground, illuminating a circular blanket lying over the forest floor. Symbols from the tarot were embroidered onto the fabric, its edges fringed. Floating beneath the lights were crystals: carnelian, rose quartz, and citrine, all spinning in circles at different heights, like a sensual solar system just for me. "Wow."

"Glad you like it, Wicked."

I spun, spotting Lynx peering out from behind a tree.

"You did this?" I asked, shocked to see him here.

"I helped, but it was actually his idea." He nodded to another tree, and Saros stepped out, umber skin illuminated by the moon's glow, making it a glittering rich brown.

If only I could.

"I just thought you deserved a special night to recharge." Saros scanned me up and down, eyes lit with amusement. "I knew you were nervous when we talked before."

Suddenly I felt very silly in my fuzzy robe and slippers. I was going to hex Hazel's scheming ass. How could she let me leave the house like this?

"And I knew you were nervous because, you know, human emotion detector," Lynx added, waving a hand over himself.

"I don't know what to say." I slowly slipped off the puffy orange gourds, stepping onto the blanket in my bare feet. "It's perfect."

"Anyway, we will leave you be. Just wanted to make sure you found the spot and got to be spoiled a bit," Lynx said, running a hand through his sandy-blond hair. He put an arm around Saros, giving his shoulder a squeeze, and they began to descend the hill.

I scanned over the spread they'd put together: snacks, pillows, bottles of water, everything I could need for a night here by myself. My gaze caught on the large cup of coffee. I knew from the steam wafting from the cup, carrying hints of chocolate and raspberry, what it would be and which of them had brewed it.

"You know, I do have quite a lot of recharging to do," I called to them, trying to stifle the quiver in my voice. They stopped walking, eyes snapping to each other before looking over their shoulders at me. "I think you should stay."

They glanced at each other, and Lynx took a step backward. Saros nodded to him, patting his shoulder before taking a few steps further down the hill.

Obviously, I hadn't been direct enough.

I cleared my throat. "*Both* of you."

I didn't *need* them to do this—I could replenish my gift on my own—but this is what I wanted. Both of them. Tonight, and maybe beyond, if it were possible. Regardless, if I let them walk away now, I'd regret it. I wanted to know what it would be like. To be theirs if even only for the full moon.

Saros looked completely dumbfounded.

I shrugged, shoving my hands in my fuzzy pockets. "If you want to stay, that is."

"I do. It's just—" He cut himself off, running a hand over his chin as if trying to figure out how to proceed.

"You don't have to touch me if you don't want to," I offered.

"Oh, Midnight. I more than want to," Saros replied as they made it back to the beautiful spot they'd created for me. The one that'd been *his* idea because he knew how hard this might be for me.

Because, despite the lack of what he could say, he wanted to say *something*.

I filled the silence for the both of us. "Then stay and let's figure it out."

Just please don't leave.

"I'm sure we can find ways to be creative." Lynx gave me a roguish grin before nodding at Saros. They took off their shirts, distracting me from whatever I'd been thinking about.

Fuck. Me.

Saros wasn't as muscular as Lynx, but he was thicker. Now, as he stood there gloriously skyclad, I realized that was true for *every* part of him.

I clenched my thighs, both of them staring at me like two predators assessing their prey. My fingers fumbled with my robe, nerves and yearning stoked deep in my core, before I finally shucked it off.

Saros's evergreens glittered in the moonlight, only outshone by his full smile. It was so breathtaking, I wished it were a permanent fixture.

Lynx chuckled, stepping closer to me and giving himself a few long strokes, precum shimmering on his tip. I licked my lips.

"There's no way she's"—he nodded to the Moon Goddess above—"not watching and ready to bless you with everything you could want. I know I would." He walked around until he came behind me, taking my hand in his and splaying it across my belly, making lazy circles that seemed to move lower, and lower.

Not low enough.

I shifted my hips, guiding our hands to my center.

Saros watched us, fists clenched at his sides. His cock somehow was more swollen than before, making me both desperate for and intimidated by the sheer size of him.

He would definitely be the largest man I'd ever been with, but Goddess above, was I up for the challenge.

"If it's better to be on your own tonight, that's also fine," Saros said, the Adam's apple bobbing in his throat. I didn't need to borrow Lynx's gifts to know he was also nervous.

"That's not why we did this for you," Lynx whispered into the shell of my ear, his gaze pinned to Saros.

"I want this." I leaned into his touch, drifting our fingers up and down my seam, keeping my eyes on the witch in front of us.

"You want our worship, Wicked?"

I nodded, unable to form words. Lynx scooped up one thigh, bracing my weight, spreading me open to Saros's gaze. Blackness nearly eclipsed his evergreen. "Every part of you will be savored under the Moon Goddess's perch until your magic is bubbling over before first light."

The warm embrace of the coppery illumination beaming down on us tingled against my skin, reflecting its shimmer with a thousand glinting facets. Pressure welled behind my eyes at the realization of how much I missed this feeling, like being cradled by the Mother Goddess herself.

A *snap* came from near my bag, and a second later a stream of lube circled toward me, running along my center. Lynx grew harder, pressing against my back.

"Just a few housekeeping things to take care of while we warm up," he said, nodding to Saros who was holding a remote. He stared where my fingers were, and when I looked down, I saw the black rose from earlier hovering over my clit.

"Can you explain your Desire?" Saros asked, brows knit in concentration, as if holding back from pressing the button in his hand and unleashing whatever wonders came with it. "When does the transference happen exactly?"

"I didn't know the answer since I was a bit distracted when it happened," Lynx clarified with a grin.

"My gift will only take from yours if you're touching me when I finish." I breathed out, eyes stuck to the rose, my Desire and my body both anxious for what came next.

"And how long does the effect last?"

"Anywhere from a few hours to a day," I answered. "Is that what you're worried about?"

"I'm not ready to burden you with my gift," he replied.

"Okay." I took a deep inhale before I spoke, trying not to sound as revved up as I was, though Lynx could probably tell anyway with his gift. "But couldn't you still be with me as long as I don't—"

"Midnight, when our bodies join together, I refuse anything less than experiencing your full pleasure while I'm deep inside of you." Saros swallowed audibly, his eyes softening. "If I stay, *that* can't happen. But if it's not enough for you—"

"It's more than enough," I reassured him. Whatever he would give me, I'd savor every morsel.

His eyes traced to where Lynx still had me spread for him, spotlighted by the lunar halo pouring from above. Then he pushed a button on the remote.

The rose licked me generously in long and heavy strokes. I matched them, pumping back into myself, keeping my attention on Saros, wondering what he was thinking—if he would *do* anything. Lynx's hand glided up and down the thigh he braced, focused over my shoulder on the black rose and my trembling body.

My legs shook, tension coiling deep in my belly as Lynx ensured my supporting leg didn't give out. His cock was poking into my back, making me want to find a way to reach it, to make him abuzz with ecstasy like I was.

A kick of pressure jolted through the rose, and my hips bucked in response. My eyes widened, shooting to Saros.

Goddess above.

"You ready for him to touch you?" Lynx asked. "Just say the words, Wicked."

Saros's throat bobbed and the color drained from his knuckles wrapped around the remote.

"Yes," I gasped, legs trembling, feeling like I'd crumble to the ground if Lynx didn't keep hold of me. "Please, touch me, Saros."

I needed him like I needed air. Another kick from the remote told me he felt it too.

Desire crackled under the surface, its particles saturated by the blessed beam radiating down on us. It slithered into the deepest parts of me, coiling up, waiting to strike.

"You heard her," Lynx said to Saros. "Come and worship our goddess."

CHAPTER 28

OAKLEY

Saros stood there like an obsidian statue. Everything about him was tense, as if he hadn't fully made up his mind.

"It's really okay if you aren't ready," I assured him.

"Yeah, you're welcome to watch what *I* do to her," Lynx challenged, sliding the hand that was supporting my thigh up a few more inches. Saros dropped the remote, the rose that'd hovered over my clit dropping to the blanket at the same time. Aside from his brows furrowing and the heavy rise and fall of his chest, he remained pinned in place.

With no floral fuckery happening, I was exposed, and Lynx crawled his fingers toward my entrance. Saros's attention zeroed in on the movement. The length of him jerked, watching Lynx nudge my hand away, delving inside me, making my eyes flutter. "So wet and perfect for me, Wicked."

I was so focused on the feel of Lynx driving in and out of me that the next thing I knew, Saros was standing in front of me, cock pressed against my belly, hand hovering just above where my jaw met my neck. His gaze darted to my lips, and he swallowed thickly. "Warn me when you're getting close."

"You could always just be really bad at it and it won't be a problem," I teased, arching my breasts toward him, wanting to close the distance.

"Oh, Midnight," he brushed back some strands of my hair, pressing a slow kiss to my jaw and pausing a moment before whispering. "We both know that isn't how this is going to go."

Fuck yes.

Lynx kissed along the other side of my jaw from over my shoulder. "How about you say *my* nickname for you when you're close?" He leaned and pressed a kiss to my shoulder as he continued to stroke me from the inside. "Say it for us."

"Wicked," I rasped, angling my pelvis so Lynx could delve even deeper.

If being wicked meant having their sinful worship until my magic boiled over, then I'd gladly be the wickedest witch of the Pacific Northwest.

"Good girl," Saros said, cradling my cheek in his hand and sucking in a breath before stealing mine with his kiss. His tongue stroked savagely, and I nipped his bottom lip, encouraging him on. When our lips separated, Saros gripped Lynx's neck, pulling him in for a punishing kiss.

My chest ached, heart pumping wildly. They were beautiful together, like the sun and a storm cloud clashing in a powerful yet strange harmony.

In one smooth movement, Saros was on his knees, hooking the leg Lynx had been holding over his shoulder, applying the same ferocious tongue technique to my clit. Lynx continued to pump into me with his fingers, kissing along my neck. His cock brushed my back as I quaked, streaking it with his lust.

"*Oh*," I whimpered, pelvis jerking into Saros's face. My body was giving into the increasing pressure, magic flowing through my veins in the moonlight. Breasts swelling and heavy, my body ached to live in this permanent high. The sensual serpent of Desire twisted up within me, ready to spring into action and sink its fangs into their gifts—

"Wicked!" I screamed, loud enough that the whole coven probably heard.

Lynx moved to the ground and Saros pressed a slow, searing kiss to my core. It throbbed, begging to rekindle what'd been snatched away before I'd cried out. Guiding me onto my knees, Saros helped situate me atop Lynx's face. Two strong, much paler arms gripped around my thighs, pinning me there.

"Ride my tongue, Wicked."

My hands grasped the blanket for purchase as Lynx fucked me with his mouth. When I tried to sit up higher on my knees, feeling self-conscious I might suffocate him, Saros's dark, calloused fingers pushed me back down. Lynx's arms tightened, clamping around my thighs, tongue darting in and out of me, lapping at me in delicious patterns, always skipping the one area that *desperately* wanted attention.

When I finally got my balance enough to bring a hand to my clit, Lynx gave me a firm smack on the ass. My hips bucked so wildly over his face that I almost fell over. Then he went to work where my body and Desire craved. The coiled pressure built in momentum until it sprang from me, feral in its pleasured haze, and seized Lynx's Empathy.

I combed through his sandy-blond waves, gripping tightly as I arched back. The coppery moon heated my body. I shook and moaned, not giving a fuck if the whole of Celestial Haven could hear.

His lust wrapped us up in rich fuchsia ribbons, the air thick with powdered sugar and the smell of freshly baked brownies. This wasn't just mine and it wasn't just the witch licking his lips in satisfaction beneath me.

I snapped my gaze up to Saros stroking his thick shaft in sinful twists from root to tip. I was desperate for him. To be filled by his cock, covered in his want, smothered by his desire and unable to think of anything else.

But I would respect his boundary around our gifts. Even so, I hated feeling like his participation was limited tonight.

"She's worried about you," Lynx said, his breath tickling my clit. I jolted to my knees, remembering the empath was still pinned by my thighs. Not that he seemed to have any complaints.

"Are you enjoying yourself?" I asked tentatively.

"Midnight, I could watch you fall apart and never tire of the sight," he said, giving himself another long stroke, a shimmering bead brewing from the tip. I bit my lip, and his eyes zoomed to the movement. Slowly crawling forward, I looked up at him, replacing his hand with my own and licking up the salty prelude. He groaned.

"Lynx, can you feel everything he does if you use your gift? And can you share that with him?"

Like he'd done with me.

He took a moment, deep in thought, before nodding with a salacious grin. I ran a finger down Saros's shaft, making him shudder.

"Shit," I heard Lynx exclaim.

This is going to be fun.

My gift swirled within me, moving smoothly, unlike the dust particles that had been trapped and itching for nourishment only a few weeks ago.

Taking him in my mouth, I hollowed my cheeks, moving up and down his shaft, licking the shapes of sacred runes along it as I did. He grabbed the nape of my neck, guiding his cock toward my throat. My eyes darted to Lynx who was looking both deep in pleasure and woefully confused at once, his brows knit tight as he breathed heavily, watching Saros enter and leave my mouth.

Their pelvises bucked beneath my touch and I'd never felt sexier. More powerful.

Which shocked me most of all.

When my body had changed, I felt strong becoming a mother. But sexy? I thought I'd left that part of me behind.

I knew that logically I could still be wanted, but I didn't believe it, *truly* believe it, until now.

"Wicked, your mouth may be the death of me," Lynx groaned, his hand stroking his shaft along with my motions.

"Of both of us," Saros rasped out from above me. I peered up at him through my lashes, savoring him as he unraveled. My own body responding to their pleasure, wetness growing between my thighs.

"She likes that," Lynx said, eyes hooded when I took Saros deeper. Then he walked over and knelt, whispering against the crest of my ear. The head of his cock was notched at my entrance. "I'm going to fuck you now for us, Wicked."

"Do it," I challenged, arching into him to inch his tip inside me. He eased himself farther until he was fully sheathed, my body clamping tightly. Goddess above, it felt incredible. I groaned around Saros, then began moving along his shaft again in time to Lynx's thrusts. I gripped what I could of him with my hand, pulsing Desire into him, hoping he'd feel as deliriously full of ecstasy as they were both making me.

Saros hissed out a slew of mashed-up curses, warmth shooting the back of my throat. Face contorting, hips thrusting out the final waves of his release...

It was the sexiest thing I'd ever seen.

My body clenched around Lynx's length, making him moan. Once Saros had begun to catch his breath and took a step back, Lynx wrapped his arm above my belly, pulling me upright while he continued to fuck me for both their pleasure.

Saros knelt in front of me, licking his fingers before bringing them to my clit. He drew rough circles and I shook like a leaf in the fall wind between them. Lynx plunged in and out of me, the hand holding me upright drifting up just as my body shifted forward in pleasure.

Oh shi—

Milk sprayed with jet propulsion straight into Saros's face.

I froze in shock, then slipped off Lynx, quickly scrambling away. Grabbing my fuzzy robe, I held it in front of myself.

Goddess, how completely fucking mortifying.

This was why I needed a nursing-friendly lingerie line.

Saros dabbed at his face with the rim of the blanket.

"I'm so sorry," I croaked out, face heating. "I understand if you want to stop. If you're grossed out."

Way to kill the mood.

When he dropped the fabric, he was smiling. Full-on smiling. With teeth! And Goddess, I would do absolutely everything in my power to see it more often. "Do I seem like I'm grossed out?"

Wait, what?

"A little spilled milk isn't getting you out of this," he said with a smooth chuckle, then he crawled toward me until his face was mere centimeters from mine. Forehead kissing my own, he clutched the robe I'd covered with and ripped it away.

"I already told you that every part of you is perfect for me,

Wicked," Lynx added, locking eyes with Saros. "Same goes for him."

Without another word, Lynx came over and kissed me deeply before doing the same to Saros, which did things to me all on its own. Then Lynx laid me down on the blanket and settled himself between my thighs, lifting my hips up. I steadied myself on my feet, using my heels to pull him closer until his cock eased into me.

I looked down, spotting a few droplets leaking from the pointed tips of my nipples. Taking a deep breath, I reminded myself this was normal; they didn't care.

"Oh, Wicked. You make the most beautiful mess," Lynx said, driving into me.

Saros's gaze went to my chest, then down to Lynx plunging in and out of my body. I reached out, grabbing his cock and stroking it.

"*Goddess*," they heaved in unison, feeling each other's pleasure. I watched the lust dance in waves of hot pink, a few paler hues mixed in. Lynx's thumb strummed my clit, and they let out a hiss. My body and fist clenched around them, pulsating with the euphoria flooding me. I was so Goddess-damned close, but I gritted my teeth against that delicate edge and gripped Saros tightly in my hand, feverishly working his cock until ropes of shimmering white shot from his tip, painting my chest and belly.

"W-wicked," I rasped, letting go of him. Desire swam to where his release touched my skin, the coppery glow of the orb above us making it glisten. He continued to stroke himself until every last drop had fallen onto me. I swiped a finger through it, bringing it to my lips and letting out a contented sigh.

"So. Fucking. Hot," Lynx hissed, still pumping into me a few times. Then he pulled out, running his hand along my chest and stomach, scooping up Saros's cum and pushing it into me with his fingers.

"Told you we loved you messy," he said, sheathing himself in me once again. "We're going to make sure the Moon Goddess sees you overflowing with *us*."

Holy wet and wild...

My whole body heated, tingling in response. My Desire pulsed under the moonlight, as if the Goddess herself approved.

Not that I needed her approval. Tonight, *I* was their goddess, and I would take every ounce of their sinful worship.

"Harder," I demanded, needing this release and the fill of him pistoning into me. Never wanting it to end but greedy for my orgasm, nonetheless.

"You can do better than that," Saros mocked breathlessly. Lynx, still feeding his partner the pleasure of every thrust as he fucked me, picked up the intensity.

I bucked my hips when something latched onto my clit. Looking down, I spotted the rose pulsing, sending shockwaves through my core. Saros sported a devilish grin, his fingers wrapped around its remote.

Another push of the button on it had me screaming loud enough to scare off any banshees wandering these pines.

"Keep doing that," Lynx encouraged. "Wicked is gonna be the loudest thing in these woods tonight."

"Yes, she is," Saros agreed with a dark chuckle.

I didn't know if I loved or hated this demonic side of him. When the pressure came in pulsing waves, making my legs kick out, the answer was clear.

Loved. Fucking loved.

My body felt like it could float right up to the moon, every inch of me soaking up its magic. I buzzed with its energy, letting myself fall slack as Lynx hissed, spilling his liquid lust into me.

When Lynx pulled himself out, Saros scooped me into his arms, laying me on my side to face him, kissing me slowly, exploringly, like he wanted to learn all my secrets directly from my lips. His shaft rested against my belly, ramrod straight and wanting. Reaching down to his lap, I began to stroke him lazily, letting my Desire drive my movements. He groaned, hips pressed into me. My body was numbed in blissed-out ecstasy, but I was still so desperate for these witches. I wanted to wring every last drop of pleasure from them both.

Lynx nuzzled up behind me, trailing gentle kisses along my shoulders. Minutes later, he lifted up one of my legs, settling back into me with slow, languid thrusts.

Nestled between them and blanketed in the full moon's glow, my magic overflowed—having never felt more cherished and wanted for just existing as my perfectly messy self.

CHAPTER 29

OAKLEY

Three days later, at four in the morning, my phone *pinged*. I reached over Aspen who was in the bed next to me, half asleep while finishing his early breakfast.

SAROS

Outside. Didn't want to wake Aspen.

Go ahead and knock. Hazel should get the door.

She'd already know they were coming anyway.

Be right out.

Once I rolled out of bed, I settled Aspen in his bassinet. Then I brushed my teeth, combing back the wayward strands of auburn clumped around the top of my head like a scraggly crown. When I made it into the living room, Lynx had his arm around Hazel. Saros stood with his hands down at his sides, eyes apologetic.

"What's going on?" I asked, bouncing Aspen with each step.

Saros took a deep breath, folding his hands into his pockets. "We wanted to come by and tell you that the evidence has concluded that Acacia was behind your sister's disappearance."

"So the case is closed, Acacia was behind the missing witches?"

"No. Unfortunately, from what we were finally able to recover from the warded files, she was looking into the other disappearances, which leads us to believe she didn't have anything to do with them," he sighed, brows furrowed a moment before softening. "The good news is that we believe your family is no longer in any danger."

Hazel's fists were clenched at her sides. If that was all they'd come and said, why was my sister still so upset? "That's not the only reason you're here, is it?"

"No," Lynx said, hand braced on her shoulder. "We're also here to give you both a heads up that there's about to be an arrest in regard to Acacia's murder."

"Who was it?" I asked.

"It doesn't matter because they're wrong. There's no way they could do that," Hazel protested, her brown eyes edged in anger. *Hurt.*

Confusion washed through me. Why was my sister so hell-bent that they were wrong?

To me it felt like a huge weight had been lifted to know she wasn't in any danger.

That *we* weren't in any danger.

Lynx kept his arm on her shoulder until she knocked it away, seemingly pissed that he was trying to calm her. "Unfortunately, the evidence says otherwise."

"What evidence?" I asked.

"The vials we collected at the scene. They were a match for the ones that were being given out at the blackout bash—the full moon formula. They had been tampered with," Saros replied, looking over at Hazel who cut him a glare, as if to remind him she still didn't believe what he was saying. "We found traces of a rare form of blue nightshade. Only she and one other person on the street ordered from the same potions mistress. The same person who grows blue nightshade."

"Who are they arresting?" I repeated, regretting that I'd not been the one to answer the door.

Something was flitting at the back of my mind... Who had I recently talked to about a potions mistress?

Just as Saros opened his mouth to say more, the banshee alarms blared outside.

It was happening *now*.

Hazel and I rushed to the window to see what was happening, and a trail of unmarked SUVs came into view.

THE NOISY PARADE OF OVERSIZED BLACK SUVS ROLLED DOWN STARRY NIGHT LANE.

One after another, they drove up Blessed Crescent, curving around its main drag. Car doors popped and swung open; dozens of boots hit the concrete. Witches wearing black leather cuffs and vests with SNO-OPS across the back began filing in, moving up the long, paved driveway.

The Supernatural Neighborhood Order had come to collect their prize.

The neighbors creaked their doors open in their pajamas, squinting to see what was going on. Everyone was in the cul-de-sac aside from the four watching from number 13's window.

That information was filed away for later.

The agent in the gray suit remained back, watching his team knock on the door. Fitzgerald Wells opened it with a smile. His wife, Aurora, a few paces behind him, paling. Unaware of the twenty or so agents gathered around the perimeter, Fitzgerald welcomed them into number 5 Blessed Crescent, and the door shut itself behind them.

The neighbors waited outside, murmuring to each other, eyes now wide. When number 5's door opened on its own, a hush came over the crowd. Fitzgerald and Aurora Wells stepped out on the porch with their hands bound, heads held high.

She didn't frown when they arrested her. She didn't frown when she noticed the others' stares, but when her gaze rose to find Atticus and Chrysanthemum watching from their windows, her lips turned down.

They were taken to the first few SUVs, where they were separated and shoved into the back seat, and the man in the gray suit climbed into the one holding Fitzgerald.

The neighbors watched in silence as the caravan began rolling out of Blessed Crescent, the crowd of witches moving back to let them through.

Ruby Cove called out to everyone outside. "Go back to your homes. I'm sure we will hear more soon," she directed. "Secrets never stay hidden in Celestial Haven."

And despite the wisdom behind her words, she really had no idea how true they were.

EPILOGUE

OAKLEY

One week had passed since the Wellses had been arrested for Acacia's murder. Ruby had temporarily taken in their two teens, along with stepping into the role of coveness. While the coven was in flux, the investigation still underway, there would be no blackout bashes or moonlucks until we knew more.

No one brought up the other disappearances.

No one seemed to think it strange that houses emptied on the row quickly.

For the time being, I focused on having Hazel back and getting designs drawn up before relaunching Full Moon Emporium.

The neighborhood was finally starting to calm down, people spending less of their days huddled in the cul-de-sac around Luna's empty coffee truck. Lynx and Saros had been called to the Council of Magical Welfare's headquarters to report to their superiors. I couldn't wait for them to return, to have a better idea what was going to happen now. Whispers about the couple had filtered around the block, with the timing of their departure, which the couple claimed was a planned belated honeymoon abroad.

Finally venturing out of the house, I pushed the stroller down the drive and onto Starry Night Lane. I couldn't help the twinge of disappointment I felt not seeing Luna's window open, no twinkling lights strung under its awning or witches enjoying their morning brews and chatting.

Once the guys were back, would they even reopen it? I tried not to worry that this trip of theirs would signify their return to Oregon, especially when I'd finally decided to settle here to build a life for Aspen and I alongside my sister.

Bright-colored leaves flitted across the breeze, and I inhaled the rich fall air. Soon it would be bustling with our Hallowed celebrations, holidays the coven, along with the greater supernatural community, took very seriously.

Supernatural schools closed up for the week and the festivities would go on for days—some more family friendly than others. This would be my first year seeing how Celestial Haven celebrated, and my first year with Aspen in tow. Last year I'd only been able to manage about half the amount of appearances Atlas and I usually made, too tired and swollen to want to run around from one event to another.

I'm sure this year would prove to be a different kind of exhausting, but I couldn't wait to take lots of pictures and see the look on Aspen's face. All the more reason I was glad to have my magic back, to make the season completely enchanting for him, like my parents had done for me. I was already plotting some over-the-top decorations for the house.

A black SUV turned onto the street, and my heart leapt into my throat. *Are they back already?* I couldn't wait to see them again in person, to enjoy whatever time we had together. To also just know what the hell was happening with their assignment.

That balloon of excitement quickly deflated, sinking to the ground as the SUV moved closer, sporting the Archon crest on the hood. This surprise was not the one I'd hoped for.

The window rolled down, and Atlas gave me a smile that sank straight in between my ribs.

"What are you doing here?" I asked, much too brusque, earning a swift pat on the back from Hazel.

It was hard enough to keep my guard up around him when I planned ahead, much less when he showed up unexpectedly.

"Had a few things to attend to in town and figured I'd stop by for a quick visit. Didn't you get my texts?"

I went to pull out my phone, finding my back pocket empty. I dropped down to check the stroller basket to see if I'd accidentally thrown it in there. It was probably back at the house... Goddess only knew where. I gave him a shrug. "Forgot to have it on me, I guess."

"No worries." He pointed to the house. "If you want, I can go park and then join you all on your stroll?"

And have the whole neighborhood see me walking around with him and give them something else to talk about right now? I think not. After all the eventfulness taking place these past few weeks, the last thing I needed was being the topic of the nosey-neighbor rumor mill.

(((●)))

Ten minutes into searching for my phone, I found it lying in Aspen's crib. Tapping the screen, I retrieved my messages from Atlas. There were a few from Lynx and Saros, but I quickly swiped them away before reading, not wanting Atlas to somehow see something incriminating.

Aspen squealed as Atlas lifted him into the air, pretending to make him fly around the house. My chest ached at the sight. Hopefully this visit would be quick and painless, just a few hours with his son and then he'd walk out the door. I could wallow in my own guilt over pushing him away later.

I leaned back on the counter. "So your text said you had something important to talk to me about?"

"There's been another disappearance," Atlas said, looking at Hazel and I.

What? Was Hazel in danger? Were we?

"Who?"

"I'm not able to share that information just yet," Atlas replied, tone full of his official Archon bravado. It was something I used to find sexy—commanding, even. I still kind of did, but right now it more frustrated me than anything.

"How is that possible?" My hands quivered, so I dropped the phone back onto the counter. "Didn't the Wellses confess?"

"They confessed to Acacia's murder. SNO-OPS is not sure how they are tied to the other disappearances, but they still believe they are."

Hazel's gaze narrowed on Atlas, still not wanting to believe it herself, though she remained silent.

"How do you know all this?" I asked, bringing my attention back to Atlas. I knew he had people looking into Hazel's kidnapping, but he'd never said anything more than that. "Some contact you have at SNO-OPS?"

"Kind of." He pressed a kiss to Aspen's head. "The project was recently passed to me."

"What do you mean?" I asked, pulse racing. "I thought Lynx and Saros were working this case with their boss."

"They *are*, and I see they told you more than they should have." He bristled, looking unimpressed. "Who do you think they all report to?"

Shit. Did I just get them in trouble?

"I don't understand," I stammered over my words, chest and neck heating.

Hazel stepped between us, putting her hands out for Aspen. "Why don't I take him outside to brew some bubbles while you two talk?"

Just as I went to stop her from going, Atlas nodded, making me concede. It was probably better.

As soon as she'd taken Aspen out into the garage, Atlas stood up, striding a few steps toward me.

"What the hell is going on?" My body heated—from his nearness or frustration, I wasn't sure. When the fan kicked on automatically, a special feature of our home system now that it wasn't in manual mode with no magic to draw from, it somehow flared with even more heat.

Atlas's gaze lifting before he arched a brow at me. "I wasn't originally handling the project, but when I saw the position was opening here—closer to you and Aspen—I put in for a transfer. I'm the new Archon for our Washington division." His aqua irises met mine, pooling with a question in their depths that he knew better than to ask aloud.

Poof! All the breath vanished from my lungs.

"What happened to Archon Lukas?" I managed to croak out.

"I wanted a change of scenery," he replied with a shrug. "He's heading up the Vermont branch. Anyway, I figured I'd stop by to tell you that while the Wellses are going to prison for a long time, whoever nabbed the others on this street is still out there."

"Are we in danger?"

"Of course not. Lynx and Saros are still going to be here working the case. Still undercover, so you and Hazel will not be able to tell anyone what you know."

They would be here longer. We'd just have to keep things a secret. We'd had to do that this whole time anyway with them being *married.*

"So you're leaving Salem?"

"Yes."

"How soon?" I was completely baffled. He had grown up in the capital, been raised within the political arena. I'd seen how much that meant to him—his family's legacy. He thrived on city life and the attention and power that came with it.

"I'll have to go back and forth for a transitional period, but then my posting will be three years, longer if I ask to extend."

"I don't understand. You have goals to become the High Archon, like your father. Like your grandfather." My heart and mind raced, trying to make this make sense. "Has that changed?"

"No. It hasn't."

"Then what are you doing moving *here*?" I had left Salem, *him,* to keep him safe. To build a life for Aspen and I the best way I could. "What does this even mean?"

"Mean for what?"

"This doesn't change anything when it comes to us," I said with an exasperated sigh, clutching the countertop behind me with my fingers, needing it for support.

This can't be happening.

He came toward me, hands bracing the counter on either side of mine, body engulfing me with the rich aroma of crisp linen and bergamot. Desire flowed through my veins, desperate to lure him closer, to close that very small distance between our bodies. I clenched the marble, smothering out the overactive libido of my newly reclaimed magic.

"According to you, there is no us. But I think I've been very clear where I stand, Oakley." His hand gripped my chin—

Flashes of nights together under the full moon, visions of us together with Aspen. Him as a toddler, throwing black petals around me dressed in a plum lace gown—

I pushed him away, that dress and Hazel's fatal premonition—too much for me to handle.

"It means I'll be around more for our son," he said, eyes softening. "I understand that doesn't mean we are going to be together. Sure, there might be part of me that hopes you'll change your mind and join me for a full moon picnic again..."

My heart twinged at the thought, knowing how I'd spent the last full moon and how much that would probably hurt Atlas.

He could *never* know.

Not when Lynx and Saros worked for him now. He could ruin their careers in a heartbeat. Not that I thought he would, but I didn't want to do anything to mess up their work or the investigation—especially since it would be ongoing.

Hopefully Atlas would find a place in Seattle or with one of the other Washington covens. Closer to us but still with some distance. There were so many great covens in the region. "Where are you going to be staying?"

"Well, funny thing... A few houses recently opened up on Blessed Crescent, and I just so happen to know the neighborhood realtor," he said with a wink.

My chest clenched. "You can't be serious."

"Deadly," he replied, a smirk playing at the corner of his lips. "Looks like we're going to be neighbors."

THANK YOU FOR READING

I hope you enjoyed the first book within the Celestial Haven series and getting to meet Oakley and her magical crew.

Each romance within this series will be told in a duet or standalone that are all interconnected and take place within the same supernatural suburban neighborhood.

Oakley's story concludes in Midnight with the Hexed, Part 2 of the duet.

Please take some time to leave a review and some stars for my witches. They truly make a huge difference in indie authors getting our books into the hands of readers.

ALSO BY L.R. FRIEDMAN

<u>The Blaze Legacy</u>

Adult Dark Portal Romantasy

Descend

Scale

Pitch: Origin Story Novella

Ascend

AFTERWORD

Celestial Haven started out as a *no plot just vibes* way to have fun while I was been deep in the world of writing my debut dark fantasy series. However, it quickly became a personal passion project.

Getting to share Oakley's journey of finding herself within the messy, chaotic, and beautiful world of new motherhood was very cathartic for me. I struggled with postpartum depression after my first two pregnancies and I've often wondered if I would have found comfort within the pages of stories like this one—seeing more postpartum heroines dealing with similar things.

This duet will always hold a special place in my heart because of the personal healing it and joy it brought me to write.

Everyone, whether a mother or not, goes through seasons where we feel more lost within ourselves than others. If you're in one of those seasons right now, I hope you have found some comfort (and drool-worthy moments) within these pages.

Thank you again for spending time in Celestial Haven.

Acknowledgments

First of all, a huge thank you to all my readers who decided to check out my first paranormal romance book. Whether you are new to my writing or are jumping over from another series, I don't take it lightly that you have chosen to spend time in my worlds.

Angelique - I could not be more grateful for all the time you've taken beta reading for me and giving me so much beautiful insight to help make my books sing. It isn't lost on me that you took a chance on a total new baby author when we started working together and I absolutely adore you.

Emmerson - From cheering me on with my crazy deadlines to talking me through scene logistics, I would have lost the small shred of sanity I clung onto if it hadn't been for your continued support.

Sarah - Without your words and friendship, I wouldn't have had the courage to write all these books. You continually inspire me to push myself and do better—even though it terrified me beyond belief for you to see my words still in their early mess. Thank you for all your invaluable help with my witches.

Chinah - As much as you keep me in line as my editor, I would be absolutely lost without you as my friend. You've been with me nearly every step of the way and really were the one who encouraged me to do more with this story than just *vibe* with it. Thanks for encouraging me through (hopefully) my craziest year of storytelling deadlines. I'll be ready to enjoy a midnight margarita with you to celebrate next time I see you.

Ashton, Aubrey, Brittani, Jennifer, Jourdan, Sam, Thea, and Vanessa - You all have been such a huge support for me since the beginning—before I'd even published a word for most of you. Thank you for being there to laugh with me, encourage me, bounce ideas off of, read my words, and bolster me when I needed it.

To my Initiates - Time to start planning another pass the book video! But seriously, your belief has fueled me on so many days when I didn't want to show up or when things got hard. You've spread the word about my books and have built such a beautiful community I consider my own safe haven.

Mom - thanks for being such a great example in motherhood, for listening to me talk about my characters, crazy kiddo stories, and for reading my books in their good, bad, and ugly forms. I love you.

About the Author

Author L.R. Friedman loves curling up with a cup of coffee while diving into fantasy and paranormal romance worlds. A Virginia native, she currently lives in Texas with her husband and three children.

When she's not writing, you'll find her enjoying tacos, dark chocolate, and the occasional glass of whiskey.

As the girl that grew up trying to find a magical realm hidden in her closet, she hopes to transport readers to beautiful, sexy, dark, and enchanted places through her stories.

For updates about upcoming releases, please visit http://www.lrfriedman.com, sign up for her newsletter, or join her group on Facebook at Books & Brews with L.R. Friedman.

CONTENT & TRIGGER WARNINGS

In the Celestial Haven duet you will find:

Explicit language, on page descriptions of sexual acts (solo play, MF, MM, MMF+), voyeurism, oral/vaginal/anal sex, use of sex toys, blood play (think vampires), public shenanigans, mild dubcon, completely fictionalized magical rituals, horny supernaturals on the full moon, consumption of elixirs and potions—including caffeinated and boozy brews.

There are themes relating to motherhood including: breastfeeding, body image struggles (not weight related), hormonal shifts, spit-up, and poopsplosions.

Kidnapping, mention of torture, murder, and death.

www.ingramcontent.com/pod-product-compliance
Lightning Source LLC
Chambersburg PA
CBHW020059310726
48970CB00002B/398